Ledoyt

Other books by Carol Emshwiller
The Start of the End of It All
Carmen Dog
Joy in Our Cause
Verging on the Pertinent

Ledoyt

by Carol Emshwiller

MERCURY HOUSE   SAN FRANCISCO

—•—

Published in the United States by Mercury House, San Francisco, California, a nonprofit publishing company devoted to the free exchange of ideas and guided by a dedication to literary values. This book is supported by a grant from the National Endowment for the Arts.

Text design by David Peattie. Printed on recycled, acid-free paper. Manufactured in the United States of America

Library of Congress Cataloging-in-Publication Data

Emshwiller, Carol.
Ledoyt / by Carol Emshwiller. — 1st ed.
p. cm. ISBN 1-56279-081-1
1. Runaway teenagers — West (U.S.) — Fiction.
2. Teenage girls — West (U.S.) — Fiction.
3. Stepfathers — West (U.S.) — Fiction.
4. Cowboys — West (U.S.) — Fiction. I. Title.
PS3555.M54L4   1995
813'.54 — dc 20   95-11056
CIP

FIRST EDITION
5   4   3   2   1

With special thanks to the Hunewill Ranch family in Bridgeport, California; the volunteers of the library of the Laws Railroad Museum in Bishop, California; and the Bartlett Training Center, Hammill Valley, California.

Ledoyt

Lotti writes, in large curlicued letters: HE LOVES ME, HE LOVES ME. Then she tears the paper into little pieces and eats them. She thinks, If ink and paper are poisonous, well, so much the better. She does get a stomachache almost right away, but when she goes out to feed the dog and tell him her troubles, she forgets about it—until she's in bed that night. The words lie like a big lump in her stomach. How can she ever get to sleep with that? She can hear Old Saddle Face and Ma talking out in the kitchen. She's old enough to stay up as late as they do, but they always tell her it's bedtime when they want to wander around out there by themselves. They're probably eating secret good things. They're probably kissing. They're a lot too old for that.

She climbs out the window, but only for a minute. Just long enough to look in on them. They're not doing anything. Their main happiness seems to be getting everybody into bed, including her, and then watching the fire. Sometimes they watch the fireplace and no fire even lit. It's as if just sitting, Ma in the baby chair, leaning her head against his knees, is what they've waited for all day.

She climbs back in. There's a lot she could be doing out there, but she decides to begin her journal instead. She's been thinking about it for a long time, but she's mostly been too tired to write. Besides, it's a girl kind of thing to do, except she's going to do it anyway. Nobody will know. The journal has a lock and she has a good hiding place where Ma will never find it.

She'll write what she just told the dog. First she writes: June 3, 1910, and then, It all began in the spring of 1902. I was six years old when he first came and everything began, first all good and then all bad. It's the bad I need to write about. He was ugly. That's all I saw at first. And scary, too, but then I got to like him—even his looks. And as soon as I got to like him, he up and married Ma. That was the first bad thing that started off all the rest.

Him as bucktoothed horse by Itti

Yesterday I watched him as he stopped in the middle of our planting. (I was working like a man. I always do. And I was dressed like a man. Anybody looking out at our fields would have thought it was a couple of men out there—just about the same size, too. Sometimes I get paid men's wages.) He had stopped to listen to the meadowlark. He was squinting up at the sky with his mouth open, which he shouldn't do because I could see his crooked teeth out from under his crazy mustache. I wonder what he sees when he looks at me? Not crooked teeth, that's for sure. I'll bet he hardly even knows I'm fourteen and grown up.

This morning there was fresh snow on the mountains. They looked sprinkled with sugar. There were storm clouds up there, too, but we knew they wouldn't come over us. They hardly ever do. They *especially* don't when we want them to. Sometimes when it's so cool and pretty like that, and when I've done a full day of outdoors work, and I'm tired and hungry in a good way, I feel happy in spite of everything—even in spite of him and Ma and in spite of their plans for me. And that's *all right,* because feeling happy doesn't change things. I'm still going to show him and Ma what it feels like to have to be me. (And that's what I told old dog Dewey.)

—•—

He adopted me and "gave me his name," you could say, but that wasn't anything I ever wanted. Ledoyt. Now everybody will think I'm French, too. I don't know what I am. Maybe nobody knows. Ma isn't even my real ma. I'm glad of that.

I t's American to be from somewhere else, and it's American to go from east to west. It's American to seek your fortune someplace other than where you are, or to be escaping something—sometimes the law, sometimes a shrewish wife or too many children, sometimes the death of a loved one or the death of one's whole family. But sometimes you might be avoiding your fortune, always moving on to make sure you're not there when good fortune is about to come your way. This is the case with Ledoyt. In fact, the last two of these. He ran away to escape the deaths of everyone in his family except his younger brother. Together they headed west—he, fifteen, and his brother, thirteen. By dint of trying hard all this time, Ledoyt has managed to escape even the tiniest bit of a fortune. It's his brother who has become a wealthy man.

Sometimes people call the brothers "Frenchies," but they're born-here Americans, equally fluent in both languages, though their French is as provincial as their English. Their grandfather was Ledroit, but as Daguerre became Dugger and Beauchamps became Beecham, so Ledroit became Ledoyt.

Earthquakes, landslides, fumaroles, hot springs too hot to bathe in, alkali dust, wind . . . these are all of home he's cared to have.

He smells of buckwheat and sage (everything smells of sage)—and tobacco.

Tennyson is usually in his back pocket, or Sir Walter Scott or Longfellow. Even before he met Lotti's mother, he felt the need to improve himself.

Most often they call him Bill, but that's not his real name. Lotti doesn't call him anything. For a little while, that spring of 1902, she called him Uncle—as was the custom then for a young person to call an older person—but now if she called him Pa, she'd be admitting he was her stepfather.

Back in 1902, Lotti's mother had a brand-new cabin and six hundred and forty acres of nice flat land. Not really big enough for a piece of desert, but it had a creek running through it that came down from the mountains. She hadn't done any irrigation except for her vegetable plot. All by herself (Lotti making play sluices beside her) she had shoveled out a wobbly, foot-wide ditch and used stones for gates. She was thinking to hire a man who could plow some real ditches and build some real gates, flood out the sage and rabbitbrush; then grass would grow, they said, all by itself. It was the law that she irrigate within three years, and she'd already lived there a year and a half.

She was satisfied with her life just as it was, or would have been if it wasn't for those men hanging around who seemed to think she needed to be married. She'd thought if she moved way out in the middle of nowhere, they'd stop coming, but they didn't. No matter that she'd told them, over and over, that she wouldn't and couldn't and didn't ever want to be married, they kept coming. They could help, they said. They could make her place thrive, or better yet, they could take her away to a nicer, bigger place that they had picked out for her or that they already owned. She did admit she needed a man, but just to work for a month or so, and she wanted one she could pay and hire or fire and tell what to do and not be beholden to for things done for free.

T-Bone Ledoyt (his name had gone from Thibaud to Tibo to T-Bone, and sometimes he was just called Bone)—T-Bone Ledoyt told Lotti's mother about his brother, how he came wandering in just about every spring and worked for anybody who needed him. He said his brother could help her out. He knew all about gravity flow and ditches.

T-Bone told her right out that his brother was a penniless tramp and that she shouldn't be shocked or frightened when she first saw him. He said his brother hardly owned more than an extra shirt and a hoof pick. He said even when there was a good barn or a room for him to sleep in, he

preferred to lie out under a bush. He said nobody knew whether he worked at all the rest of the year, and if anybody asked, he wouldn't say. Just made some joke or other. Never ever said where he'd been either. T-Bone said, "Poor old Beal is scared stiff he might amount to more than a peck of turnips someday after all."

To make sure this wasn't just brother talk, Oriana Cochran asked other neighbors about him. One told her, "Men like Bill Ledoyt are as rare as clean socks." But everybody said she shouldn't expect him to stay around if he happened to take a notion to leave, which might be mighty sudden, right in the middle of anything. Someday she'd up and find the horse and plow out somewhere all by themselves and no Bill.

They said, "Got so poor he had to sell his horse to buy a saddle and then had to sell his saddle, and that's the exact truth of it, except he never seems to want to own anything, anyway."

When his brother came around that year, T-Bone told him there was this Mrs. So-and-So who needed somebody, mostly for ditch work. She couldn't pay more than for the spring season, but she was a good cook and there was a dry place for a man to sleep, "not," T-Bone said, "that you would give a damn." She was pretty, too, "not that you would give a damn about that either." Beal said, "I'm not that far gone yet." She had a little girl and she called herself "Mrs." Cochran, but everybody knew better or thought they did. T-Bone wasn't the sort to tell tales, but he thought his brother ought to know the lay of the land. It seemed most of the men around found her all the more interesting because of it, though the women didn't. T-Bone's wife was too French to care.

T-Bone said how bachelors, and those who pretended to be, came from all over—rode all day sometimes—just to sit at her table, eat up all her food, and do a bit of courting. Mrs. Cochran was said to be awful particular, and she'd said right out that she would never ever marry anybody. T-Bone said, "You'll be alike in that. But you know how I feel. I wish you'd settle down before what you keep doing is the death of you."

And Beal ought to know, he said, that no man can offer to help her up or down from anything without she doesn't flinch away. And she won't look a man in the eye. Beal should be careful not to get too close and scare her, "though not likely you would."

Almost as soon as that Ledoyt brother arrived at Mrs. Cochran's, the men who hung around knew something had changed. In a week or two they stopped coming—except for one. He was a big redheaded Scot who thought to set himself up with a redheaded wife and get himself a dozen or so redheaded children, all pure Scottish. He was rich, too, and knew himself to be particularly handsome. He was sure that one of these days, Mrs. Cochran would wake up to her good fortune in being sought after by him. It wasn't possible she wouldn't.

Of course *all* those men felt they were more worthy of winning Mrs.

Cochran than that tramp Ledoyt. But though out at the elbows and down at the heels, Ledoyt was, even so, looked up to. There was something of the big brother about him, though those might seem odd words to apply to someone so bony and raggedy and not particularly tall. Perhaps it was the way he held himself—as if sitting on a horse even though he didn't own one. Or perhaps it was that ironic smile of his. Or perhaps it was merely that fancy, overgrown mustache. But standing up straight and looking ironic didn't impress the redheaded Scot, who not only had a mustache that matched in size and magnificence the ones each Ledoyt brother had but it was an orange one besides.

The Scot came out with his fancy harness horse and sulky on purpose to show up the hired hand and teach him a lesson he wouldn't forget. It seemed to him that Mrs. Cochran had looked at the hired hand and that the hired hand had looked back at Mrs. Cochran as though they had a secret. (They did have a secret, but they hardly realized it themselves.) That hired hand was a vagrant. Everybody knew it. The Scot didn't want Mrs. Cochran making a big mistake. There was no way that she could be liking Ledoyt better than himself: worn-out, foreign-looking man, too dark, too French, hair all over him down to his knuckles. It wasn't seemly that someone like Mrs. Cochran, so pure Scottish, so fair skinned, so red-headed, should care anything at all for such a person.

—•—

If it hadn't been for the big Scot, those two would probably still be just looking at each other.

Odd. She couldn't figure it out herself, but only this man and almost at first sight. Well, yes, at first sight. The only possible person who could have changed her mind after she had decided never to come close to any man ever again. It was hard to avoid the suitors in this place where there were still so few women, but she knew she wasn't going to marry any of them, no matter that they were persistent and no matter that having a man around would surely make life easier. She was not going to let anyone touch her ever again if she could help it. Every time she thought of . . . of that (she had no words for it she could even let herself think) she felt weak and sick all over again. Except now, when she thought of Mr. Ledoyt.

—•—

Chickens clucked and scurried the moment Dewey started barking. She straightened up from her washboard, saw him walking (walking!—who would be walking but maybe a Paiute?) out past the junipers and the baby poplars she had just planted—a wobbly, half-limping walk. She was wet with washing water all down her front. She was sweating. Her hair was coming loose from its Psyche knot. (Except it always did anyway.) She must have looked a sight, but it hadn't mattered. He'd smiled that self-mocking smile she got so used to later, and she saw that this odd, ugly man, who took off his hat and revealed a bad haircut—even worse than most—thought her beautiful.

He didn't look like any of the suitors. They were always freshly shaved and at least partly dressed up, for her sake. She found out later he couldn't have dressed up if he'd wanted to, hardly having more clothes than were on his back: one extra shirt, one extra pair of long underwear (he'd ridden right through the seats and the inside of the knees), two pairs of extra socks that were almost more holes than socks. He said he didn't want her washing his things for him, but she went into the shed where he slept anyway and found them and washed them and darned them. She knew he didn't want her washing them because he was ashamed to have such worn-out things. She stopped reading in the evenings and began to knit.

She also began to bake a lot of pies. She made dried apple pie and raisin pie. She had mincemeat she'd put up and was saving for Christmas, but she opened those jars now. When she ran out of those, she made mock apple pie out of crushed crackers or red bean pie. She made vinegar pie.

---

1 cup sugar	5 tbsp. vinegar
1 cup cold water	2 tbsp. lard or butter
2 tbsp. flour	

Mix and pour into pie crust.

If you can hold your hand in the oven and count to twenty, it is just the right temperature.

Bake until the crust is brown.

He looked so overworked and underfed—she wasn't going to be a party to that. But later she would say, "I can't do a thing with him. He hardly sits down. Sometimes he just seems to pretend to eat."

——•——

The first time she brought him his midday meal, out where he was working, she could see he didn't want it. She almost went right back home so he could throw it away secretly. But she forced herself to stay just so he'd eat something and rest for a minute.

First thing she said was "I'm sorry," and he said, "Why ever?"

She couldn't say what she really meant, which was I can see you don't want it, so she said, "To have made you stop. Right in the middle."

"This is fine," he said and squatted down but didn't sit. He looked as if he was about to get up any second. She wanted to say, Please sit down, but didn't. (This was before she knew about his bad hip and that he couldn't sit flat on the ground.) He ate, she was sure, out of kindness. She'd brought him fried chicken and apple pie, and still he stopped his work—his plowing out ditches—and ate only from kindness. Well, at least he ate.

Next time—and she would see to it that there was a next time: he ought to eat whether he wanted to or not; if he only ate out of kindness, then that was all right—but next time she would bring a wet towel for him to wipe off with and twice as much lemonade.

Walking back she was thinking how he wasn't really ugly. Not at all. Maybe a little bit funny looking. A big-Adam's-apple kind of man. Sort of like a grizzled, bony little boy being led around by an oversized mustache and a cigarette.

But she knew she was wrong and getting more wrong every minute. Seemed all she could see was the look in his eyes. Except after her experience with tall, handsome, rich, and educated, this opposite kind of man seemed safe. Even the first night he was there (and this had never happened before no matter who stayed over) she slept through the night and didn't wake up worried. She couldn't remember the last time she'd done that—she'd been that anxious for so long.

His brother had told her most likely he wouldn't want to sleep inside in the shed she'd fixed up for him, but he did. Mr. Tibo Ledoyt had said his brother liked to be out in the air and light, rain or shine. The shed had only one little window. And the bunk was narrow. Mr. Ledoyt had said his brother liked to spread out. But Mr. Beal Ledoyt never said a word. Just slept in there. Maybe he was just being kind again, but she did like having him close by.

The shed was a lean-to set up against the cabin so that his bunk was just the other side of the wall from her cot. She could hear him moving around, the bunk so narrow he often bumped the wall in his sleep. When he smoked, she could smell it. Now and then she'd hear him having a nightmare, grunting so loud he'd wake himself up. Afterward he'd smoke again and she would put her pillow close against the wall, breathe the smoke, and sleep.

She was thinking maybe everything would be all right—at least for a little while. She was careful not to say or do anything that might scare him off. She knew she'd be lucky to have even a few months of him. But surely he'd let her know when he was going to leave. Though maybe not. Some people hate good-byes, and he seemed like one of them. She'll have to see if she can read it in his face so as not to be too surprised and disappointed when he's suddenly not there.

But she should be grateful to him no matter what happened because he'd already changed her whole view of the world just by walking in. All her fear and disgust: stallions, geldings, and, almost every time they're standing still, bulls . . . down way beyond their hocks. Mares even . . . even mares! . . . What they called "winking" . . . with that other eye. Desire—if you could call it that—need, greed, taking, mounting . . . everywhere you looked. Frightening. Disgusting. Or had been. In towns you weren't quite so compelled to notice. You could almost pretend it wasn't happening, but on ranches and farms, all over the barnyards and pastures . . . It seemed like that's all there was to the world, and maybe that *was* all there was, that and birth to go with it, and death. Those men coming around, grabbing at her or wanting to, helping her up or down from carriages and holding on to her longer than was necessary. Staring those meaningful stares that were supposed to be telling her something she refused to hear. And here was another male creature who wanted something, though he never made a move or said a word, but all of a sudden the whole world looked different because she felt the same way about him, and all the more so because he wouldn't make a move.

So there was love all over out there, too. Horses were always paired up with some special horse friend, whinnying out to each other, waiting at the gate for their friend to be turned out to pasture before they'd go off, and little horse love bites, their lips so soft and sensitive. If one paid attention—and she hadn't until now—friendship and love were all around.

—•—

From the start, Mr. Ledoyt had looked at her as if thinking hard. He'd stop in the middle of smoothing down his preposterous mustache with the knuckle of his first finger and just look. She could tell her cheeks were flushed. Surely she's too old—and too . . . soiled . . . spoiled—for these kinds of feelings.

And all this time she hadn't wanted to be touched, but now she wanted to be yet she knew for sure he wouldn't. Once he reached across her to take a heavy bucket of milk, his arm against hers, his breath—his sigh it was—his big sigh so close she felt the prickle of it on the back of her neck. (She could have handled that bucket perfectly well by herself, but she knew it was important to hand it over to him.)

—•—

She liked how he muttered to the animals all the time. You'd have thought he was a talking man, but he wasn't. In fact she heard him tell Lotti she wouldn't be able to see—really see—the sunset unless she kept quiet about it.

—•—

He brought her spring flowers (lupine, mule ears, paintbrush, mariposa lilies, iris . . .) but he brought them so discreetly she hardly knew when. They appeared in jars or glasses in odd places. She would discover them when she was alone and he out in the . . . pastures—by now they had started to be pastures. She knew she shouldn't thank him or acknowledge them. She did venture to say how the mariposa lily was one of her favorites, but afterward she was sorry she'd mentioned it because then he often brought them. They only grew off in the foothills, and he would have to go out of his way for them. Strange to think of someone like him making a special trip for a lily, getting off her old horse to pick them. She hoped it meant something. Well, of course it did, but it didn't look as if anything would ever come of it even so.

So that big Scot, Big Andy, trotted over in his fancy sulky, didn't go near the cabin, trotted straight down along the river, tied up under a cottonwood, and walked out to fetch Ledoyt from his ditch. Ledoyt tried to talk him out of it. It was easy to see who would win, but to Big Andy it wasn't a matter of winning—he always won—it was a matter of right and wrong. In fact it was a matter of what was downright disgusting, and unless Ledoyt left the place that very minute, he'd learn better within the next five.

Side by side, as if they were friends, they walked down along the river so as to be even farther from the cabin.

Lotti always hovered around Ledoyt. Half the time she pretended he was a wild animal, and the other half, she was. This time she was stalking him. She saw it all. Six years old at that time, Lotti was as happy as she'd ever been. She had fallen in love with the hired hand and had asked him several times if when she grew up, he would marry her. He always said, "Aren't I a little bit long in the tooth?" or "Who'd want to marry me?" and Lotti'd shout out, "I do!" Sometimes he'd say just plain, "No," but Lotti didn't believe him because he always let her watch him work and even let her help, and in his spare time (of which there was hardly any) he had put up fifteen bottles of root beer. They were ripening in the little cool cave behind the house. He'd made a swing and hung it from the overhang, and it hardly took him any time at all to do it.

When he first came, Lotti didn't like him. She didn't like his snaggle teeth. She didn't like his worn-out clothes. She didn't like how he always looked as if he should have shaved even when he just had. She didn't like his eyebrows. She told her mother that his voice sounded like a rattlesnake. He didn't even have a horse, and everybody who was anybody at all had a horse. Even *they* had a horse. She hid from him, wouldn't eat when he was at the table, yet she stalked him—always knew exactly where he was—drawn by his strangeness and even by his scariness.

One evening, after he'd been there six or eight days, Mr. Ledoyt sat sipping coffee and Lotti finally came out of hiding and stood at the far side of the table. She began to inch toward him—so slowly—as though to fool even herself that she could be doing such a thing. Closer and closer, until her hip almost touched . . . and then touched . . . his knee. Oriana dried the same plate over and over, hardly daring to move, not sure which of them might spook first. A whole drama being played out, yet hardly any motion to it, taking a dozen minutes, maybe more, he pretending not to notice, until, finally, Lotti leaned her head against his shoulder and he lifted her onto his lap. She fell asleep quickly after that, as though she was at long last comfortable. Oriana thought she would feel the same way—at last comfortable—if she dared to lean against Mr. Ledoyt.

After Lotti fell asleep, he put his cheek on the child's forehead and shut his eyes. Oriana wondered if he was unhappy, and she felt, even more than before, the danger of scaring him away. And yet that time seven years ago, she had been the one who ran away, and without a word, neither then nor later, nor a backward glance.

—•—

After that, Lotti said the things he said. She said, "A good horse is never a bad color." She said, "You ate so much the dog will starve." She said, "Don't let nobody catch you walking unless you're looking for a horse."

—•—

Now she thought that, even though he was smaller and thinner than the other man, he would, for sure, win the fight, or any fight.

Ledoyt, after a few falls, stayed down, but that man didn't think he'd given him half enough of a lesson, so he kicked him several times. "Never kick a man who's down," they always said. Ledoyt hadn't even kicked one who was up, though that was the French way. He'd fought "American" style. Years ago he would have gotten angry—that he had fought so scrupulously fair and then been kicked when he was down—but he has been beyond that kind of anger for a long time. And then, being scrupulously fair is his nature; he hardly thinks about it. Besides, he knows only too well that the French are looked down on and enough so already without him being accused of not fighting fair. Maybe he would have won if he'd fought with his feet (at least it would have kept the big man away from him) but maybe not, anyway. And he's beyond caring about winning, though he might have cared if Mrs. Cochran had been watching instead of Lotti.

(He always knew when Lotti was stalking him, but he never let on to her that he knew. Here by the river there was some real brush for her to hide behind. Usually she had to make do with some scraggly mesquite or sagebrush.)

He curled up, trying to protect his balls and his stomach. He got a couple of broken ribs but he didn't lose any teeth.

———•———

Lotti knew she should have been going back for her mother, but she couldn't stop watching. She'd not seen anything like it before. Two grown-ups! And not a play fight either. She'd seen cats and dogs. At first the men were as wild as that, with animal grunts and growls. Ledoyt had come in fast, thinking that was his only chance against this much bigger man— come in fast and stayed fast, so Lotti, just as when she watched the cats and dogs, couldn't tell what was happening. The big man got a bloody nose right away, and Lotti thought that was a good sign. But then Ledoyt started getting knocked down. Even so, Lotti couldn't believe he would lose. How could he? He was such a magic man, could make quarters come out of her ears and had even brought the newborn calf back to life that they thought was dead, by holding one nostril closed and blowing into the other. (She and Ma had thought he was doing a bad and crazy thing when, first, he'd twirled the calf around—he said afterward, to get the mucus out of its nose. And he'd shown them how the hooves were soft at first.) Lotti kept expecting him to get up at the last minute. She didn't go for her mother until it was all over and the big man had trotted away in his sulky. Even then she waited, watched him retch, fascinated. She'd not seen a grown-up man do that. She watched until he lay quiet, his face in the dust, looking like a rag doll might, tossed away into a position no human being could be comfortable in.

That was one of the first things she wrote about when she was four-teen and began her journal, which was to be the story of all the bad things and how this was the start of them, how right after this fight, everything went wrong. She wrote how her mother knelt in the dust with him and how he told her mother, in an angry tone of voice that Lotti had never heard him use before, to go away. How he retched again, and her mother held his forehead and he kept saying for her mother to go and she kept saying she wouldn't leave him. When he was finished being sick, her mother held his head against her breast and called him, "My dear," and he said, "No!" and he said she didn't understand at all who he was, and she said she did. He said he couldn't let her, and she said she would anyway and that he couldn't stop her. She was crying, though Lotti had never seen her do that. Pretty soon everything was switched around and he was the one holding her mother.

He had closed his eyes and looked as if he was in pain. At the time, Lotti thought it was because of the bruises he'd gotten and being sick and the split lip and all, but now she doesn't think so.

Lotti writes: That night Ma wanted for him to sleep on her cot where she thought he'd be warmer and more comfortable, and she said she would sleep by the fireplace, but he wouldn't do that. (Not right then, though it happened later. Ma tricked him into it. I'm sure of it.) He said he'd bring the blankets in from the shed and sleep by the fireplace himself and he'd be plenty warm. But I don't know what difference it made, anyway, in Ma's cot or out of it, because I know it for a fact that they both slept in front of the fireplace. A couple of nights in a row it was, and then they both moved into her cot, which was hardly big enough for one. Of course they moved in there to get away from me.

Because he threw up so much, Ma wanted to go for the doctor, but he wouldn't let her. He never wants anybody to get a doctor. For other people sometimes, but never for himself. Ma made him valerian and chamomile and white willow bark tea like she always does when anybody hurts. She put wine in it, too. That was before we found out he couldn't hold his liquor—not even a little bit. Maybe that was one reason he ended up in her cot.

Ma helped him tie up his broken ribs with strips of torn sheeting. I saw his naked chest. He's the fuzziest man I ever did see. Even all over his back. I don't know why Ma bothers knitting him sweaters. I never have figured out how he knows where to stop shaving down his neck.

He did lighter work for a few days, in the kitchen or the vegetable garden or repairing the harness. He and Ma would sit, knees touching, on the front step, peeling potatoes or stringing beans. He never minds woman's work. A lot of cowboys won't milk cows, but he will. Of course he's not exactly a cowboy. Like he always says, he'll do most anything that needs doing.

I remember how strange it was after that. Ma, who never cried before all this (that I knew of), had tears in her eyes practically every time she looked at him, but she was laughing, too. It made me feel funny. But then everything after that made me feel funny.

—•—

He fell down three times during that fight. Those, added to the times he fell down on the way back to the cabin, make exactly five times in all.

—•—

I should have known. I should have *known* they were in love way, way, way before all this happened! Even before the fight. I was told. Right out. I should have listened. But that was when I was still happy. That's when I was calling him Uncle Beal and Uncle Bill both. He'd talk in a squeaky voice for one and a low voice for the other. He has a raspy voice anyway. Before the bad things began and all that love started going on around here, I would sit on his lap and lean my head against his shoulder and I could hear his voice rumble all through his body. I called it a rattlesnake voice because it rattled and because in the beginning, I was afraid of him. I thought he looked like a rustler.

—•—

A few days before he had his fight, I fought. I fought to make him be my uncle, I fought to make his love for Ma not true, I fought as hard as I could, and I won, and I thought that made everything all right.

His brother, Uncle T-Bone, and his brother's wife, Aunt Henriette, had left their big girls at home and ridden over with their only boy, Henri, who is my age but smaller than me (though not anymore) so the fight wasn't even fair. They had to get up before dawn to get here for noon dinner. They stayed overnight, but they camped down by the river where we had a picnic (practically in the exact spot where he would have his fight and throw up all over it). They came to say hello to him and to see how he was getting along in his new job after he'd been here a couple of weeks. They brought a whole French meal, with what they called coq au vin (which is just plain stew as far as I'm concerned), some funny long loaves of bread, sweet butter, tarts, and cheeses that tasted funny and that Aunt Henriette said were only pretend French. And they brought snails! I'd never heard of that. Ordinary, everyday snails! Even Henri wouldn't eat them though I dared him to and he dared me. Ma ate one. (She was just trying to like everything for his sake.) All Ma had to do was make coffee and vinegar lemonade.

> Snails collected for eating must be purged of any off-flavor or toxic materials from previously eaten food. Put about a half inch of damp corn meal in the bottom of a container. Put snails in the container and cover with a ventilated top. Place the container in a cool, shady area and let snails purge themselves, by eating the cornmeal, for at least seventy-two hours.
>
> University of California,
> Division of Agricultural Sciences Leaflet 2222

We carried everything down to the stream and spread an oilcloth under the aspen and cottonwoods. That was the first time I ever ate those French things. They tasted strange then, but Ma learned from Aunt Henriette how to make all that stuff herself—except the snails, thank goodness. (The things the French eat! You'd think they were Paiutes.) I pretended to like everything just like Ma did (not counting snails) because of him. When I think back, I do remember how he was looking at her all the time to see how she liked those things, as if it was important to him that she should.

He was different with his brother and Aunt Henriette. That was the first I'd seen him like that, he and Uncle T-Bone cutting up all the time and giggling. And Aunt Henriette was hugging him and kissing his cheeks. In fact I thought Aunt Henriette hugged him and kissed him a lot too much even for a French person. (Aunt Henriette is straight from France. Uncle T-Bone sent over for her and paid her passage even though he'd never met her. That was a long time ago, but she still doesn't speak right.) You could see she liked him a lot, but then she held Uncle T-Bone's hand and you could see she liked him, too. They were the only people I knew of—up to that time, that is (afterward, right here, that's all I saw)— but they were the first people I knew that touched each other so much. And Aunt Henriette even held Henri's hand, and Henri let her. He would lean against her in a way a boy as big as six mostly wouldn't be caught dead doing. I wouldn't let anybody hold *my* hand and I'm not even a boy. (Well,

I guess I did let Old Him do that some at first. I leaned against him and I sat on his lap a lot back in those days. I remember how he would build the ditch gates in the barn where it was cool and shaded and then drive them out to the ditches in the wagon. I'd stand between his knees and we'd both have our hands on the reins, his on top of mine. Sometimes I forget how nice it was *before*.)

They were speaking this funny mixture of English and French and then apologizing to Ma for doing it and then doing it again. I felt left out, as if everything was a secret, like when grown-ups spell things so you won't understand. But I first felt left out when Henri jumped on Old Him right away, rode on his back, played bucking horse, got twirled around. He hadn't done that with me, but after a few minutes of doing it to Henri, he did—rode me piggyback and twirled me around, too, until we all got so dizzy we couldn't stand up, even Old Leather Head, and Aunt Henriette said he should stop or he'd make us all sick, and besides, she said, "In five minutes—*cinq minutes*," she said, "somebody will start to cry. It always ends that way." She said it probably would be Uncle Beal who'd cry first of any of us. (Whether she said Beal or Bill, you couldn't tell the difference, though sometimes she said Béàl.)

At that picnic was the first I heard Aunt Henriette call him Mr. Aggravation. But she also called him her favorite brother-in-law. Then she said he was her only brother-in-law but that, if she had twenty-nine, he'd still be her favorite. Aunt Henriette always says funny things. She calls him and Uncle T-Bone *"les deux moustaches."* That was the time, too, when Ma and I found out he couldn't sit down on flat ground because of his hip. He and Uncle T-Bone dragged over a log so he could stretch his leg out in a special way. Maybe that's the reason Aunt Henriette calls him "poor old thing," sometimes even to his face.

Uncle T-Bone only looks a little bit like him, though they're both dark and they both have the *exact* same mustaches. I think Uncle T-Bone wants to be like him, but he can't. Uncle T-Bone is only two years younger, but he hasn't got one single gray hair—even now—and Uncle T-Bone's stomach sticks out so that his pants hang down below it. I hate that. Uncle T-Bone is getting bald.

After we ate, the big people just sat around and talked—still going on as if they couldn't keep French and English straight in their minds, which I guess they couldn't—so Henri and I went back to the cabin and Henri said he knew a secret he wasn't going to tell, especially not to me. I said I'd show him where the bats were hanging upside down behind the shutters if he would. I wish I hadn't.

He said he heard his ma tell his pa that Uncle Bill was in love with my ma. I said it wasn't true. Besides, how could his ma know a thing like that, especially since they'd only been here hardly a couple of hours? Henri said his ma said she could see it right away and that his pa said she was right. His ma said she couldn't stand to watch it because Uncle Bill was acting like he always did about anything that had to do with women, and he was suffering. His ma said nothing would ever come of it, and she was sorry for my ma. In fact she said she was sorry for my ma either way, whichever happened.

I said it was easy to see Uncle Bill wasn't suffering, because why were they all laughing and carrying on so much then? Besides, he was *my* uncle, not Henri's anymore, because he lived here now, and I pounded on Henri. (I even knew back then it wasn't fair because I was bigger, but it was important to me.) I pounded on him until he said, "All right, all right, he's yours."

Back then when I was six, I thought because I'd won that it was true and he was mine, but a few days later everything changed. Not for the better.

It was that evening after the picnic that Oriana changed her mind about almost everything concerning Mr. Ledoyt. First there was how relaxed and homey he was with his brother and his brother's family, and then how they all looked up to him so, even though Mr. Tibo Ledoyt was considered by everybody to be the successful brother. And there was Henriette calling Mr. Beal Ledoyt "Mr. Aggravation." That was a different view of him, and she could see that it was true. But later that evening, something else had happened that changed her mind about him even more.

After his brother and Henriette and Henri had gone down to their tent by the stream, she and Mr. Ledoyt and Lotti were still caught up in the excitement of the visit. Lotti said "Uncle Beal" every place she could insert it in the conversation. She made a song out of it, chanting to herself, over and over, "Uncle Beal, Uncle Bill; Uncle Beal, Uncle Bill." She insisted that only Mr. Ledoyt put her to bed. She was so tired she fell asleep the moment she lay down, though you'd have thought, seeing her jumping up and down just two minutes before, that she'd never get to sleep.

Oriana had almost finished cleaning up the kitchen area when Mr. Ledoyt came back from tucking Lotti in. It was getting dark, and he had leaned across her to take the lamp from the windowsill in front of her to light it, and then thought the better of it and put it back unlit. He stood behind her, not quite touching, as she finished the last of the wiping up. She knew something was about to happen. She wiped her hands on her apron and wondered what to do next. Where to turn? She stood a moment by the dry sink, not doing anything, but nothing happened. Finally she said, "You have a nice family," but she couldn't find more voice than a whisper. But then a whisper fit with the twilight. And he must have not been able to find any voice at all because he didn't answer. She went to the open door and stood there, and he followed, almost as close behind her as he'd been when she was at the sink. She stepped outside and he did, too.

No moon. Stars beginning to come out. There were four or five bats streaking around, looping and diving. Oriana began to wonder how far Mr. Ledoyt would follow and how long he could keep this up. She began to think it was funny. Henriette had changed Oriana's view of him. Henriette teased him—didn't take him seriously. Oriana wanted to tease him, too. She thought of zigzagging slowly, or perhaps at different speeds, all over their sandy desert of a front yard just to see how long he would keep this following-a-foot-behind-her up. She moved out to the little stick of an apple tree she'd planted not so long ago. He followed. Something *was* going to happen.

Once she'd seen a buck follow a doe almost this same way. The doe was grazing—seemed not to be paying attention. The buck wasn't eating. He stalked her, stiff legged, tense; almost, but not quite, trembling. He never for a second took his gaze from the doe. This went on and on. She'd left before it ended.

She crossed to the opposite side of the yard to the chicken coop where the chickens were still making settling-down noises. She leaned forward against one of the rickety posts that held the chicken wire. She looked up at the stars, hardly seeing them, not caring how beautiful they were. She was only aware that Mr. Ledoyt was close behind—that he must be looking at her. She decided not to traipse around anymore, and stood still for what felt like ten minutes. She was so aware of her own breathing she thought she would faint. Afterward she thought she should at least have pretended to. Then there was the sound and flare of a match. He was about to light a cigarette. She turned, saw the glint of the match in his eyes, and he looked as if he was watching the glint of it in hers. He stared at her until the match burned his fingers. He had to strike another because he'd forgotten to light his cigarette.

But whatever it was that had been about to happen wasn't going to. She went back to the cabin, walking with purpose this time. He still followed—seemed pulled by the same wires as before, but near the door he turned away toward the shed. She didn't trust herself to say good night. She didn't know what her voice might do. Perhaps he felt the same way because he didn't say it either. She'd have felt even worse about what had happened—or rather, what hadn't happened—if she hadn't heard Henriette call him Mr. Aggravation and Monsieur Agaçant.

So it was all up to her, then. He wouldn't, couldn't, didn't even when he wanted to. And since she hadn't fainted when she should have, she would have to figure out some other way.

But maybe that was one reason why she liked him, that he left it all up to her, never made a move and wasn't going to. He gave her plenty of time and space to get back to feelings she had closed off for so long. Even the frustration—that he came so close and yet never quite close enough.

He had been thinking to stay a while longer. She needed help and the place was just beginning to shape up. With him around it could amount to something. A small half-ranch, half-farm like this was just what he liked best. One man could manage it alone. Lots of times he had looked at her and thought, Why not? And settle down for good? And he'd seen that in T-Bone's eyes, too, as clear as if spoken out. Henriette's, too. Well, she was always thinking something of the sort whenever a skirt walked past and he looked back, but with Bone it was different. Except it shouldn't be Oriana. He wouldn't impose himself on somebody he really cared about. Actually not even on anybody he didn't care about. Monsieur Agaçant (that was true), Mr. Tramp, Mr. Drunk, Mr. Smoker-of-Loco-Weed and anything else handy . . . Even T-Bone didn't know what depths he'd sunk to.

Lotti writes: Old as she is, my so-called mother is thought by lots of people to be beautiful. Her hair is a flyaway pinkish mass. (I call it a mess and she does, too.) And of course she still has the freckles that she hates but that everybody else seems to like. (Except me.) Every now and then—well, not after he came—she tried bleaching them. Sometimes with buttermilk and cucumbers or with freckle cream she sent away for. The cream just turned her face red all over like a sunburn, and nothing happened to the freckles except they sort of got lost for a while in all that red.

Ma doesn't look like she belongs here at all, she's so pale under her freckles, but I have the complexion called olive and I don't sunburn. I have Indian kind of hair. I'm already taller than Ma is. I'm about as tall as he is. The way I've grown is one more proof that Ma isn't my real mother. I don't know why she bothers to pretend it.

Ma called herself a widow back then, but she just made that up to make herself look good. Of course Old Saddle Face wouldn't have cared if she'd been married before or not or if I was her real child or not. As far as I know, he's never asked any questions. And he likes everything about Ma just as it is, as though she was—is still—the yardstick by which all good things are measured. She feels the same way about him—though sometimes she gets irritated with him. I've even heard her call him beautiful, though everybody knows there's absolutely nothing beautiful about him. (I did get to like his looks after I got used to him, but I know he isn't the tiniest bit good-looking.) He laughs when she calls him that. He'll say, where did she get her ideas of beauty? And she'll say, "From looking at you," and he'll say he was afraid of that. That's how things are between them. Sometimes he calls her, *"Mon chez moi à moi."* When I got to know more French, I knew he meant that she was "home." And it must be true, because even though he kind of runs away for a while sometimes, he always comes back pretty soon. Ma still doesn't believe he'll stay. She thinks he's like he used to be. I know him better than she does. And I know her, too, better than she knows herself.

My so called Ma

Lotti

He calls himself a *navet*. Sometimes turnip head. I guess me calling him Leather Head or Horse Face doesn't add much to those. He called Fayette *"mon vieux,"* even when he was just born. You could learn French from all the things he calls people. That's partly how I did learn it. But I tried hard to learn fast because when Uncle T-Bone and Aunt Henriette and their children came around I didn't want them to have any secrets from me.

He used to tease me and call me "buzzard bait" sometimes, but he hasn't called me that since I got breasts. I knew even before that bosoms were important. The bad thing about them is that then I knew I really had to be a woman for sure and would have to stay that way forever. When I was twelve or so, I had some sort of idea that I wouldn't have to grow up to be either sex—that I'd stay as I was, a kind of in-between nothing. If I couldn't be a man, then that was the next best thing.

And there are other things about women! I couldn't believe it when Ma told me. I thought maybe she was trying to scare me, except she looked so embarrassed when she talked about it, I knew it must be true. (I was scared. And angry, too.) For a while—well, even now I can't see how anybody can stand being a woman. They call it "the curse" but Ma doesn't want me to call it that. In her day they called it all sorts of silly things, like "falling off the roof." The curse seems more like what it is. If Ma had her druthers she'd not call it anything, that's easy to see. I'm still not used to it. All that washing out of rags. I hang them behind my bed so he and Fayette won't know. Thank goodness, when I'm working really, really hard, like out at Grandpa Jacob's, it stops. At least I don't have to *act* like a woman. And I never do. I'm not flighty. I never complain. I'm as brave as anyone I know except maybe Old Horse Face. I don't talk too much and I don't talk about dumb things like knitting and food. I talk about hay and oats and cows. I read all his government bulletins. Ma wouldn't think of doing that. She only did it a little bit before he came, but not after. She leaves all that up to him now.

That other stuff . . . I suppose that's maybe funny to write about in a journal. Except what do I know about what people write? I've never read a single journal. Only heard about them. I guess I'll write whatever I want to. Nobody's going to like it anyway. Ma, stay out! (You can't find it anyway.) Later on I'm going to put in how Fayette was born too soon. I suppose they think I don't know what went on. *Everybody* knew about it. I heard talk. If Ma does things like that, she can't be telling *me* what to do. I don't think they're even ashamed.

Female Debility and Irregularities

The system of the *female* is the finer and more complicated, having to perform a double work, (child-bearing), yet confined to the same or less dimensions than the male. To perform this *double* function of sustaining her own life, and giving life to her species; it becomes necessary in the wisdom of God to give her such a peculiar formation, that between fourteen and forty-five, she should have a sanguineous (blood-like) monthly discharge from the organs of generation, known under the various names of monthly sickness, menses, catamenia, courses, menstruation, &. Why it should have been so arranged or necessary, none can tell. We are left to deal with the simple fact; and it would be just as wise in us to say that it was *not* so, as to say there was no one which *planned* it, or any other thing, because we cannot see and fully understand the great first cause.

Dr. Chase's Recipies, or Information for Everybody
Dr. A. W. Chase, M.D., 1866

━━ • ━━

When he gave me this diary for my thirteenth birthday, he said thirteen was a lucky number and I thought, Well, that's news to me. I know he just said that because my twelfth birthday was so bad after I got myself burned (which I'll write about when I get up to it). I don't even remember if I had a twelfth birthday, though I suppose I did. At the very least Ma cooks something special and knits a pair of socks. The only worse thing to get than socks is an apron.

I do like writing things. It's about the only "ladylike"—if that's what to call it—thing I do. I didn't think Old Him noticed. They know I draw. That's how Ma used to get me out of her way when I was little, sat me down with paper and pencil. That's how I got started writing. I could put drawings on the front and write secrets on the back, and then I would burn them in the stove and nobody would know.

Even though he knew about my writing, it was odd for him to give me this diary. He usually gives me something cowboy. He gave me his old hat. Even before he gave it to me, I used to put it on in the evenings, and I'd put on his smelly old boots, too, and clump up and down. (This was when I was little and things were still good around here, which wasn't but a little more than a month.) He'd be wearing slippers he folded out of newspapers. After he showed me how, I'd make them for him. I made so many they piled up and Ma said to stop. She said we needed the newspapers for the outhouse.

So he gave me this diary a year ago, but I can't use it for a diary, the days don't match up anymore, but I'd never have wanted to use it for that. I don't really know what to call what I'm writing. A history maybe, like I said before, of all the bad things. The absolute truth, by Charlotte No-Name. I've always known that name Cochran had nothing to do with me. For all I know, my name isn't even Charlotte. Sometimes I like not having a name, it leaves open a lot of possibilities, but mostly I keep wondering what my real name is and if I'll ever, ever know.

At first I was saving the diary for just what he'd said: lucky things and good things, but nothing good happened. I did start a few pages with things that were a little bit on the good side, like black mountains striped with snow in their crevices, and about arrowheads I found, and how we went off picking currants in the foothills and how I didn't pick any but sat in the shade of a big, gnarly juniper and wrote in the new diary. (After I got burned they let me get away with not doing lots of things I should have been doing. Sometimes I pretended it hurt when it didn't, but mostly it *did* hurt, a lot for a long time, and after it began to stop hurting, it itched like anything. Sometimes it still does.)

I got bored writing that kind of stuff pretty quick, so then I thought of writing things that weren't true, making up a nice life for myself with adventures and hardships and a mother and father. The mother would be an Indian but not a Paiute. They're too dumpy. The father would be a white man and look like me and be very tall. He didn't marry my mother, but he loved her the best. (My so-called mother never married until Leather Head came along. Like I wrote, I hear things. Sometimes people would just wink and leer and think I was too little to know what they meant. Those men that used to come around—some of them weren't even trying to hide what they thought in front of me. They thought I didn't matter.)

And then I decided I'd write nothing but the truth—all the bad things just as they really happened, and then whoever reads this journal (probably just me since I'll be the only person who knows where it is) will not be reading a pack of lies.

If I'm going to be so truthful I'd have to say I thought Old You-Know-Who was the ugliest man that ever came courting Ma, though, of course, he hadn't come courting, and I remember thinking, Thank goodness for that! He was too raggedy to be seen around us. I thought he ought to eat outside or in the shed. We had a lot of fancy things. Maybe not exactly a lot, but we had good books (some hand-colored), we had a family Shakespeare with the bad parts taken out, we had a pump organ. I couldn't reach the foot pumps then, but I could play "The Moonlight Sonata" if somebody would pump for me. He liked those books. When he first came, he looked at them most all the free time he had.

Even back when I was little, I could tell right away that his big mustache hid a lot of defects, and I told Ma *exactly* what they were, but she wouldn't listen. His eyebrows are so bushy he sometimes has to push them out of his eyes. Or Ma will do it for him, lick her finger and smooth them down. It's disgusting. (Once I called him Old Horse Face right in front of Ma and she got really mad.) I had many forebodings because she liked him from the start and I thought he'd steal everything we had. I told Ma that, but she said, what did we have to steal besides a few books and two silver teaspoons? And as far as she was concerned, he was welcome to them. He didn't try to win me over to his side as most of Ma's suitors had tried to do (unsuccessfully, I should add), and he never talked that kind of hearty way some people do when they're talking to children. He never asked me dumb questions like, would I marry a cowboy when I grew up? I was grateful for that. In fact, that's what made me begin to like him.

After we got to know each other he changed a French song into English—a reading song that helped me with my learning to read, but I found out later he wasn't the greatest reader himself. (Recently a lady told me he doesn't speak the best French and that I shouldn't imitate how he rolls his Rs with the tip of his tongue nor the way he pronounces all the *N*s.)

Once when we were all out at night together, he taught me and Ma how to tell time by how the Big Dipper circles the North Star. He said the Indians say the Milky Way is a mass of spilled white beans, not spilled milk like we say. He said they never had milk until us. He said what we call the Seven Sisters, they call Coyote's Daughters.

—•—

He always says, "Even if you don't make a choice, you're makin' a choice." I thought I had made a choice a long time ago, but it was one of those just-drifting-along choices. I've decided now. I won't be going east to school. I'll go, but someplace else. In the West for sure, and I won't go alone. It's not going to break anybody's heart if I disappear out of their lives, but I'm taking the apple of his eye.

The truth for Ma!
What goes on under
his mustache
Lotti

After the fight and after those first few nights by the fireplace, Oriana brought Mr. Ledoyt into her cot, not only because he'd be more comfortable there than sleeping on the floor but as part of her plans. It took some persuading, but afterward, when he asked her to crawl into the cot with him, that took almost no persuading at all. (It was the tears in her eyes that made him ask her to come. Those tears were real and false at the same time.) She wanted to hold on to him every way she knew how, even if that holding on might only keep him around a few extra months or weeks. In spite of what Tibo (Oriana prefers not to think of him as T-Bone) and Henriette seemed to wish would happen, she knew he wasn't the kind of man who would want to marry, else why had he looked to be so drawn to her all this time and yet never made a move? They wanted him to marry and settle down, but if she cared about him at all, she couldn't ever mention such a thing. There was a chance, though—she hoped there was a chance—that he might become so attached to her he would marry—except, of course, even married he might not stay around. She could see him marrying for her sake and then taking off in his usual way when that had to be. But she wasn't thinking beyond right now. A little while would be enough. Besides, she was already a fallen woman, and it wasn't as if people didn't know it. And somehow, someway, she had to undo what had happened to her. And that could only be with someone she really cared about.

When he asked her to come into the cot with him, he told her she was, as he put it, "safe" with him, that she'd always be safe with him. Besides, he wasn't that recovered yet anyway. But she'd seen signs—felt, that is, signs that he was recovered enough. And "safe." What did she care about "safe"? "Safe" wasn't going to undo anything of what had happened. With "safe" she'd never find out what love was all about.

(She had pulled the curtains to her alcove and pinned them shut, though she knew that wouldn't stop Lotti from knowing what went on. In fact, it would probably make her all the more curious, and if she was curious, there'd be no stopping her, but it was a gesture toward decency she had to make.)

She crawled in and he wiped her tears on his mustache. He said, "Now I finally know what this thing is good for." Then he groaned.

She said, "What's wrong? Are you in pain?"

"No. It's you. . . . It's being this close to you."

"It's all right. I . . . want you to."

"You don't know what you're saying. Don't say that."

"Why not?"

"Because I want to, and if you keep on saying it, I will."

"Everybody probably thinks we already have anyway."

"But I want to do what's right for you."

"You're such a good man."

"Mrs. Cochran—you ought to know this—I've done everything bad you can think of and a lot of things you can't possibly think of. I've smoked everything and drunk everything and done everything bad there is to do and ten times over."

"You're the nicest person I ever met and you don't even know."

"Not so. Not so."

"Oh, yes. Do. Do."

Then it seemed things would happen smoothly and no problems, but . . . the ragged breathing . . . close in her ear . . . reminded her. Maybe she couldn't, even after all this wanting to. But then he turned away and said again, "I don't want to do anything that isn't right for you," and that reminded her that this wasn't the same sort of man at all, and maybe she could. "It *is* right," she said. "You keep deciding everything isn't right for me. You didn't even want me to be in love with you. Maybe you still don't want me to be, even now."

"I do. I want you to."

There had been times when she'd been breathless with wanting him to touch her, but now, as he turned toward her again, kissed her with the same energy that other man had, made the same gesture, pushing up her skirt . . .

She would have to open her legs. That man had forced them. She'd fought. She had thought for a few moments that she could keep them closed, but he was too strong. There was nothing she could do. And now, as then, she couldn't breathe. Everything she'd tried to forget came back: the fringed velvet drapes, the dark green and gold . . . Stifling, stifling. And the chandelier. All through it, she had looked up at that, wishing it would crash down on them. It had glittered, even in the twilight. Even unlit it glittered. She hated cut glass. Glittering glass kept coming back in her nightmares.

She shouted, "No!" Lotti would hear, but what did she care? "Please. I can't." She shouted that name she wanted to forget and thought she had. Mr. Ledoyt had said she should push him away if he did anything she didn't want him to and he would stop. She thought she'd never want to do that—not with him—but just as he'd said he would, he stopped. He was trembling, but he stopped. She thought, Poor man, even as she began to hit him. Poor man, that I should do this at this very exact moment. She knew she was hitting him on his bruises, on his battered face, probably on his broken ribs. He didn't defend himself at all. She wished he would. She wished he would stop her. Each time she hit, he grunted. It sounded as if she *was* hurting him. She both cared and didn't care and she thought, He knows. He's guessed it all. But she kept on hitting and she knew she was hitting the person she cared about the most in the world. The only one she'd ever cared about and maybe ever would. Then she began to cry, but it wasn't like any crying she'd done before. Great gasps. She was suffocating. And she had been all this long, long time and hadn't known it until now.

When she could finally catch her breath, she cried in a different, more usual way—cried because she'd hit him and hurt him and cried because maybe she'd never be able to do what she ached to do and maybe never be able to give what she wanted to give and then he would leave her, sooner than he might have. "It's not you," she said, and he said, "I know." She said, "You're the only, only one . . ."

"You've had a bad time."

"But I should have . . . I shouldn't have . . ."

"It's over. It's all done with now."

He made her lie down again and pulled the quilt up around them both. "But what if I can't . . . I mean, *ever!*"

"It's all right."

"What I mean is, what if I can't ever be . . ."—she almost said "a wife to you," but she stopped herself in time—"I mean, be a woman to you?"

She was thinking, If I can't he won't stay, but she said, "I won't let you stay. It isn't fair."

"Now you're being like me—deciding what's good for everybody else. We'll see. We'll go slow. Rest now."

Then he was nicer to her than she knew how to be to him. The people she was used to, the Scots, were not like this. Was it because he was French? Or because he was just himself, Mr. Ledoyt? She hadn't thought a man could be this way, especially a man who never said a single word about love. (She was the one who'd said all the words.) It was almost as though his touch was to make up for what he couldn't say.

She fell asleep exhausted, he curled up around her, his lips against her forehead. He had loosed her hair. It fell across their faces. It tangled in his fingers.

She woke first, after a few hours. The lamp, the wick set low, still burned. They hadn't thought to blow it out. He had turned a bit away, yet was still so close his profile took up her whole view: big Adam's apple, salt-and-pepper mustache, the scar where a rope had snapped back and he'd almost lost an eye. Usually he had a devilish grin and—whatever it is that makes an ugly man beautiful, but now, at rest, he looked sad. She wanted to make him happy. She wanted to give him everything she had to give and herself most of all. She moved closer so that her cheek touched his prickly one. She was still enfolded in his arms and tucked in tight by the quilt, but she untangled herself so she could put her arms around him, and he woke and pressed closer.

It happened, then, so naturally—as though it was the only possible next thing to do. And more than once, though she thought it must hurt him some. Afterward he said he'd broken ribs before and those times had been worse. He told her how he once got trampled by a herd of cows that broke through a chute. She said maybe what she'd done reminded him of that, so it ended with a laugh.

—•—

Their sweat—mostly his—had mingled, over and over, through her dress and his longhandles. (Daring all that she had dared, she hadn't dared undress to put on her nightgown.) Next morning she heated water and moved the laundry basin in behind her curtains. She bathed first and he after, in the same water. They didn't look in at each other. They carefully avoided that. The fact that they busied themselves someplace else while the other bathed made it all the easier for Lotti to peek in at each in turn.

They'd had to get up at dawn with Lotti. She didn't seem to have slept much either. She was more jumpy and irritable than Oriana had ever seen her, and she wouldn't look at them. There was no possible way that Lotti hadn't heard and maybe seen, too, but Oriana couldn't make herself feel bad about it, though she knew she should feel bad. She had so much else to feel both good and bad about that she could hardly think or care about Lotti at all. Mostly she felt dazed with joy, because he was—well, a moral man, so maybe . . .

Earlier, when they lay by the fireplace, and Mr. Ledoyt had been groggy with the drink she'd made him for the pain, he'd said, "You going to marry me or what?" And she'd said, "Either one or both, but I don't know if you're asking." But then she said, "Ask me in the morning, in the sober light of day," but he didn't.

—·—

Mr. Ledoyt . . . *her* Mr. Ledoyt fell asleep that evening right after supper, sitting, facing the unlit fire. (Twenty minutes before, Lotti had collapsed at the table, her head almost in her plate and her spoon still in her hand. Mr. Ledoyt had carried her in to bed. She had spilled her supper all over the oilcloth as if she was two years old instead of six and a half—on purpose, Oriana knew—and she'd hardly eaten any of it, even the rhubarb pudding.)

After cleaning up, Oriana sat, squeezed into Lotti's little rocking chair that was almost too small even for Lotti, and studied Mr. Ledoyt as he slept, and felt bad all over again that she had hit him when he was so bruised already—studied his hands, streaked with rope burns, with their dirty, broken fingernails, not at all like her father's pale, plump hands—studied how he was completely white where his hat covered his forehead. Under that weathered, brown look, he was a pale man, always dark circles around his eyes. He seemed, in an odd way, fragile. Perhaps he wasn't, as she'd thought him to be, her savior, but instead she was his. When she tied up his ribs for him, she'd been surprised at how many old scars he had. His body had embarrassed her. A man with that much hair all over him seemed even more naked than one with less. And Lotti was right, of course, it was easy to see that his mustache hid defects—buckteeth and a bit crooked—but she liked him all the better for them and had from the start. Pulling off his boots for him had embarrassed her, too, especially because he was wearing the socks she had knit. How thin he was! Though when Henriette and Tibo had come over, Henriette had said he'd never looked better in all the years she'd known him. She said he looked rested for a change and downright fat. (How could she say fat! And when did he ever rest?) Henriette had told Oriana when they were alone that Oriana was good for him and she was glad he was here, and she hoped he'd stay a long time. "Except," she said, as though to warn her, "of course he never does."

He woke and found her, there by his knees, curled up in Lotti's little chair, looking as if she loved his every wrinkle and scar, and she did, too, and there was nothing much to do about it now. Things had gone too far in spite of all his resolutions. Maybe partly that drink she'd been making him for the pain and for his stomach. He had decided, but it had happened anyway. The worst that could. Up until last night he would have found some way to leave; even after being held in her arms all night long like a baby, even after saying God knows what after that drink, he could have left.

But happened! Things don't just happen! Except, earlier on, they had to her, that was easy to see, and not in a nice way. But for him, now. Any place along the way he could have stopped and didn't. Tried, but not hard enough. She'd said, even last night right afterward—even this morning— that she'd never hold on to him, that he could leave whenever he had a mind to, and he had said he was staying, so that was that. *Probably* that.

Now he reached to pull her close so that her chin rested on his knee. He said, "It's me." Those were already their special words. Last night, when things finally came out right for her and she could, he'd said, "It's me, Oriana, it's me." Now he said it again, and she said, "It's you," as though he was a miracle, and at least right then, he felt himself to be a miracle, in spite of what he knew he really was.

———•———

He had masturbated almost every morning and almost from the start, hearing her just behind the wall. He hadn't been there more than a day or two before he realized that the lean-to where he slept leaned up against the cabin right where her bed was. He could hear when she went to bed and when she got up. He liked to get in bed before she did and lie in the dark and smoke and listen and try to guess what she was doing. In the morning it was usually Lotti's "Maa-aa," sounding exactly like a lost calf, that woke her—and him, too. Sometimes she would hum to herself. Once he heard her cry. So quietly he wasn't sure at first. That was the night after T-Bone and Henriette and Henri had come. He knew she cried because of him.

The day of that picnic she had looked so flushed with pleasure—open and talkative and yet shy at the same time, her hair going wild all by itself, frizzing out, bursting from its knot as usual. That night he had let himself come too close. Breathing down her neck. Out in the starlight. He had been thinking again, Well, why not? Only at the last minute he had walked away and saved her from himself—for the moment—and caused her pain.

Some repayment for all those things she'd done for him. He'd had to convince her over and over that he wasn't working too hard, that he was eating enough. All those pies, and then all those socks—and sheets! There were sheets on his bunk. When had he last had sheets? He had been hoping she'd knit a sweater before he left. It would be something that would remind him of her even better than socks. Now that it was decided and done and out of his hands, for sure there'd be a sweater. Probably, knowing her, a whole passel of sweaters.

This was all very well for him, at his age. Maybe the best that could be, but for her? Except she *was* thirty-three. Older than he'd thought. And he was, at least for the time being, making her happy. He could see it in her face now, as she looked up at him, her chin on his knee, her arms around his leg. If he could just keep himself in line . . . And then here they were, kissing again. For about the twenty-seventh time that day.

Word of the fight got around. Everything always did, and almost as fast as it happened. T-Bone and Henriette heard about it two days after it happened. Back in town, that man had boasted how he'd beat up on one of the Ledoyt brothers, the one who was a no-good tramp, and no trouble at all to do it. And maybe now old Bill Ledoyt would know where he belonged—which was in the gutter—and stay there. Everybody knew it couldn't have been a fair fight. Even though they would always have favored a Scot over a frog, it wasn't right, a two-hundred-and-twenty-pound man against—what? A man about one-forty at the most.

T-Bone was worried about what might have happened to his brother, so he and Henriette came by—without any of their children this time. They brought a ham and French bread again and tarts. They came on horseback this time. Henriette wore a split riding skirt and didn't ride sidesaddle, though she used to back in France. To Oriana she looked stylish and rich. She wasn't pretty, but she had such a nice rounded-out figure. Oriana felt skimpy in front of her. Too small all over. Maybe her breasts weren't big enough to be attractive to Mr. Ledoyt. Maybe she was too sunburned and too freckled, and then her hair never ever was anything but a mess, but Mr. Ledoyt reached out to hold her hand. Right in front of them. On purpose.

Oriana saw the glance that passed between Tibo and Henriette. There had been lots of glances on their first visit, too, and Oriana had suspected that they knew even then how she felt about their brother. She couldn't hide it, though she tried. (She didn't realize it was Beal they were thinking about. They'd watched him watching her, helping her when she didn't need help. *"T'as vu c'que j'ai vu?"* they asked each other afterward.) Now they looked at each other and laughed. Mr. Ledoyt hadn't said a word about marriage, but Tibo and Henriette seemed to take—well, *something* for granted. Tibo said, "So it takes getting beat up to finally get you bulldogged," and Beal said, "I guess so," and Tibo said, "I wish I'd known that before." And Lotti ran straight out to the tool and buggy barn and they didn't see her the whole rest of the day, though Oriana went looking, and later Henriette and Beal did, too. She didn't even come out for lemonade and brioche. Afterward Beal found the harness axed and hacked—slashed almost beyond repair, but he managed to repair it.

—•—

A few days later, Beal started work on a bigger bed, and right after that, a new room. Oriana thought that must mean something about his intentions.

otti writes: They have sinned. I know it for a fact that my so-called mother had the first baby before she should have. They couldn't hide things from me. I practically saw it all, even though I was only six— seven when Fayette was born. I wasn't inclined to count up months back then. (I didn't even know she was going to have a baby. I just thought she was getting awful fat.) But after Fayette was born I heard things. I used to hide under tables a lot. I could creep around quiet as a lizard. He called me that sometimes. That's my Indian side coming out. But even back then I knew what they were doing and that they shouldn't have been doing it.

I can't see and hear everything that happens the way I could when Ma and I only had one room. It was a pretty large room—at least I thought so then—and had parts that were divided by curtains, so I could easily keep track of what went on. I knew *everything!* Now that we have our big house with six rooms, I can't keep track no matter how hard I try. I did a lot of pretending to be asleep back then, though I'm not sure that was necessary. They always forgot about me. That made me mad, and I thought, All right, then, if I spy on them it serves them right.

And I did see them, right in the cabin, that first time that Ma pinned her curtains shut and they slept together on her cot. Well, I didn't exactly see them *actually* doing it, but I *almost* saw them. (If they ever get hold of this journal, which they won't, they won't like reading this. So if you're there and reading it, I don't want you to like it, anyway.) I hadn't really meant to look, but I heard funny noises. I was worried already, what with all that talk before about concussions and doctors. Of course they'd been kissing all the time when they thought I wasn't looking, but there wasn't any place *to* look that they weren't in it hugging each other and laughing for no reason. Ma especially. Even when they weren't smiling, they looked as if they were. I could have run away right then and there, instead of pretty soon now, and they wouldn't have noticed I was gone for a week.

When Ma pinned her curtains shut, I knew even more than I already knew that I was supposed to be left out. And then they started whispering. I hate when people have secrets. It seems like my whole life is full of nothing but secrets, including how did Ma get me? Who are my parents? And then Uncle T-Bone and Aunt Henriette talking to him with a lot of French words sprinkled in. All their children understand, even the littlest ones, but Ma and I didn't—at least we didn't then.

I wasn't going to peek, but after I heard Ma shout out and then I heard these funny noises, I made myself an eyehole at the edge of her curtains, and I saw Ma hit him and hit him, and I saw him just letting himself be hit. I felt bad that he didn't even lift his arm to protect himself. I could tell she was hurting him. He grunted every time she hit. How could she do that? I thought she wasn't that kind of person. She never hits anybody. She never even slaps me like some people do their children. And why would she do a thing like that after they'd been kissing practically all day long for two days? He must have done something awful bad to her. Except I didn't think he was that kind of person either. The only good thing about her hitting him like that was, I thought, now he'll like me the best for sure, and that made me feel better. For a minute or two. Then Ma turned away from him and leaned over and started not being able to breathe. I thought she was going to die, and all of a sudden, even though she isn't my real mother, I didn't want her to. And then I started feeling as if *I* couldn't breathe either. But he didn't seem to think she'd die. He moved up close behind her—but not too close, as if he knew she needed room for air. He kept his hand on her, and when she began to be able to breathe again, he did come close, and she turned toward him, and it got to be the usual that they'd been doing all the time, only he was the one doing most of the kissing. I could tell he hadn't stopped caring for her. It was almost as if he liked her even better. I watched for a while, but I got bored. The whole thing bored me. And it still does. It didn't look as if they were going to do "it" anyway, so I went back to bed, but I couldn't get to sleep for the longest time.

He wanted, especially after that fight fiasco, to do something special, spectacular even, for Oriana or in front of her. She thinks well of him, but what has he ever done to deserve it? Get beat up is all. Dig a ditch. Here there are no ways to show off the skills he knows best. There are no beeves, only two tame Jersey cows, the new calf, and one balky old horse named Dormant. (Dormant wasn't mean spirited, and after he'd worked with her a couple of hours, that nag is fine. She'll even move for Lotti. Lotti picks up all his tricks in a hurry.) Usually he's content to be himself, whatever that is, though he knows he's not exactly husband material. But he'd like Oriana to see a different side of him than milker and pea sheller. He's thought of ridiculous things to do, like climbing to the top of one of the pines in the foothills. Or lift stones. Build a dam. She'd say . . . No, she'd never say it, but like as not she'd be thinking it: "Haven't you anything better to do than climb trees?"

(When they have their honeymoon—at home but without Lotti there—and take some time off from the chores for a picnic in the foothills, he does do that—climbs up maybe a hundred and thirty, hundred and forty feet. Like a boy again—trees, cliffs—back then he'd try anyplace that looked impossible. But he'll feel foolish afterward. Wonder why he did it.)

It's stupid for a man his age to have such thoughts, or maybe it's because of his age, but then what has he ever done to impress her? But get himself beat up? And throw up. She wouldn't leave. Not exactly the way he would have chosen for them to have their first embrace—that she would be holding his forehead.

And he's never especially tried to be nice to Lotti, yet Lotti likes him. Or did. God knows how she feels now. But in the beginning she stared at him as if he were completely alien, which is exactly how he feels himself to be. Alien to both of them. Hairy gorilla among the teacups—though they only have but two nice teacups.

And Oriana had liked him right off. It seems such an unlikely thing for her to do. He's not good at any of the things he thinks she might admire. He can't even talk straight—in English *or* French. Sometimes it's as if in front of him, she pretends she's not such an educated person, but it comes out. She has more books than he's ever seen in one place except a library, and how often has he been in a library? She plays Bach on the organ. Even Lotti plays Bach. He's heard of Bach. Just barely. Lotti, six years old, already knows more than he does.

But then Henriette is an educated person, too, a lot more than T-Bone, yet she does love T-Bone. And she always has been just a little bit in love with him, too. She even says so. Though she makes a joke out of it, he knows it's partly true. And it's all right because she's happy with T-Bone, and she knows she has the dependable brother and the wealthy brother and the easy-to-live-with brother. She says that, too, but the way she says things, nobody ever gets angry. Best he shouldn't be trying to show off but trying to be easier to get along with, whatever that means. Till Henriette came along and started calling him Monsieur Agaçant, he hadn't thought much about it.

He does do heavy work out with the irrigation ditches, but it's not the kind you'd especially want to get watched doing. Nothing much to it in terms of skill or guts. Alternates dusty to muddy (muddy before he put the headgates in). Mrs. Cochran watched him some. Brought out dinner at noon though he kept telling her he'd just as soon do without. He's used to only two meals a day and prefers that. It was sometimes a long walk to where he worked, and he had Dormant and the plow out there scooping ditches. Now and again he moved to different spots and though you can see a long way across Mrs. Cochran's valley, she sometimes had trouble finding him. When she didn't come, he figured he'd got himself lost. It was easy to see she wanted to come and wanted to fatten him up. Brought vinegar and molasses lemonade and that newfangled peanut butter stuff. Sometimes fresh-baked pies to tempt him. He'd rather she didn't.

Anyway, better than climbing trees would be to pipe the water up to the overhang. Maybe put a pump right inside the cabin. But maybe first add a room. It's been hard with just one room and Lotti there, though that's not so unusual. Except for the fact that they're not married, and that's a big difference. But he and T-Bone grew up looking down on their parents from the loft, until their father closed it off. Wasn't so nice and warm up there for the boys after that, but it was their own fault. At least it was his and T-Bone's. The other boys were little.

Once upon a time, two oldest sisters, then himself, then T-Bone (though he wasn't called T-Bone back then), three younger boys, two parents, and a graveyard with only three dead babies—he, seven years younger than the biggest big sister, but the oldest boy. That seemed the hardest of all to be. Kind of like the king's son, heir to everything including trouble. Every chore not done, somehow not done by him. Every accident, because he wasn't watching. Every younger child in mischief, due to his goadings or his dares, though it wasn't—not ever—true. And he was just about the only one of them to ever get whipped.

"*En faire un vrai homme,*" they said, but why was he the only one that needed to be made a man? He supposed they thought they were making a "real woman" of Christianne by working her to death. He and that biggest big sister, the oldest of them all, had to stick together.

It was nice how T-Bone always hated when they thrashed him—always brought him something afterward. Sometimes he'd milk the cow and bring milk. Still warm. Sometimes just a drink of water. Once he gave him his rusty old pocketknife, one he'd found and that he cared about. Christianne did things like that for him, too. He never cried—not even once. At least that.

Poor Christianne. The whole family sick at the same time and Christianne nursing all of them. She got so tired, she told him, lots of times she didn't think she could stand it one minute longer, and yet she went on. Even so, as Maman lay dying, Maman was saying, "*Sauves mes garçons. Sauves mes p'tit gars,*" as if Christianne didn't count. And to Maman the girls didn't, except if they could save the boys. And then Papa, angry at Christianne for letting Maman die, as if it was Christianne's fault. Angry at her for everything. Angry that he was dying, though hard to tell if he drank himself to death or if it was "the fever" killed him. When Beal himself was sick, Christianne would put cloths across his forehead even after he didn't need it, just so she could come up into the loft and hide there—sit with him and rest a bit when she felt discouraged. Whatever was good in life, he learned from her.

How could Christianne die? He should have saved her. She had saved him two years before when everybody died except for the three of them: she, T-Bone, and himself. Back then, when he was sick, she'd promised she'd never leave him. He was as sick as he'd ever been, then or since; even so, it was one of the clearest memories he had of anything. He had such a high fever he felt exhilarated for a while. Saw a great white-domed city all along the ceiling of the loft: turrets and towers, in sunshine with thunder. There was a heaven after all, and he could see it and feel it and hear it. But then the city turned scary. The same city as before, except he was terrified. There was a hell, too, and it seemed it was exactly the same as heaven. He must have made a racket because Christianne came up, slapped his face to wake him—slapped him hard several times, and it felt good because it brought him back to what was real. Even with all the sickness and all the deaths, one after another, real was better. It was then that he told her not to leave him, and she said she never would. *"Je n'te quitterai jamais. Jamais, tu sais,"* but two years later, she did. (After that vision, and then even more so after Christianne died, he lost his religion. He'd prefer—if he could make himself believe in anything at all—to believe as the Paiutes do, in Coyote or in Great Clown. Now *there* was something it made sense to believe in, Great Clown in charge of the world.)

When she died (not of anything anybody knew about—even the doctor), he was the one in charge. He was the one to nurse her, to sit up all night, to do for her what she'd done for him and for all of them all at the same time. She died anyway, no matter that he tried. The day before, he recognized that look on her face and knew, and knew that she knew, too. Sometimes he wonders, what if he hadn't fallen asleep this time or that or the other? Maybe she'd still be alive. She'd promised him she'd never leave him, but maybe *he* was the one who hadn't helped her enough for her to be able to keep her promise.

The day after she died—that was the first time he got drunk, he and T-Bone. He hadn't wanted ever to be anything like his father. He'd been thinking that from the time he was three, but there he was—here he is. . . . They stayed drunk a long time, too, drunk and sick and drunk and sick and drunk and sick, until there wasn't anything left to drink, he, fifteen, T-Bone, thirteen. First thing after Christianne died, T-Bone ran off and hid. He knew where T-Bone was, but he would have liked to go hide, too, so he left him alone. Washed her. Not very well. Just her hands and face and feet. Didn't dare do more. Washing her feet seemed strange enough. Like he shouldn't be doing it. He dressed her in her best. Carefully so as not to see her body. Part of the time he had his eyes shut. He laid her out. When she died he didn't even wake T-Bone. Just sat. Hours and hours went by as if no time had passed at all. He can't remember T-Bone waking up, or how he'd told him, or *if* he'd told him. It was building the coffin that he remembered, and doing a good job of it, too. The best thing he ever built up to then. Dragging it to the porch. Putting her quilt in for her to lie on. Lifting her and laying her inside. T-Bone still not there to help, but he was glad he wasn't.

He'd thought to leave right after that. All by himself. Let T-Bone do the best he could with what was left to do—or not. But he had to be the big brother Christianne would have wanted him to be. She never shirked what had to be done, no matter how hard and no matter who yelled at her. Unjustly. *Always* unjustly. So, for her sake, he stayed, and he and T-Bone got drunk.

Christianne was more of a mother to him than his mother. She'd always seemed big to him, but looking back, he knew she was just a little girl, hardly a year older than Lotti when he was born. She teased him about how there was nothing she didn't know about him. About how she'd changed his diapers from the start. Boasted that when she was only seven, she had walked him up and down all night when he had colic. He knew nobody else in the family would have done that. Twenty-two when she died. Most likely she would have been married by then if she hadn't had him and T-Bone to look after. "We three," it was, for almost two years. They could run the farm by themselves. Everything was, more or less, all right. In lots of ways better than ever. There were times they talked and laughed and danced to their own pounding and stamping and whistling most all night, but they still got everything done the next day that needed to be done. We three. And then just two.

So he and T-Bone ran away west with nobody to leave behind. They came to this very same valley, roamed around in it, working at the soda-ash plant, logging, mining quicksilver and wolfram, and ended up cow-boying at Jacob's. At Jacob's they gave him his first shave. He must have been pretty fuzzy by then. Downy. Scared him and T-Bone half to death. They didn't know what was happening. (By then his brother was T-Bone, and by then they called him Bill.) Wrestled him down. They had to wres-tle T-Bone down, too. T-Bone was trying to rescue him from six or seven grown men. They tied him to a chair real tight and came at him with a straight razor. Of course after they came close with that razor, you bet he held still. It was one they'd all chipped in and bought just for him. He hasn't lost it yet. Later he got to T-Bone himself before anybody else did. Bought him his first razor. T-Bone was so worried about what some gang of men might take a notion to do to him, he sure as hell kept himself nice and smooth.

Later on, when he saw how good Jacob was to T-Bone and how much Jacob liked T-Bone and how T-Bone liked it there, he did what he'd been aching to do all along from the minute Christianne died. He left. By himself. Went crazy-wild by himself. Drank, whored, fought—simply in order to hit and (especially) be hit. He doesn't like to think about it.

When he finally came back, T-Bone was still there but with a place of his own and, pretty soon, a mail-order wife who turned out to be not pretty but fun and good and loving, and then children. T-Bone had done fine—more than fine—and he was proud to have him as a brother, but surviving was all he himself cared about, though maybe not even that. He'd done dangerous things on purpose, and sometimes gotten so drunk he thought he'd not wake up at all and hoped he wouldn't.

He hadn't told Oriana anything about having had a sister. About having lost his family and then lost Christianne. And Oriana had never told him anything about what had made her hate being touched by any man (except for him). (He didn't expect it when she took his helping hand right off.) Everybody made jokes. And made jokes about Lotti. Now he'll be in those jokes, too, no doubt. He knows the gist: Frenchie, frog who doesn't know how to hold a fork, and beautiful redhead; gorilla and—not deer, more deer mouse, though as to rodent teeth, that's more like him. Drifter who doesn't own one single thing, weds—yes, weds . . . It's a terrible idea, considering, but he will ask and she will say yes. Would have said it the day he walked in most likely.

But he won't be mentioning marriage for a while, though he worries she might worry that he doesn't want to. He's wondering when would be the right time to ask and the right place and how to say it. It has to be done properly. And maybe he should try to get a ring. One that would be a step or two up from a cigar band if he can manage it.

It wasn't hard to imagine what had happened to her—why she didn't have any relatives she ever spoke of or why nobody ever wrote to her.

Disgraced, that's what she was. Not so different from himself. (He wasn't disgraced exactly, but he was a disgrace.) When she'd hit him, right at that particular moment, he was sure of what had happened to her. He let her have her panic and then gentled her like he would a frightened horse. She'd said, "I can hit you, but I couldn't hit him," and he told her he was glad to be the one she could.

And he is actually happy, though he distrusts happiness. How often has he ever been happy for more than a couple of minutes? Happiness is for people like T-Bone. Maybe for Oriana, too, if he can make it so. Strange how she wants him as much as he wants her. She's like good-woman and bad-woman all rolled into one. Daytimes she's happy in a quiet way, but nighttimes she's as if gone loco—as if only *that* can take away the pain of what had happened. Sometimes she cries even as he's loving her. Says she never thought to ever be happy—never thought to ever know what love was all about.

She's happy even though Henriette keeps saying how difficult he is to get along with. Tells Oriana she's sorry for any woman who might end up as his wife. Says for Oriana to pay him no mind when he won't answer and pay him no mind when he won't eat. Says she shouldn't bother repairing his clothes, he'll look like a dirt farmer anyway, and "God forbid he should ever show himself inside a church." Well, Oriana doesn't go either. And she doesn't mind anything about him: that he's sweaty, comes home covered with dust, that he's too big for her cot, steals the blankets though he doesn't mean to, that he snores. . . .

Home! Indians say if you know where home is, you know everything you need to know.

Except for those few years just after he'd left T-Bone alone in California, he's always thought of himself as an excessively moral man, but now, just like that time when he went crazy, he doesn't give a damn what's right or wrong. And Oriana doesn't either. It's wrong with Lotti there all the time. There's no way she can not know about it, but they let themselves forget about her. Lotti knows that, too.

After the fight, Lotti didn't want to go to bed at all, and this went on and on for days. He would tuck her in and sing and talk for maybe half an hour, and she'd seem to be asleep, but the minute he'd leave her alcove, she'd pop out. They knew it wasn't just the fight—maybe not the fight at all. After they'd decided to let themselves be in love (he's still not sure just how that came about; it's all mixed up in his mind with the pain and the drinks that made him feel so warm and drowsy) they couldn't—well, they *didn't* keep their hands off each other. Lotti seemed to be everywhere, staring at them. They could understand her feeling left out, so they did everything they knew to do to include her, but she wouldn't let them. When they asked her to come sit with them and help peel potatoes or sit with them in front of the fireplace, she'd say, "I know you wish I wasn't even here at all," and there was some truth to that. She looked to be the same scared little animal she'd been when he'd first come and she would hide behind the bureau or pull the curtains to the alcove where she slept and then peek out at him.

—•—

He has been thinking that someday he'll ask Oriana to make love without him in his longhandles and her in her nightgown. Someday make love skin to skin. "Flesh of one flesh," as God or as nature intended. He hopes she won't be shocked if he asks her to. Neither had expected to have that

honeymoon, a gift from Jacob and Aunt Jenny, but they were to go on home by themselves for ten days without Lotti. That could be the time. Maybe even more than once. She'll likely say, "As Indians, as savages," but maybe she could put up with being a savage for a day or two. But if she doesn't want to, he won't push her.

———•———

He will build a dam during that honeymoon—a dam for no reason except to move stones for the pleasure of it—and he and Oriana will bathe naked in the pond it forms. To see her, in his pond! . . . The first time they do it, she will blush all the way down to and through her breasts. (She had blushed, too, back when she'd helped him tie up his broken rib. He had reached out and pressed her cheek into the hair on his chest. Done it mostly to save her from her own blush.)

———•———

That pond of his will become a favorite place for all the children, both his and T-Bone's. Trout will swim there.

otti writes: I have gone on with the first worst day of my life, which was the day they started kissing all the time. Now I go on to that other worst day, their wedding day. (There's a third worst day. That was when I set myself on fire—though in a way, that wasn't such a bad day as you might think. At least something happened, and I was very brave. I never made a sound. It is he who bears the scars of that day more than I do, or at least more visibly than I. I go all over goose bumps whenever I see those scars that are proof that he has, and willingly, suffered for my sake. I used to think things would come out all right in the long run because of what he did. I thought maybe he was just waiting for me to grow up and get bosoms. I knew they were important—but then Ma went and used hers on him. Now I know things won't turn out right, and I don't even want them to anymore.)

Their wedding day hurt worse than that fire.

No wedding bells will ever ring for me. I always knew that, and I don't want them to. When Ma married him, it was Grandpa—my so-called Grandpa Jacob's dinner bell they rang. When I was little I thought theirs wasn't a real marriage because of that and of not being in a church and because they had a lawyer marry them instead of a preacher, but I guess it really doesn't matter. It has lasted all this time, as if it's to go on and on and on till, as they must have said to each other, though I wasn't there—on purpose I wasn't there to hear it—death do them part.

I couldn't stop the wedding, but I could at least slow it down. I was only six, otherwise I'll bet I could have really stopped it. First I tried my saddest wails. Of course I'd already tried that lots of times before and nothing much had happened, except they did try to please me in all sorts of other ways but I refused to be pleased. I had also already tried being strong and silent and like an Indian about it, but they didn't even notice. Now I screamed and screamed. I hadn't done that before, but I was desperate. I knew the wedding was really happening. I didn't believe in it until I was right in the middle of it—not until Old Snaggleteeth was standing there next to Uncle T-Bone looking just about as raggedy as usual, and my so-called mother was walking up to him holding my so-called Grandpa Jacob's elbow. I started screaming when I saw that. I fell down, rolled in the dust. I knew I was acting like a baby, but I didn't care. In fact I got the idea from seeing one of the little ones who were there turn all red and have a tantrum and then turn blue. I was hoping to turn blue, too, but I don't think I did. Finally Uncle T-Bone lassoed me! In front of everybody! (I used to kind of like being lassoed by those men at Grandpa Jacob's. Some of the younger ones did it all the time, except when they were lassoing mullein or each other. But now, after what Uncle T-Bone did, I can't stand to have somebody do that.) Uncle Bone took me all the way up to the headgates. Everybody was saying, "What on earth ails that child?" Some of the old ladies said I was "possessed." Ma didn't say it. She doesn't believe in being possessed. I guess I should be grateful for that.

Probably Uncle T-Bone is the closest to a real relative Ma or I will ever have, but I have no real relatives and thank goodness for that. I mean thank goodness none of *these* people are relatives of mine. Uncle Walt, Uncle Tom—all those men who work for Grandpa Jacob. I just call them uncle. And Grandpa Jacob—all he is is the old man that hired Ma to clean and cook. He did ask Ma to marry him. I don't know what I'd be calling him if that had come about. He wanted to give us a home and a name, and he really does like Ma. I think he really loves her. He always likes to come visiting for no reason. Ma told me about him asking her to marry him when I was maybe only four years old. Back then she didn't have anybody to talk to but me. She still does that now and then—tells me all sorts of things she probably shouldn't, but not like she's talking to me at all. I think she's lonely sometimes even now. I hardly ever bother listening, though every now and then I hear things I do need to know about.

My so-called ma has no real relatives either. All I've been able to find out is that she ran away from someplace in New England. (She never talks about the things I want to know. Why would *she* run away from it and yet want *me* to go back there to school? And since when was I ever a decent student? Well, I know why and they probably can't wait for me to be gone.) Ma started in some fancy school but never finished. But I don't know why I should care about her life. She isn't even my real mother. We look so different she shouldn't try to pretend I'm hers. Sometimes I think there must be Indian blood in me. I would like that but Ma wouldn't. Ma might not know anything about it. I don't know where or how she got me. Not in the East, that's for sure. A while back I thought there was Indian blood in him, too. The French are like that. They marry Indians and don't even care, but dark as he is, I realize now he's much too hairy all over for that.

Uncle T-Bone told me, while we were up by the headgates, that someday I'd be sorry for what I was doing, but I haven't been sorry yet. In fact I wish I'd done more. If only I'd been as old as I am now, or maybe if I'd thought to set myself on fire *then* instead of later, I could have completely stopped the wedding.

They had all been saying, and for a long time now, that that "Mrs." Cochran ought to pick out a man from those who wanted to marry her and become an acceptable "lady," though, of course, they hadn't exactly meant that particular Ledoyt brother. And they had all been saying, for an even longer time, that T-Bone Ledoyt's tramp of a brother was too old to go on living as he was and should settle down. Everybody was glad that both these things were finally happening. Those two were liked, even though one was suspected of being a fallen woman and the other was a vagrant. Just about every fancy-free man around had courted her some, and everyone was glad to see him when he turned up for spring work, and here they were, finally going to be respectable. (He was younger than he looked and she was older than she looked, so it wasn't such a May-September match as, at first glance, it seemed.) But some did wonder where her brains had got to. Wasn't she stooping just a mite too low? There were plenty of decent Scotsmen among the men who wanted her. Better she should have picked most any one of them than some French trapper's grandson. Except it was easy to see she loved him—to distraction, by the looks. Exactly the most dangerous kind of love. She'd be sorry when she found out all the book learning he didn't know anything about. Some tried to tell her right then and there, but her eyes just glazed over right away. Perhaps she had been taken in by the fact that he spoke two languages fluently (though both in a countrified way) or simply by the fact that he was kind, which, they thought, wasn't anything to base a marriage on, especially not for somebody like Mrs. Cochran.

Everybody wanted to have a big party. Jacob wanted to give the wedding at his place, and T-Bone and Henriette wanted to help with it. Others, who'd tried to help Ledoyt over the years, thought if they did something for his bride-to-be he couldn't very well object to that. People would come from miles around.

—•—

Though they'd already been lovers for a month and though he knew it was time for him to settle down, on the morning of the wedding Beal turned pale and threw up. T-Bone was tying his string tie for him when Beal jerked his collar loose again ("*Qu'as tu donc?* You're white as a sheet") and ran outside. T-Bone, right behind him, stayed back until he'd finished. Afterward they sat behind the house, Beal on a stump and T-Bone on an upside-down bucket.

"*Mon ami . . . Mon bon ami . . .* You don't have to, *tu sais.* You can take my horse and hightail it out of here. I don't want you to, Lord knows, but you should go if you must. *J'arrangerai les choses pour toi.*"

"*Je reste.* I want to."

"Well, I know you do, but I don't know if you want to be *married* and I don't know if you *ought* to be married."

"I want to."

"It's your last chance to go."

"I'm staying."

"Wait here. I'll get you a stiff drink."

"Not too stiff. You know me."

T-Bone wiped the sweat from his brother's forehead and straightened him out a bit. Retied his tie. "*Voilà, pauv' gars.* This is about as good as I can do with what's at hand. If she wanted looks, she should be marrying the snubbing post instead."

"*Je sais. Je sais.*"

———•———

Said: "I, Béàl, take thee, Oriana, forsaking all others, for poorer and in sickness and injuries, for the work and the heat and the dust and the loneliness . . ." And he'll often not be there. Hire himself out for haying, branding, castrating, ear notching. He's fast. They do a hundred a day. Afterward they fry or roast some of those piles and piles of "oysters" over the branding fire, telling jokes that women wouldn't like to hear.

> Wash the oysters. Take off all the extraneous membrane. Cut the gland part-way through. (The outer membrane shrinks and the oyster will open as it cooks.) Dredge with flour and fry in bacon grease.

Balls! Back in those days they knew what it meant to have them or not to have them.

—·—

Or he'll be gone on his once-a-month drunk.

—·—

Said: "With all that I have and all that I am, I do endow thee," thinking, Endow thee with nothing. Thinking, at his age he ought to have done something, learned something, have at least a little something to give.

—·—

Told T-Bone: "I won't take any of Oriana's land. That will all stay in her name and in Lotti's." And T-Bone said, "I wish you'd stop making rules for yourself." But he never did take any of Oriana's land.

—·—

The soft, sexy velvet of a horse's nose reminds him of her.

—·—

At the party afterward he ate nothing—except for that one bite of wedding cake *she* fed him—but he danced a lot. Everybody except T-Bone was surprised. After hearing his monotone mumbling, which he seemed to think was singing, and seeing him limp, they'd not expected him to be so adept at dancing. Those who thought they knew him well had shouted, "Look out, everybody, Ledoyt is going to try a waltz," but after they saw him dance they wondered how and where and what other women had taught him. Mrs. Cochran didn't wonder. She had a past herself. After what she'd been through, she couldn't believe her luck.

—·—

So somehow, and even though he'd never really asked her to marry him, the wedding had taken place.

Dancing: The fashionable promiscuous ball, protracted far into the night, or even till the dawn of morning, in a heated atmosphere, and to the sound of voluptuous music, is injurious to both health and morals. It merits all the condemnation it has ever received.

It seems impossible to exclude from these gatherings men who are unchaste in thought and impure in life. And how can we consent to have our virtuous sisters or daughters subjected to the delicate and skillful manipulation of those whose touch, whose very look even, is charged with a magnetic influence that excites unhallowed desires?

As a means of physical culture, it favors the development of the muscular system, and is promotive of health and cheerfulness. When practiced for this purpose it is the best indoor exercise.

The People's Common Sense Medical Adviser
R. V. Pierce, 1883

They danced till dawn: waltzes, jigs, reels, square dances, line dances, round dances, polkas—all four and five times over—and Beal and T-Bone had danced some fast-footwork Frenchmen's dances they'd learned when they were boys, and then Beal danced with a beer mug, full to the brim, as his partner, and Oriana thought, Do I really know anything at all about this man? Lotti laughed like a maniac, and when he stopped, she kept yelling, "Do it again. Do it again." She had been red-faced and wild and always in the way, but she'd seemed happy—too happy. Oriana suspected she'd been at the beer, but she wasn't going to say a word. She didn't even want to think about Lotti. Someone else could deal with her.

(Two fiddles, one fife, one mandolin. For Oriana's sake, Jacob had got together a fancier wedding than the usual.)

It was light enough for them to blow out the lamps. Lotti was asleep and Oriana thought, Thank goodness. Some people were dancing still and with as much vigor as if it was the first dance. Oriana went off for a moment, and when she came back, Beal was dancing slowly by himself. She knew he was very drunk, which wasn't surprising since he hadn't eaten all day and part of the night, too. (There was plenty of homemade beer around, though people—Oriana, too—were advocating temperance.) She watched him from across the room: her beautiful, ugly, scarecrow man, still as raggedy as ever, though she'd done her best at patching up his clothes. His black pants were almost white in spots. You could see all the things that were usually in his pockets outlined whether they were there or not: the pocketknife with hoof pick, the tally book he always carried, though there with her, he didn't have any stock or any fences to keep track of. She wondered what he used it for. Perhaps he wrote down ditch and gate problems. She saw even "that" that she had no words for, outlined in the lighter, faded black. For just a moment Oriana thought, Mine—*all* of him mine, but she hushed her own thought right away. It wasn't seemly.

By that time in the morning Mr. Ledoyt looked even more disreputable than usual, since he was a man who looked as if he needed a shave almost right after he'd done it. Her parents would be shocked just looking at him, though they'd probably never have to do that. They'd dislike him as fast as she had liked him. She wondered how he'd be all slicked up. Probably pretty much the same, even with a decent haircut—still and always a farmer sort of man.

He wasn't exactly dancing. He was turning in circles with his eyes shut, arms half raised as if waiting for her to come back into them and dance again, and she did. He kissed her a drunken kiss in front of everybody. Not the sort of kiss as when they'd been pronounced man and wife (almost a whole day ago by now), though that time, too, they'd gotten plenty of catcalls. But his kiss was the kind you shouldn't do in public—or so she'd always thought (sometimes she even worried about what was right to do in private, except she did trust Mr. Ledoyt to know)—and at the same time that they were dancing much closer than they should have been. The musicians changed the music to something slow and sentimental, and everybody yelled and whooped and clapped. Oriana felt herself blushing even as he kissed her. She wasn't sure whether she ought to be embarrassed or not, but she was proud that he wouldn't stop. Then they sent them upstairs to the privacy of Jacob's bedroom, "before," they said, "something happens right here and now that shouldn't," and that made

Oriana blush all the more. All Jacob's young hands seemed drunker than they should have been, to be saying such things with ladies present.

At first Beal wouldn't let go of her so they could leave—Oriana kind of liked that, too—but he finally did, and she and Tibo helped him upstairs to his room and put him to bed. Tibo undressed him down to his long underwear and tucked him in.

"*J'ai tout gâté,*" Beal said.

"*Mais non,* you haven't spoiled anything. Look at her. *Elle est complètement folle.* For you. Beal! *Voyons.*" But he had curled up and covered his face. "*Béàl? Allez, vas, pauv' 'ti' bonhomme,* go ahead and cry. It'll do you good."

—•—

The others bedded down on the floors—girls and women and babies in the house, boys and men in the barn. Ledoyt was so drunk they might as well have slept dormitory style, out with everybody else, though Oriana was glad to be alone with him so she could hold him as he cried and listen to his drunken monologue by herself. It would be years before she would hear him like that again—that crazy mix-up of drunken French and English. He said, "Orianà," in a way that made it sound like a French name. He said, "*Ne me quittes pas, ne me quittes pas,*" over and over, and "*J'en mourrai.*" She wasn't sure if she understood or not: *amour, mourir*—they sound so much alike.

—•—

They all slept only four or five hours and then had a big going-away breakfast party with biscuits and gravy and pancakes and bacon and eggs, and after that those two went home loaded with cold chicken, a side of bacon, jars of pickled beets with hard-boiled eggs in with them, jars of sauerkraut, and a chunk of wedding cake. . . . The others went back to dancing.

Of course there was Lotti to be dealt with. Before they left, Beal spent half an hour with her until T-Bone said, "*Mais ça n'en fini pas,*" and he and Jacob and one of Jacob's cowboys pried her off Beal finger by finger and held on to her until they left. She made a show of running after them, but they were way too far by then. She sat out in the sun by herself for a while, shaded a bit by sagebrush, and then came dragging back an hour later.

Lotti writes: It took three of them—Uncle Walt, Uncle T-Bone, and Grandpa Jacob—to pull me off him when he and Ma tried to leave the morning after the wedding and after the big party, which wasn't even over when they left. He talked to me alone for a long time, but I didn't hear one single word he said. I had by then pulled his shirttail completely out. I tore his clothes. I remember to this very day how he was all askew when he walked back to my so-called mother. At the last minute he gave me his wedding string tie. (It was all he had on that was different from what he usually wore.) Then he gave me his special pocketknife that had a hoof pick in it. I suppose these were the only things he had handy. I threw them in the dust. I stamped on them. I did like that hoof pick a lot. It was one of my favorite things. Even as I threw it away, I knew I'd come back and try to find it, but Uncle T-Bone picked it up and gave it to me later.

They went off to have their honeymoon alone at home—without me. They had to get back to the cows and chickens. (Somebody else watched over them for the time they were gone.) I had to stay behind at Grandpa Jacob's. If I had to be someplace not with them, I'd rather be at Grandpa Jacob's than with all those children speaking French. Besides, I knew Grandpa and some of his men from before.

I remember Ma hanging on to his arm with both hands as they drove off, and I remember the clucking of the chickens and the mooing of the cows—beef cows this time—that were their wedding presents. You could hear the mooing and clucking a long ways off even after you couldn't see him and Ma anymore. I suppose—at least I hope—that they could hear me, too.

—•—

Everybody was saying that he would never have taken any of those beeves and chickens if they were just given to him and not to Ma, too. They said that if people started giving him things just for himself, he'd have run off for two years before they got to the second hen.

He saw her, his new wife, when he opened his eyes in the first pale predawn light. She was stirring at last night's campfire and making coffee the way he'd taught her, using his battered can and laying a willow wand across the top to keep it from boiling over. She was still in her shift—she'd slept in that—so all in white, though she'd not been in white yesterday when they were married.

This was a special spot. They thought of it as theirs, though people knew about it. Another creek flowing down, as they all did, east out of the mountains, each rimmed with trees, making a thin green stripe across the desert. Willows, aspen, cottonwoods . . . There was another creek south of this one at Jacob's, and another north at Oriana's cabin. Here there was a half-cave hollowed out by wind and water. A week or two before, they'd made themselves a bed of fir boughs there, dried out now but still a good bed. Somebody else had slept there since and scratched THANKS on the rock wall. Beal had bought Oriana a small derringer, and because of that THANKS, he put it under his rolled-up jacket and shirt that he used as a pillow. The horse and chickens would have given them first warning if any person or thing came near.

And it had been the chickens in their crates on the wagon that woke him up. Watching her at the fire, everything inside him seemed to turn upside down. It was as if *now* was the real wedding. Yesterday he'd been numb, dazed—*drunk,* actually. He should admit it. But now, here among the aspen, with the sound of the stream, the coming of the dawn, like a ceremony, tingeing everything the color of Oriana's freckles . . . Sometimes all this had seemed so wrong—for both of them, but especially for her—but, at least at this moment, it looked like the right thing to have done. It was as if the dawn was saying—well, that it *was* dawn and things begin. And he did love her, though maybe he never would manage to say it. He found it hard enough calling her by her first name. "Oriana," like a secret intimacy between them. Easier to talk about love in French. In

French he was a different person. A little bit. Politer. Talkier. Odd how that was. Except he hadn't ever said he loved her in French either. Now he watched her, felt love, but when she brought the coffee, he shut his eyes and pretended to be still asleep, so she was the one, again she, who touched her lips to his mustache and said it. He pretended to wake up. Hoped his smile would show how he felt. If he kissed her, that would show more. If he made love, that would show even more. If he would say, "I can't tell you—I can't," she might say, "Be quiet. I already know." To speak would never be necessary. Perhaps later on, he could buy her something instead of saying anything.

—•—

The first thing he ever bought for her was glycerin and rose water because good as it was, he thought she shouldn't have to use the cow's "Bag Balm" on her poor raw red hands.

Lotti writes: I really did have a good time at Grandpa Jacob's, though I pretended not to. I complained all the time and cried when anyone important was looking at me. There was an old lady there who helped Grandpa out. He'd lost his wife a long time ago, and this old lady had recently lost her husband. She did the cooking and cleaning up. Ma did that for Grandpa Jacob and his men before that old lady came. Grandpa hated for Ma to leave, but he liked her so much he helped her get her land anyway. Grandpa's men built our cabin. My first memories are of us there at Grandpa's.

Everybody called that old lady Aunt Jenny. I spent most of those ten days in the kitchen with her. She was the one who started me out making all those things for Old You-Know-Who. I knew it was just to keep me busy and out of her way while she worked (I was used to that with Ma), but I liked making those things anyway. I asked her if she thought he still liked me at all, even a tiny little bit, since I'd made such a big fuss and since I'd torn up his only decent shirt. Except it was old and worn out anyway.

She said, "Who?" like she wanted me to say Pa or at least *something*. But I just said, *"Him!"*

She said, "Of course he does, but making things can't hurt." And she said, what was his favorite dessert? "You know," she said, "what they say about the way to a man's heart."

I really did start to think, for a little while when I was there at Grandpa's and didn't have to watch them be in love with each other all the time—I really did think that maybe pretty soon, after he got to know Ma better, for sure he'd like me best.

We made all sorts of things I knew he didn't have, and anyway, he didn't have much of anything. We made inside-out sheepskin slippers. We made a bootjack and lined the V of it with leather, though his boots were in such bad shape they hardly warranted the trouble. Aunt Jenny taught me how to make gingerbread. That was one of his favorites. Except he's the kind of person who likes most everything. Though there are other times when all of a sudden, he doesn't like anything. That drives Ma crazy.

Aunt Jenny talked all the time, but it was fun talk. Not like some people. She said, back in the olden days, men would ride fifty miles just to come and look at her, and she wasn't even pretty like, she said, my ma is. They'd sit and stare and stare, not having seen a white woman for months, maybe years. Once a man came a hundred miles. All he did was stare for two days and then rode back to where he came from. At first it bothered her so that she could hardly do her chores. And she worried because she didn't know what those men would end up doing. But nothing happened except just once. She wouldn't tell me what. She said she hadn't ever told anybody and she wasn't going to start with me, and anyway I was too young. She didn't know I already knew everything by then, though I did want to know what she wasn't telling me just in case there was something I'd left out.

It was Aunt Jenny who told me to stop drawing pictures of houses burning down, so I switched to runaway horses instead. Their manes and tails flew up and trailed out like flames. After, I'd throw the pictures in the fireplace or the stove and watch them burn up.

They'd hardly been married three months before Beal was off working for Tibo—or so Oriana thought, but Henriette came trotting over with Beal's change of clothes and his bedroll and told her he was gone and had been for a week. Work had slackened off and suddenly he wasn't there. She and Tibo thought maybe he'd gone home, but then they heard he wasn't here either.

Oriana didn't want Henriette knowing that Beal would do such a thing so soon after their wedding, and she didn't like Henriette knowing about it before she did. Except, of course, Henriette knew, much better than she, that he'd always been this way. She'd even warned her. She probably even knew that one of these days he'd leave her for good.

"I wish you'd told me right away."

"We didn't want you to worry yourself, and we hoped he would have appeared by now."

Even though Henriette had ridden half the day and fast, trotting most of the way, she still looked as cool and collected as she always did. That upset Oriana all the more. She had only been doing the usual things around the house and not even the laundry, and she knew she looked hotter and more harassed than Henriette would probably ever look.

"Maybe he'll never . . ." Oriana couldn't say it.

"He always does."

"Five years from now, maybe."

"He loves you. *Tu le sais bien.*"

"Why doesn't he ever say so, then?" She was saying all the exact things she didn't want Henriette to know about.

"I knew he was in love with you the minute I saw you two together. I never saw anybody hovering so much. It's a wonder you could breathe at all."

She knew Henriette was trying to make her feel better, but she felt upset even about that.

"Maybe not hard for you to see."

"Oriana, don't. You'll be as irritating as he is if you don't be on guard. Beal is just being Beal. You know that. And it's not other women. T-Bone says he's not cared about *les filles* since he was a crazy boy. And it's not necessarily drinking, either. He just goes off."

Then the tears came in spite of herself. Henriette hugged her, called her *"ma soeur."*

"Henriette, I said to myself a thousand times before I married him, and a thousand times after, too, that I'd be grateful for every little bit he could manage to give. Maybe this is all there is."

"*Pauvre petite.* I guarantee it's not."

"I . . . *we're* . . . having a baby."

"He told me."

So Henriette knew everything. She always did. "*I* wanted to be the one to tell you."

"Please. Oriana. It's going to be all right, and I'm staying here with you until he comes back, and it won't be for any all of five whole years."

—•—

He came walking in three days later, bringing a gift: an ungainly silver pin of an owl, wings spread, in its claws some prey or other, maybe fish, maybe snake. It was ugly. He had no taste whatsoever. (But she already knew that.) And it was brutal—like his life was sometimes, castrating all sorts of things, notching ears. She'd seen him use the end of his lariat as a whip, dragging it behind him as he rode and then snapping it forward on some poor beast's haunches. He was uncouth, too. She'd heard him cursing when he thought she wasn't around—words she'd never known existed. She'd seen him spit. She'd seen him squatting in the dust with a couple of Paiutes as if he was one of them. But she had known all this almost from the start, and he was—he really was—a polite and honorable man.

But just about anything at all would have been a better gift than this pin: cloth (she'd have liked that), flour, bacon, nails, leather—they needed *everything.* And he didn't have one bit of money left on him, not even a penny. Did he think this atrocious pin made everything all right?

Henriette handed him a basin of warm water and pushed him into their brand-new bedroom. (It still smelled so sweetly of fresh-cut pine and cedar. Oriana hadn't slept—together with Beal—in that new room more than a few days before he'd gone off to work at Tibo's, and all this time he wasn't even there and she hadn't known it.) Henriette told him he smelled like a stable. She said, "Throw out your clothes, but the next time you live in them for near a month, get somebody else to wash them for you before you come home, because Oriana isn't going to do it." Oriana wouldn't even have thought such a thing, let alone said it if she had.

After the door to the bedroom was shut and they could hear him washing in there, Henriette looked at the pin and said, "This is awful." The truth again, which nobody but Henriette would say. "This is even worse than anything T-Bone ever got for me." She started to laugh.

Oriana felt better about things right away.

"Well, he's trying, poor old thing," Henriette said. "I suppose he's doing the best he can."

"Poor old thing"—Oriana was beginning to understand what they meant by that.

—•—

Later he will give her a pincushion shaped like a little shoe—a silver shoe with red velvet inside it for the pins. Henriette will say it looks like a whore's shoe, even though Henriette has a pair of shoes for dress-up a little bit like that herself. She calls them her San Francisco shoes, though she got them from Monkey Ward's. Without Henriette, Oriana would hardly know how to deal with these gifts.

—•—

She first heard "Poor old Bill" when Jacob and Tibo were visiting her. That was before she'd even met Beal. That's how it all got started. It was unusual for both Jacob and Tibo to be at her place at the same time. What if Tibo hadn't come bringing hay? And what if Jacob hadn't come to buy eggs and butter? And what if they hadn't stayed for noon dinner?

Jacob had said something like "What about poor old Bill? Is he still runnin' off before he gets paid? I probably owe him from a couple of years back."

Tibo said, "When he decides to go, he goes, paid or not." And that had piqued her interest.

Jacob said, "Isn't it about the season for him to be wandering in? He'd be a good one to come help out Mrs. Cochran here."

She remembered Tibo had perked up at that. She thought he must have started thinking about his brother getting married to her right then and there.

But it hadn't been Tibo's doing. Or anybody else's.

Lotti writes: He's not really what you'd call a hard-drinking man, even though he got drunk on their wedding day. I think it happened by mistake. It doesn't take much. He can't even hold his liquor as well as I can. I sneaked quite a bit of beer at the wedding. Nobody noticed. I *needed* it. It made things seem a lot better—for a little while. I've stolen from his bottle every now and then, and not so long ago either.

By now everybody knows exactly what Old Saddle Face is going to do and that he'll be gone for a day or two and come back sick. He walks off with his greasy old saddlebags over his shoulder just the way he walked in on us that first time. Walks, even now that we have horses. I don't know why. Nobody ever asks. Especially not Ma. She kind of tiptoes around him all the time, and she always says, "Don't bother your father with things like that." ("Your father," she calls him! To *me!*) Maybe he walks because he likes to think back to when he was, as he himself says, *un vau-rien,* and could just wander around and didn't have Ma and me and Fayette and the little ones to look after. I feel exactly the same way—all these people around all the time. . . .

In the saddlebags he carries his rotgut and some coffee and a tin can to make the coffee in and drink it from. He won't take food. Ma wants him to, but she doesn't dare mention anything about it or slip something in secretly. Everybody knows what he's going to do, but nobody admits they know. Even Gabby and Briant know. I don't know how we all know.

Ma doesn't like that those saddlebags are always hanging in the cow barn in plain sight, ready for him to take off. She mutters things to me. If Aunt Henriette were around more, Ma would talk to her instead. They get along fine, even though Ma keeps saying, "I can't believe she said that." But she likes it. It's as if Aunt Henriette says what everybody else wishes they had the gall to say.

Even after all these years Ma worries every single time he goes off—

that he'll not come back at all, on purpose, or that he'll be too sick to come back, or that he'll get himself lost out there. A man like him could never be lost. He can go without sleep or food. He can throw cows down by their tails like the Mexicans do. He could walk around on a broken leg if he had to. He almost already did. He broke his toes and wouldn't take his boot off for a week till he'd finished what he had to do, in case they swelled up and he wouldn't be able to get his boot back on. Ma kept saying, "Isn't that just like him!" in an exasperated way. It *is* just like him. When Christy died he was as if made of iron. I didn't even dare talk to him, he was so strong. I don't believe I said a single word to him that whole time—not until he came back from being gone a couple of months. Ma was like she didn't know what was going on.

I didn't dare track after him that time, and anyway, he left in the middle of the night. Even when I was only six I could follow him so quietly he never knew. After he made me my bow and arrows, I took them along. I shot at him a couple of times. He knew I didn't really want to hit him. He knew if I'd wanted to, I could have, but he told me never to do that to anybody even if I meant to miss. I did it again anyway. I *think* he got mad, though it's always hard to tell. That was the one and only time he slapped my bottom. Hard, too, but it didn't hurt. I told him that. First I ran, but he caught me in no time. He can move pretty fast for a man who limps.

I tracked him that very first time he went off to get drunk. That was even before he and Ma got married. He didn't go as far as he always goes now. It didn't take very long before he was looking like that time he got beat up, lying as if thrown away. He didn't come home that night, though he was only about a half hour's walk away. I could have told Ma where he was, but I thought I'd let her worry. She kept going out to the little hill behind our cabin and looking off all around. And then she took Dormant and went for a big circling ride until it was dark. Horses can see in the dark, and they know their way home. She could have stayed out a lot longer, but she didn't know things like that then. I did, though. She cried when she came back. She tried to hide it, but I could tell. That was the first time he was away all night. I know she thought he was gone for good. She always thinks that—though I have to admit, now and then it does seem like that, even to me.

When he comes back after those drinking bouts, he always looks terrible. I don't know how a person as tanned and leathery can manage to look so green.

He never says a single word about it when he comes back. Neither does Ma. It's like they pretend it didn't happen. She gets very busy after those times and pretty quiet, and looks like she'd rather not think about it.

He is everything her parents despise and had taught her to despise. For a while their lessons had taken, and she'd thought herself better than all the good people who had helped her. Not only because of her background and education but because she came from the East, and not just any East but New England, where Hawthorne and Thoreau and Emerson had lived and where they founded the Unitarian Church. She was proud of having been a member. She had thought of herself as—at least compared to most people—an intellectual. Her father kept saying they were in the top 2 percent and that she had an obligation to marry properly and bring up educated children. She was an only child. Her father had expected her to equip herself to become a proper mother of lawyers and judges.

So she had thought herself as better than Jacob even after all he'd done, and better than his sister Hazel, who had done the most for her, back when she had nobody—back when she was frightened and practically starving. Thank goodness Hazel's was one of the first places she'd looked for work when she got to Cincinnati. She'd helped in Hazel's boardinghouse and given piano lessons on the side to some of the ladies who stayed there. That was lucky, too—that there was a piano and people who wanted lessons. And it was lucky that there were no men. She needed women. And they were all good to her, but especially Hazel. When she'd gotten big and awkward, Hazel would have her lie down in the afternoons and not do any heavy work like making beds. What difference did it make that Hazel had never even finished eighth grade? They could talk, too, and like Beal, Hazel had guessed it all and had accepted her, even sullied as she was. Hazel was one of the smartest people she ever met. Wise is a better word: fat and tall and ugly and wise and good. It was Hazel who had gotten her the job here in California with her brother Jacob. Hazel told her to go on out where nobody knew how Lotti had come to be and told her Jacob would never ask, and he never had. Nor had Beal. It was

Hazel who had taught her to cook for a dozen people so she could handle the job at Jacob's ranch.

But especially, how could she have kept on being such a snob after what that Shakespeare-spouting, cello-playing (all those sonnets! all those sonatinas!)—what that lawyer had done to her? She didn't even want to think about Shakespeare anymore except maybe for Lotti's sake (and except for those lines that seemed to be about how she saw Beal: "What eyes hath Love put in my head, Which have no correspondence with true sight!"). At least that man had left her Bach and Longfellow.

Her father (like everyone, she thought of him as "the judge," even as she called him Father)—he would have put her out of the house for good if she hadn't run away before he had the chance. No, no, she had run away because she knew he had the power to force her to marry that man who was his friend. He could argue anybody into or out of anything, especially her. He would have made her see the "logic" of it.

She had never been in love with that man—not ever—but she had trusted him, and sometimes she had thought herself lucky to have such a tall, good-looking lawyer as a fiancé. Everybody had said so. Behind her back they were probably saying, "It's about time." (She was twenty-five.) He was very like her father and seemed such a proper, straightlaced man. She'd been surprised . . . shocked . . . People she knew didn't do this. That kind of thing was done by (she thought then) people like Hazel and Jacob and Beal—as ignorant of morals and manners as they were of letters and learning and arts and poetry. It was supposed to all go together, learning and morals—but here now, Mr. Ledoyt, as honorable and in some ways even as courtly as any man she'd ever met.

Even after all that had happened with that man and all the good things with Jacob and Hazel, only when Beal came did she really change her mind about what was worthwhile in a person. Here was a shabby failure of a man, yet so full of lore and skills and kindness and good humor. Life around him was fun almost no matter what happened.

Funny to think about that country wedding at Jacob's where she wore the best she had, which was none too good, and yet how happy she was. Beal, such an odd bundle of bones and angles . . . He'd never do what that man had done. When he'd wanted her naked in the pond, he'd asked so tentatively. Her mother had taught her how to dress and undress under her nightgown back when she was so little she could hardly dress herself to begin with, so she'd wondered if it was wrong to do it, but she was glad she had, and done it more than once that time when Lotti was at Jacob's. Naked—both of them. At first she hadn't thought that he was going to undress, too. She felt embarrassed all alone out there. The aspen that fringed the riverbank seemed full of black-on-white eyes. And then *his* eyes—he, a dark figure all in blacks and grays, barefoot on the shore . . . But then . . . and she should have known he wasn't the sort to leave her out there all by herself. . . . He never touched her, both of them out there naked. She was glad of that. That was the first time she'd ever seen a *completely* naked man.

So both of them there, and the sound of the river bubbling over the rocks of his dam, the wind in the aspen . . . She couldn't feel spoiled and soiled and ugly anymore—not right then anyway. If he loved her and loved her body, and if this breeze and if this cool mountain water, and if there was to be his baby (she suspected that, even then on their honeymoon), if all this, then she must have been made pure again.

She had needed for him to be . . . going all the way and that they not be married. He wasn't the sort of person to do that. It took persuading, but she wanted everything to be exactly the same as before and yet entirely different. She had to do it all over again and make it right this time. She needed to be taken but by somebody that she cared about and who cared about her. "Taken." That's what that other man had done and with kisses that were attacks. She would never ever, ever again have wanted to do . . . with that other man—even after they'd married. She had to run away.

It had happened in her own living room. How had it come to be that she'd been left alone with him? Even the maid must have gone. She can't remember. That man must have known. Could he have arranged it? Her parents trusted him. But what about her father? Where was he? How could he have let it happen? But maybe it was all her fault. Had she teased and tempted him and not even known it?

At first she'd been too confused and frightened to struggle. She'd tried to talk him out of it, but she had no words for what she wanted to say. Who would have thought she'd ever have to talk about things like that? For a while she couldn't believe it was really happening. Then she did try to fight him off. He was a big man. (Lotti got her tallness from him and her handsomeness. Handsome! What good is handsome?) He hadn't needed to hit her in order to hurt her. He never left a mark, but he had ways of twisting her arm and pressing her wrist and elbow, even her knee. (Trust a lawyer to know such things. Beal's hands, rough and scarred and callused, never hurt.) That man had liked her struggling. She could tell. She stopped. It wasn't doing any good anyway. He'd said, since he was about to be her husband, he had the right, and she should get used to that. He said it wasn't healthy for him to need her and not have her. She should know that about men. And did she want him to go to whores? Now? Just weeks before their wedding? He said it was her duty. He said, "Service" . . . like an animal. She supposed, if he'd known about Lotti, he'd have said she had "settled." Then, just when she thought it was finally over, he started again. His hands were everywhere. He had fondled—But that's not the word for it. He'd been careful not to tear her blouse.

Even in the middle of it she felt he had the right. He was an important man, and anyway, he was a man and men had rights. Her parents felt the same way. They'd be angry. At *her* most likely, not him. She couldn't tell them, anyway. Nobody talked about things like that. Besides, they wouldn't have believed her. She hadn't cried afterward. In fact she hadn't cried until Beal was there.

She had cleaned up the parlor, picking up things she'd knocked over trying to get away. Thank goodness there wasn't much blood, and it was mostly on her shift. Then she took a bath. Over the next couple of days she took bath after bath after bath, but it didn't help. His hands had been . . . everywhere. She itched all over. She was surprised when no rash popped out.

She wanted to change her face, her hair, her clothes. She wanted to wear only browns and grays. She wanted no friends or anyone who might see something in her eyes. She wanted no love and no pity—no thoughts of her at all by anybody. She wanted to be someplace far away where she could pretend it hadn't happened—where she could forget all about it. Never have to think of it again.

She didn't run away right at first. She could hardly think beyond the next bath. She had no money. But then she stole all she could find in the house: Mother's kitchen money, Father's hidden twenty-dollar gold pieces. She even stole from the maid, money and a skirt and shawl. She left her jewels and clothes up in the maid's attic room. She hoped her parents would let them stay as gifts from her. She took no luggage. Just a box with bread. She felt unworthy of cheese or butter or ham. Everything tasted like dry bread anyway. She couldn't swallow. She felt she needed neither sleep nor food.

She thought of Canada, but the next train went west. She had money for as far as Cincinnati.

———•———

And Beal *had* "taken" her exactly the way she wanted to be. Once or twice he had reached for her in the middle of the night, hurried, needy. It was over in a few minutes. She'd felt, for the first time, really his. She'd felt bad for him that he owned nothing and would take nothing and yet wanted to give things to her. Here it was her cabin, her little barn, her horse and wagon, her money put by (a little), her Jersey cows, her stream, her land—and he insisted that it all stay hers as though he might be gone someday. She knew better than to try to give him any of it. He would be offended. Might run away. But he had, a time or two, taken her as if she was his property. She liked that he felt he could do that. It was unlike him just to take, and he really hadn't. He'd said, "Please," and she'd said, "I love you."

———•———

That man never would have made a decent father. It's Beal who's a real father—was a father to Lotti almost from the first days, or as soon as Lotti would let him be one. She herself hadn't been a good mother, especially not at first, but not later either. She had given the baby her favorite name in hopes that would help, but it hadn't. Poor Lotti, scrawny, premature . . . She had hoped the ugly thing would die, and for a while at least, it looked as if it would. (Who'd have thought she'd grow up to be such a handsome child, striding around as if she was a boy or, more like it, limping a little as if she was Beal?) Lotti must have been seven or eight months old before Hazel had told Oriana she had to act like a real mother for Lotti's sake. Told her, "Then was then and now is now." (Hazel said that a lot. Mainly just to her.) And "it's not this baby's fault." Hazel said she should put out of her mind, once and for all, how Lotti came to be. (She thought she had, but when Beal first tried . . . , she knew she hadn't.)

Actually it's Beal who taught her how to be a good mother, and even now, and though she tries, he's still a better mother than she is, always willing to listen and take time, knows all sorts of games and songs and can invent new ones on the spot that turn chores into fun, and he's quick to praise and quick to thank—except there are those times when he drifts away from everybody.

—•—

For a Nursing Baby

Take one quart good flour; tie in a pudding bag tightly as to make a solid mass; put into pot of boiling water early in the morning and let boil until bedtime; take out and let dry. In the morning, peel off and throw away the thin rind of dough. With a nutmeg grater, grate down the hard dry mass into a powder. Of this, one to two teaspoonsfull may be used, by first rubbing it into a paste with a little milk, then adding a pint of milk and bringing it to a boiling point. Cool and give through a nursing bottle.

White House Cook Book
L. P. Miller and Co., Chicago, Philadelphia,
Stockton, Cal., 1887, 1889, 1909

Except the first time she told him she was pregnant, she couldn't tell for sure if he wanted to be a father or not. She had overslept and he had let her. She hadn't heard him get up. He'd left a cup of coffee and a glass of milk by the bed. The milk was still warm from the cow, so he'd done her milking. She couldn't face either the milk or the coffee. She threw out the coffee (she couldn't even stand the smell) and made tea. She felt queasy, and it wasn't the first time lately. She knew what was wrong, but she was afraid to tell him. Though he'd mostly stayed around so far, it might be the last straw.

She lay down again—she thought it was for just a moment—but then here he was, cheek to cheek with her. "What's wrong? Are you all right?"

"No. Yes. Of course." She was groggy with sleep. She could see the clock beyond him on the bedside table. (That table was just a wooden box she'd covered with blue and white muslin.) They'd forgotten to wind it. Yet again. They often forgot these days. (She never had until they started sleeping together.) For all she knew she'd slept the whole day away. It felt like it.

She said, "I have to tell you something, but don't be angry." His mustache tickled her neck. Lightly. He was doing it on purpose. (*Baisers de papillons.* Butterfly kisses. He'd learned that from his big sister. The real way was with eyelashes.) So was she going to tell him already? Saddle him with one more burden? Bind him with one more chain? But she needed to tell it and needed to know what he'd think about it.

"If I'm angry I'll bite your earlobe." His teeth were on it already.

"Please. It's not a joke."

She thought to say "we," but then she thought she'd better not. "I'm," she said, "*I'm* having a baby." She would take all the responsibility. She'd brought up a child by herself before. She didn't want to do it alone, but she could. This time it would be all right because she wanted this baby, and no matter where he might be off to, she was Mrs. Ledoyt.

He sat up slowly and looked toward the window. She couldn't read his face.

"You're upset. Aren't you."

"No. I have to think."

"What did you expect would happen?"

"I guess I always thought T-Bone would be the one to have children, not me. Besides, we only just got married."

"Yes, but . . . before . . . Being married isn't what does it."

At the very beginning, just three days after he'd come to them, he'd saved the calf they thought was born dead. He'd breathed into its nostril, and then when it turned out the calf was all right after all, he taught it how to nurse, talking to it the whole time. He'd called it *"Mon p'tit."* He said, "Go to," when it finally did nurse, and then he'd turned toward them, her and Lotti. (He'd been covered with mucus and worse—another thing she hardly had words for or at least any words she liked to think about. His hair was plastered to his forehead with slime.) He'd looked up at her suddenly, straight in the eyes, and something wonderful had passed between them. Perhaps that was the moment when she'd really fallen in love. He must want this baby. How could he not?

She said, "I want a little boy just like you."

"Poor thing. Besides, they've already got one pretty much like that over there at T-Bone's."

"I want you to be happy, too."

He said, "Move over," and lay down beside her. Said, "Be careful. Of yourself."

otti writes: They are still in love. It wears me out. There're still those secret half-winks and the raising of the eyebrows that you'd think were just twitches if you didn't know better. (Mostly he's the one that does those, not Ma so much.) Aunt Henriette, even after all these years, still calls them, *"les amoureux."* Sometimes after supper, I'll be doing the dishes, the children will be in bed, and Ma will go and sit on a footstool between his knees. They'll be facing the fireplace, whether there's a fire lit or not. She will lean back and he will lean forward and they will put their heads together. I watch but they don't know I do, and I see him touch her breast as if he owned it, even sometimes inside her dress.

But *I* think there's a lot less highfalutin stuff than love in it. *I* think they keep on being close because they were so old when they got married. They probably knew it was their last and only chance. I don't know of anybody else that got married so old. Ma was thirty-three and he was forty. You'd think they couldn't still have children. You'd think they wouldn't want to or want to do *that* anymore.

I think he had to stop wandering around sooner or later. He wasn't getting any younger (he says that himself), so why not stop here, only a day's ride from his brother's place and with a person some think is pretty, and with a person who already has a cabin and some land? Except he left all her land in Ma's and my name, and everything is on her land, all the oats and hay and the new house and the old cabin, too. I suppose they expect me to take care of the little ones if something happens, but I've had my fill of taking care of them already, so maybe I will and maybe I won't.

He's got land of his own now, but it's steep, raw land that the government said he'd not be able to graze cows on. He said they would graze there even though it's a 60 percent grade, and they did, so he knows more than the whole government.

But it's the little ones that die off, not Ma and Old Him. A brownish photo of one of the dead ones, in her coffin holding wild iris, is on the table next to Ma's side of the bed. It's in a silver frame he bought for her. The other dead one was born dead. I guess it's just as well they didn't have a chance to get a photograph of him.

Those two dead babies are buried over at Uncle T-Bone's and Aunt Henriette's next to their four dead ones. Ma says she doesn't believe in souls, but even so, she wanted those babies where they'd have company. She said she knew that didn't make sense, but she wanted it anyway. From other things she's said, I think she feels comforted that she's not the only person who ever lost a baby. *She's* the one who needs the company—of people who have gone through it. All six of those children had funny French names, even Ma's and his. There's Hypolite, Fleur, Adorée, Ulysse, and then ours, Didier and Christianne. No wonder they died. (Why does Ma let all her children's names be French? You'd think she wouldn't because French is not a good thing to be around here. Of course we can't get away from being Ledoyts now, even I can't, but do they have to rub it in?) Ma never goes over there to look at the graves. Lots of times she visits but not out to where the graves are. I think she's glad they're not close by us.

Both times those babies died, he made the coffins in the middle of the night right after it happened. That's how I knew they were dead—from the pounding and sawing sounds out in the tool and buggy barn.

Over at Uncle Bone's they haven't had a baby since the last ones died and that was five or six years ago. I wish he and Ma would stop, too. I can't imagine what they're thinking of. And at their age!

Fayette, their oldest, lives. That wiry little dark one has followed me around since he first could crawl. I hide. I fool him. I used to leap out—I still do—and scare him. Finally they forbade me playing peekaboo, but when they were out of sight I did it anyway. Then when he'd cry, I'd pretend I was comforting him. Of course after he could talk, that changed, though not as much as you'd think. I had ways of convincing him not to tell. For a while, when I said I'd eat him up, he really believed I would. I'd pretend to do it, my face on his stomach. I liked the damp, baby smell of him. I really did feel like eating him up.

When Fayette was born, Aunt Jenny came and stayed over for a while before and afterward. Old Saddle Face was gone, and I think he'd been gone a pretty long time helping out someplace. Fayette was born in the spring, so there was a lot of work to do all over. (We hardly had any beeves of our own back then, so ours were already up in the hills, and we didn't have hay of our own yet either.) He'd thought to get back in time.

Even more than Fayette being born, I remember when he came back a few days later. Afterward they told about how he rode all night and all day and all night to get here. Wore out three horses and even wore out Uncle T-Bone's mule that they said you couldn't wear out. Rode in to Uncle T-Bone's on a tired horse and took the mule and didn't say a hello to anybody—that's how they tell it—even though Uncle T-Bone was standing right beside him as he saddled up. Uncle T-Bone tried to get him to come in and eat something or at least have coffee.

It was hardly dawn when I heard that mule trot up. I heard him before anybody, but I didn't call out to tell Ma. I knew first thing he'd do would be to loosen the cinch no matter how much of a hurry he was in. Maybe even unsaddle. He always told me to do that no matter how tired I was, so there was plenty of time. But then Ma and Aunt Jenny heard him and Aunt Jenny ran out to stop him from coming in. I came out, too. Aunt Jenny told him he had to wash up first and that he should keep quiet, but he walked past her like she wasn't there. Almost knocked her down. He walked past me the same way. Practically stepped on me. (Lotti, the invisible. I've pretended to be that sometimes, but I don't like it when it seems to be true. Except I'm going to be really invisible pretty soon—at least invisible to them. And with Fayette gone, too, I guess they'll finally sit up and take notice.) Then Ma ran out, though she wasn't supposed to get up, and hugged him until she was as dusty and sweaty as he was. Her nightgown was a sight. And they didn't just forget about me, they even forgot about the baby, but not for long. I never did see a bigger fuss made over such a tiny, ugly, scrawny, wobbly thing that always had a stomachache. Nothing to him but a head of ragged black hair sticking out every which way.

We were still living in the old cabin then, but we had the new bedroom tacked on. Ma stayed in there with him pretty near a whole day and night while he slept and slept. She only came out to give the baby to Aunt Jenny sometimes. I hardly knew what to do all day long. He didn't even say hello to me until the next morning.

Now that baby is in my power. Eight years old and *still* in my power. I can make him giggle or I can make him cry, whichever I feel like. It's strange that he keeps on liking me in spite of what I've done—and still do.

Often he'll do exactly what I tell him to, even dumb things like when I told him to climb the juniper. (He was four, maybe five then.) I gave him a leg up to get him started. He got stuck. I knew he would. I was the one who went back and got Old You-Know-Who to come help. I wasn't going to be the one to climb up and help Fayette down, though I could have done it. I'm not like a girl. I'm not afraid of anything, especially not heights. I climbed that same tree when I was little. I got up even higher than Fayette did and came back down all by myself and never told anybody but Dormant. Though maybe I wasn't *quite* as little as Fayette was when I got him to do it. Who knows how long Fayette would have been up there if I hadn't gone to get help? But I waited until he got good and scared. I made him think maybe I wouldn't go for help at all. I told him he might have to stay up there all night. I could see he was going to cry. I told him he was nothing but a girl. That made him really cry, so I told him he was even *more* like a girl. I said the more he cried, the more he'd be a girl.

He didn't tell how it was me who got him to climb up in the first

by Lotti

place. He never tattles. I don't know how things would be if he did. Sometimes I think Fayette looks up to me about as much as anybody on this earth. It's as if he was born liking me, and nothing I do can make him change his mind.

Back then I kept telling him there wasn't one single thing he could do that I couldn't do better, and that's still true.

I call Fayette Horse Face like I used to call Old Him when he first came—to myself—but I call Fayette that to his face. He hates that. Sometimes Ma hears me. She gets about as angry at that as she does about anything.

Fayette was smaller than any baby he'd ever seen at T-Bone's, but Aunt Jenny said he was all right because he had his toenails. A woman-fact. He is left out of those secrets. He knows the same kinds of things about animals but not about people.

He had felt the baby moving inside her while they slept, his front to her back. When she was big, that was her favorite way. He would have one arm under her head and the other across her stomach. The first time he felt the baby, Oriana was asleep and stayed asleep. He didn't say anything. He was too dumbfounded. Didn't speak of it afterward either, he and whoever it was linked in a secret intimacy. Toward the end he often felt him moving. He could hardly bear it. What do people do? Everybody going on as if it was the most natural thing in the world. You'd think they'd all go crazy, but they seem to hardly notice. Or they hide it. That's what saves them, pretending it's ordinary. Oriana . . . Except it's part of her body. There was a contentment in her all through it. She slowed down. (She said she felt like a happy squash, and he'd said, "In French you'd feel like a cabbage.") But nothing is . . . *nothing* is ordinary . . . not the smallest leaf.

(Sometimes, his lips on her neck, he can feel her life's blood beating there, or with his head on her breast. After he got beat up, that's the way she held him, and he could feel her breathing and beating against his cheek.)

Once he'd tried to tell her how he felt. That was early on. Maybe their honeymoon. Tried to tell her it wasn't only the beating of her heart against his lips, but everything . . . everything beating and needing. Or not just need. Even as he was saying it he didn't know what he meant and especially why he had to promise so forcefully that it wasn't just this need.

She said she didn't understand a single thing he was talking about, but whatever it was, she liked him saying it. She probably thought he was trying to tell her he loved her. Perhaps he was. He had thought he might as well let her think it, but it was more than that.

When she got big, he had become shy with her. Or perhaps just more shy, though he was sure she never knew he felt that way. The bigger she got the shyer he felt. She was taken up by something he couldn't know. It was like the woman-secrets, but more than that. He tried to be in her life every day, doing as much of her work as he could and keeping Lotti busy. When he had to go off and leave her so near the end to do a job he couldn't afford not to do, having to leave made him shy, too. Closed him down some. Aunt Jenny came right on over, though it wasn't time yet.

He'd been shy with Oriana the first time he touched her breast. (That was back in front of the fireplace. The second night when he'd felt a little better.) He needed to find out if she would welcome him. In *that* way. He was afraid she wouldn't, considering what she'd been through, and afraid, once he tried, there might not be another chance, but he had to risk it and what better time than when he was groggy with the drink she'd made him for the pain?

Now he will do what she doesn't want him to: drink away a whole day and night. Because of this baby. Drink away even joy. Or especially joy. She, after all his worrying, lives yet, and this little bit of five-or-so-pounds' worth—it lives. It suckles. It even has a name.

> Babies under six months old should never be played with; and the less of it at any time the better. They are made nervous and irritable, sleep badly, and suffer from indigestion and in many other respects.
>
> *The Care and Feeding of Children*
> L. Emmett Holt, M.D.
> Appleton and Co., 1894, 1897, 1904

Sometimes Oriana stops in her work, stares out at the mountains or close in at the hummingbirds that sip from the flowers she planted especially for them—bee balm, penstemon, columbine, shooting star—listens to the tiny flickering sounds of their wings, thinks how Mother would love these birds and the flowers. Someday Mother might be looking out this very same window. Not likely she'd be doing dishes, though.

She seldom thought of her mother when she was unhappy, but now that she's happy she does. Thinks, Mother, look, this kind and witty man, and our black-eyed pixie of a boy who hops or runs or jumps wherever he goes and never merely walks even though he only learned how not so long ago, and now another baby on the way. And look at Lotti! So handsome . . . Of course they'd see right away who the father was and they'd understand and forgive.

But they wouldn't. They'd be even angrier that she hadn't stayed and married who she was supposed to marry and given Lotti the father she was supposed to have and the education and wealth that was her birthright. All that was true, and it was her fault poor Lotti had none of that. Her fault, too, that Lotti wouldn't even want it, she was so spoiled by the life she'd had to live so far. All they'd see here is a rundown farm and a rundown man who looks a dozen years older than he is. They'd not like to see her milking cows and doing the laundry. They'd not like to see her rough, red hands and her always sunburned face, her desert-dry lips. They'd wonder what had happened to her piano playing.

(Beal had wanted to get her a piano, but she wouldn't let him. The old pump organ was good enough, and she hardly ever played it anymore anyway. Beal wanted to get her everything she looked at twice. She had to stop him. He was a man who made money fairly easily once he set his mind to it—always had, just hadn't felt any reason to keep it. Now he wanted every extra dollar and every not-so-extra dollar to be used for gifts for her.)

Sometimes she thinks maybe someone else has gotten word to her parents. Now that she's happy, it wouldn't be so bad to see them, even if they didn't like anything here. Maybe Hazel or Jacob would have found their address and written to them. Maybe Henriette. She's always meddling, and she's so forward you never know what she'll do next. Then Mother would appear on her doorstep when she least expects it. (In her daydream, always without her father.) Mother wouldn't like Mr. Ledoyt or the farm at first, but Mr. Ledoyt would win her over soon enough. Mother was very proper, but she could sense real worth when she saw it. But perhaps she couldn't. Sometimes Oriana suspects she's making up this mother. Except Mother could have changed. It's been a long time. And Mother would surely love the mountains and the flowers, and in spite of his funny French name, she'd love her little grinning grandchild. She might arrive in time to be here when this new baby came. They would have to give her Lotti's room. Oriana could clear out all the horse things and arrowheads and odd-shaped rocks. Take all the drawings down. (Lotti didn't *always* burn them up, thank goodness.) Frame the best ones. Mother was particular. She'd inherited some of that herself. Too much, in fact.

Maybe her parents miss her by now. They might just be waiting to hear. At least Mother might be. One of these days she'll write to them, a real letter, not just in her mind. But maybe she wants to write to her mother about her happiness because she has nobody to tell. Most of all she wants to tell Beal—how nice it is to be married, and how glad she is it's to him, and how glad she is that he's still here—but she doesn't dare. She always just says "I love you" instead, for fear of reminding him of what he's done and promised and built, and the land he's bought, and how deep in he is. Best he not realize it. And then, she doesn't want him to think she's hanging on. That might scare him most of all. It isn't that he doesn't love her—at least it doesn't seem as if he doesn't—but a part of him, she's sure of it, doesn't want a home or money or people who are tied to him.

F ayette was two and a half when they had Christy, and the minute Oriana laid eyes on that baby, who looked so much like herself, she understood how that rape wasn't her fault at all. Not any part of it. She would kill if anybody tried such a thing with this girl-child. She would make up to Christy in happiness for what had happened to herself. She wouldn't be distant and scary like her own parents. Christy would come to her right away with anything, there'd be that much closeness.

Beal hadn't told Oriana much about his big sister Christianne, except that she'd died at twenty-two and that he'd tried to save her but couldn't. Tibo had told her more than Beal had about how much they'd depended on Christianne. Oriana had suggested the name Christianne in case it was a girl, and Beal had liked that.

She thought he might be, as she was, undoing something—making up to Christy for what he hadn't been able to do for Christianne. From the start, there was something special going on between them. She thought maybe the restlessness he often had, whether he seemed happy or not, might stop. Restlessness was the wrong word. That was how he was every day—inside anyway. She always thought, Wound tight, even though he looked composed and never lost his temper. But then a stillness would come upon him. It was after that that he'd run away—for a night or a week. After Christy was born she thought that might be done with for-ever. She'd thought it once or twice before, but now she thought, For sure he'll stop, and maybe he would have.

He stayed close by as much as he could. He'd done that after Fayette was born, too. The way she'd heard it and seen it, men didn't usually care that much for tiny babies. She'd even heard Tibo say, "They're not worth their feed till you can set 'em on a horse." (Of course, they sat them on horses when they could just barely sit up.) Tibo brought over their tiny saddle when Fayette was born. He said he and Henriette wouldn't be needing it anymore. She'd wondered about that. Henriette was still young.

When Tibo needed Beal's help, he didn't want to go. He even thought to say no, but the brothers never refused each other, so he went. But then he tried to come home almost every other day until Oriana asked him not to, for his own sake. All he did was sleep anyway, usually with Christy sleeping on his chest and Fayette snuggling up beside him. But Beal said even so, he wanted to be there with all of them. Once he went to sleep at the table and fell out of his chair.

They had the perfect family. They both felt it, though they never spoke of it. They could see it in each other's eyes. Here they were, lucky at long last; first they'd had each other, and now these perfect children, and this new house and his new-bought land up in the hills where his beeves fattened. And their children were safer than other children because they were so isolated. Lotti had never had measles or mumps or chicken pox or diphtheria. All she'd ever had was whooping cough. Fayette hadn't had anything. Christy, though she looked as if she'd crept out from under some rock in their sparkling river, was more vigorous and healthy than she seemed, and she was, now at nine months, out of the danger zone, though who ever really was? Jacob always said, "We're all just hangin' by a string." ("Strang," he said.) She should have been thinking of that.

Christy's first word was Pa. She said it over and over, along with Papa and Pop-pop. When Beal came in, she sounded like a series of little explosions. She'd hold up her arms to him and screech and he always picked her up. He called her *"mon coco"* and *"mon p'tit poussin."*

They looked strange together, the pale-skinned, pink-headed baby girl and the weathered dark man. Oriana would look at them and think, Mother, look, our little girl . . . Look at her pulling on this dark man's mustache, even on his bushy eyebrows, even on the hair of his chest. . . . But of course Mother would be wondering why he had his shirt unbuttoned, and where was his tie? And Christy pulled too hard. Oriana said she'd never learn not to if he didn't stop her, but he said she'd learn all too soon. Oriana knew she said this when she felt left out of their closeness, but she knew, too, that he needed all those Papas, and he needed how Christy's whole self wriggled and bounced when he came in. He needed it more than she did. Of course in the end it only made things worse.

She died of blood poisoning. They hadn't even noticed the scratch on her foot or the red line along her leg—not in time—only how fussy she was. Perhaps if they'd noticed . . . They burned her foot with alcohol bandages. When the doctor came he said that's what he'd have done, too.

Convulsions: Keep the child perfectly quiet with ice at the head, put feet in a mustard bath, and roll the entire body in large towels which have been dipped in mustard water (two tablespoonfuls of mustard to one quart of tepid water).

The Care and Feeding of Children
L. Emmett Holt, M.D.
Appleton and Co., 1894, 1897, 1904

Two days after the doctor came, Oriana had gone out to get ice so as to cool the water for bathing the baby. They thought she might be about to have convulsions again. Usually Oriana hated to go into the ice cave because the sawdust in front, where it was warmer, was full of odd-shaped, rubbery eggs. She had no idea what they were, but now if she'd come across a whole nest of newborn rattlesnakes, she'd have hardly noticed or cared.

When she came back, Beal was on his knees on the floor, sitting back on his heels, hand over his mouth, and she knew. He looked almost as if he was praying, though knowing him, she knew he wasn't. He'd once said, if he hadn't prayed for Christianne, he wouldn't pray for anybody. Seeing him on the floor, clutching his jaw like that, she went to hold him and be held, but he warned her away with a fierce gesture and left.

All night long he hammered and sawed and sanded, making an extraordinary coffin, fine and smooth and varnished, with mitered edges and offset nails. Such a little coffin. . . .

While he worked, she washed and dressed Christy and then sat listening to Beal, out in the tool and buggy barn. Lotti had bolted herself in her room as usual. Oriana thought she ought to go tell her, but then Lotti could climb out the window any time she felt like it. Oriana hardly had the energy or inclination to go find her. And she must have heard. There wasn't much that Lotti didn't know almost before it happened.

Even Fayette knew. She was holding Christy's hand when he crept out and climbed into her lap. He pulled her hand away from Christy and cuddled up, sucking his thumb and patting the line of lace at her breast. She was wishing for the warmth of Beal close to her, but Fay in her lap was the next best thing. Rocking him, she dozed off herself.

Beal was as if struck dumb and half blind. He did chores—any chores, his, hers, Lotti's—whatever he happened to see to do, as if think-ing or planning was too much for him. Nobody dared talk to him. Tibo came over, but even he didn't dare talk to him either. Tibo kept saying, "I don't know. I don't know what." Oriana thought he must be wondering, as she was, what Beal would do next. Even Henriette hardly said a word. Henriette kept hugging her. At least there was that.

Oriana had sent Lotti, nine years old then, to tell them. She could see Beal was of no use for anything of that nature (God knows where he'd have ended up), but she wondered if Lotti could do it and if she knew the way. Lotti said, "Of course I can. I've been almost all the way over there lots of times and you didn't even know it. I never went on in, though. I didn't want to get talked French to. They're just trying to make me feel bad. I *don't* feel bad, but I don't like it anyway." Oriana didn't say, as she usually would, "It's not on purpose to tease you. That's how they talk."

Henriette arranged for the funeral. It was not to Oriana's liking, but she was glad it was done for them. The talk of God was comforting, even though she'd have liked more about nature instead. And she always loved the old songs: "Rock of Ages," "Gather by the River." (Someone she'd never met came and played on her organ. They had moved it outside under the Lombardy poplars.) But when they sang the children's song, "Jesus Loves Me," she couldn't listen anymore.

Tibo was so good to her, as if to make up for his brother's lack. The way he hovered over her was so like Beal used to do, but why couldn't Beal have brought himself to be a little bit closer? Even if he'd just held her hand through the service. But anger was useless and unladylike—immoral at a time like this. She wouldn't let herself feel it. She'd hold herself together by herself if that's the way it had to be. She had thought so often —and even before they'd married—I'll just take whatever he has to give, but this time all he had to give was nothing. In fact it felt like less than nothing—as though his presence was an empty hole where a person should have been.

It was a comfort to know that Tibo and Henriette had been through it. She hadn't understood till now how it must have felt. And four times! All their boys except Henri. Jacob, too. He'd lost his whole family a long time ago. Wife and three sons. He often spoke about how he didn't have a single child left to leave his ranch to. He always said Oriana's family was his only family now.

—•—

Then . . . and there were no preliminaries . . . (They were in bed the night after the funeral.) The first she knew he grabbed her arm. Grabbed her with a crazy man's grip. So cruel she couldn't believe it was him, and she called out as if for his help. He rolled her over, jerked at her nightgown, pushed her legs apart with his knees. It was just like that other time—the man who'd fathered Lotti. He pinned her arms up over her head as if she was fighting him, but she wasn't. She would have come to him willingly, glad to be close in any way. Besides, it was her duty as a wife and his right as a husband, though she hadn't ever thought of that in terms of the two of them before. Rights and duties had nothing to do with them.

Before the funeral he would lie every night staring at the ceiling. She couldn't tell if he slept at all, but probably not. Both of them lying tense and alone. She did want to touch him and be touched, but now this shocked her—that he could do as that man had done, forcing her, pounding at her. . . . She had to keep thinking again, It's you, it's Beal, as she had that first time when it had worked out finally, and she could, after all, do . . . be a real woman for him. (Sometimes, before, he had been violent with desire. Always tender at the start and always tender after, but wild in the middle, though never this wild. She had liked that wildness. It gave her a sense of power—woman power—over him and his body. But this was different.)

But then, in spite of herself . . . And she shocked herself: Christy dead, the funeral just this morning, and she felt this . . . dreadful, shameful pleasure, his rage as if her rage, his energy and fury, hers. Even the pain, a relief from that other pain. But she was ashamed, both of her rage and, especially, of her desire.

Afterward he fell asleep instantly. On top of her. His wet breath in her ear. Deadweight, but so alive. The feverish, beating, breathing life of him . . . Stomach to stomach so that she couldn't breathe any other way but in rhythm with his own.

She knew, for sure, at last he slept. She pulled her arms out from under him, held him, one hand on the sweating back of his neck, one hand on the sweating small of his back. She slept, finally, too, uncomfortable but comforted. They would be all right. Time would heal. Everybody said it would.

nine years old

⁓•⁓

The next morning he was gone. She didn't even know if he'd left soon after, or in the middle of the night, or when, she'd slept that deeply for the first time since Christy. And he left without a horse or bedroll or any extra clothes. Left with no food and without the heavy sweater she'd knit for him. The nights were cold. Didn't he want anything along to remind him of her but the patches in his pants? She had bruises and soreness to remember him by every time she moved. She had the marks of his fingers on her arms where he'd held her so tightly and—she hardly dared let herself think about them—teeth marks.

Always before, when she was angry with him, she could tell herself she had no right to feel that way since she knew very well who she'd married and had married him anyway. But now, no matter how hard she tried, she did feel angry. She couldn't talk herself out of it.

First thing that morning she walked all round the house and saw his tracks heading straight out into the desert—into the middle of nowhere. Then her anger left her and she feared for him, in his state. She set Lotti to cleaning the lamp chimneys with old newspapers. Lotti said it was a girl's job. Normally Oriana would have said, "I know it," or "Beal does it," and there would have been an argument, but this time she didn't answer, and this time Lotti started right in. Oriana saddled up, sat Fay in front of her, and followed Beal's tracks, but lost them where the ground got hard and salt-crusted.

—•—

After two weeks, post office money orders began to come. No letter, of course. She couldn't imagine him ever writing a letter, even under normal circumstances. The first came all the way from Gardnerville, and the next from Virginia City, and after that they came from Winnemucca, five hundred miles away, and she knew he hadn't gone by the narrow gauge. Every week, fifteen dollars. Sometimes twenty. That had to be all his pay. What was he living on? And did it mean he was never coming back? She could tell Tibo was worried, too. He kept saying, "It'll maybe take him a little while." But Tibo didn't know about that night and how Beal might be feeling about it.

"You didn't run away when your children died. Never once."

"No, but I never was like him. He and Christianne, you know. They were so close. I wasn't in that. And then, after everybody died, I grew up having him to help me. He had nobody."

Tibo called him Béal. He and Henriette always said his name that way when they felt most intimate and loving. When Christy died, they called him that a lot. When Oriana and Beal had married, Beal had said to the lawyer who married them, "It has to be Béal. Call me Béal for the ceremony."

—•—

Lotti left a drawing in plain sight for a change. She often kept her drawings secret, except for Fayette. She even let him watch her as she drew, and he never got tired of it. For that bit of time, Lotti would leave off pestering him, and Fay would go so far as to lean against her shoulder.

This drawing she had propped up against the kitchen cabinet where it not only couldn't be missed but was in the way. Oriana moved it aside, out of harm's way. She wasn't sure if it was a gift or not or if she was just supposed to see it and say something. It had a complete background: their long, low house and trees and, in the distance, snowcapped mountains. In the foreground was Lotti's mustang, Strawberry. Lotti had cleverly smeared the pencil marks to simulate the roan color. It couldn't be a gift. Not with Lotti's mustang. Or could it? She ought at least to say something, but she hardly had the energy or the inclination. Well, she would. She would find a minute and say, "Very nice," sometime when she felt better and could think, but not right now.

—•—

After nine weeks the money orders stopped. She hoped it meant he was on the way home, though she feared the opposite. But walking and hitching rides—even if he really was coming home—it would take a long time.

Then, walking—and it was almost exactly like the first time she'd seen him, this thin—as thin and tired and ragged as he'd looked on her first view of him. He looked so bad she thought, My God, he's done nothing but work hard and drink hard and smoke and not eaten at all!

She was hanging up the clothes. She had two clothespins in her mouth and two in her hand, along with Fayette's nighttime diapers. She must have looked a sight, just like that first time he came walking in, but he was all cleaned up and freshly shaven. He'd probably stopped and washed at his pond—for her sake. She thought all over again, What a funny-looking man. He took off his hat in that exact same gesture as before, respectful, honoring her, but this time without the self-mocking smile. He looked cautious. Unsure of how she would receive him.

The clothespins fell from her mouth. She dropped the diapers in the dust and then stepped on them, she felt so wobbly. They stared at each other—it seemed for a long time. She was thinking somebody should say something.

Finally she said, "I'll have to do these over," and he said, "Yes."

She said, "I got the money," and he said, "Yes."

She said, "Thank you," and he said, "Yes."

She bent to pick up the diapers in order to avoid his stare and because she was trembling and didn't want him to know. She shook the sand from them, shaking harder than she needed to. Why didn't he say something?

She'd tried. Or why didn't he reach out to her? Even in rage? Except there was no rage left in him.

Then she said the exact thing to turn him from her, and she knew it would, and would hurt him. It seemed to pop out of her mouth by itself. "We're . . . having another baby."

He turned his back, but she could see the muscles of his jaw working. She shouldn't have said it like that, and she shouldn't have said it now. She should have waited for another month or so. Maybe even more. He already felt bad enough.

And she ought to know by now that she was the one who would have to say the first words and make the first move. She was married to a man who easily told other men what to do but who was so tentative with her he could hardly make a move until he knew for sure she wanted him to. Even "that"—except for the night before he left—he always found some way of asking.

She could faint and he would pick her up and she would be in his arms and nobody would have to say anything. That occurred to her not only because she was reminded of that other time when she thought she should have pretended to faint—but it occurred to her mainly because she felt so dizzy and nauseous she thought she might be going to anyway. But feeling nauseous made her think of the time she'd held his forehead when he threw up after losing the fight. That was the very first time she'd put her arms around him. So she said what she'd said to him then, and it was almost as hard to say as it had been, but she wanted to just as much. She said, "My dear," and she said, "My love," and she took a step toward him. But then, and for the first time in her life, she *did* faint.

She woke on their bed with him putting cool cloths on her forehead and saying, "Please." And when he saw she had come to, he said, "You went down *so* hard! I tried to catch you. Are you all right?"

But she had his rough, sandpapery fingers pushing her hair from her forehead. She had his lips on her eyelids, her neck, her earlobes. How could she not be all right?

He said, "I'm the one that hurt you. I'm always the one."

"You were in pain."

"So were you. My God. I've done . . . I bit you. Did I really bite you? And this baby!"

She said, "We'll get through it," and she thought if they could do it together, they would—*she* would, anyway, as long as he stayed.

After a while he went to make her fresh coffee and then he finished hanging up the clothes. Lotti and Fayette came back from playing cowboy on the half-grown lambs. When Fay saw Beal he started jumping and yelling, shrieking really, and running around in circles. (Beal said he'd done the same when he was little.) Strange, though, happy as Fay was, he wouldn't go near Beal. As though he thought he'd disappear again. Oriana knew how he felt. Lotti acted as though he'd never left and as though nothing had happened—kept her distance and looked watchful, just as she usually did.

That night he said—for about the fourth time over the years they'd been together—exactly what he'd said on their wedding night. "Don't leave me. Please don't ever leave me. *Ne me quittes pas.*" And she thought, as she had each time, What an extraordinary thing for him to be saying to *her.* Perhaps he thought he'd come back someday and find her gone. Perhaps he thought it would serve him right if she was. She always said, "I'll never leave you. You know that," but this time, though she said it and right then in his arms she felt it, she wasn't quite so sure she might not, someday, go. While he was gone, Henriette had said, "It's about your turn, isn't it? You maybe surprise him one of these days and turn up missing." Then she said, "*Certainement* he's a pretty good man, as men go, and when he's not in some mood of his, he's more fun than most (not counting T-Bone, of course) and I do love him dearly, but, Oriana, I don't know why he hasn't yet driven you completely loco."

Except Oriana could never bring herself to leave Fayette. If she ever ran away, she'd have to bring him along. Not a bad idea actually—but she couldn't run away from this new baby, on its way no matter where she went.

—•—

He had brought her dried apricots. For once something useful. When she told Henriette, Henriette said, "And finally something with good taste, too."

—•—

Those first days after he was back, he couldn't seem to get enough of touching her, helping her, and she thought, Things will be all right with him now. Not all right with Christy dead, that would never be all right with either of them, but he'll be ready to go on and they'll comfort each other, and after a time the pain might fade some, though right now she didn't want it to. As if for Christy's sake, she kept thinking, I want to feel the pain. Except that sharp, sudden agony that caught her unawares—how long would that last?

But things were not all right at all. He hovered. When he wasn't working, he was underfoot. He watched her, almost as he had in the beginning. He asked over and over, "What can I do?" and "Is there anything you want?" It seemed he wanted her to ask of him some Herculean task. It made her think of the time he'd climbed the tree up into the tiny top swaying branches, so high it scared her and she had wished he wouldn't do that, and of the time he built the dam for no reason, though it turned out to be a good thing after all. Those were the sorts of things, she was sure of it, he wanted her to ask of him. Or even fight. Maybe fight Big Andy and get beaten up all over again. She knew what she wanted, but it wouldn't be hard enough to suit him, and it might not help anyway.

He had taught her to like being close and to need being close, and now he wouldn't. At first she thought he wouldn't, and then he tried and couldn't, and after failing twice, he didn't try again.

He used to look at her with secret signals, little half-winks or tiny raisings of the eyebrows. Now he looked as though just seeing her pained him. It was too bad she still had the mark of his bite on her shoulder. One more thing to make him wince. Sometimes at night it seemed he might be trying not to cry, but it could just be coughing.

She told him what she wanted. "Another honeymoon," she said. "It doesn't have to be more than a couple of days, but I want the two of us away alone, and I want a bed of pine boughs and for us to be looking up at the stars and you naming them and telling me about them and about Coyote."

"I'm finished with the stars."

"But can we go? Jacob would love to come over. He loves being grandpa." She hoped that when they got out where they'd been when they first married, and before that, too, and where he'd been so . . . so the opposite of now, it would make him able to be . . . a husband again.

On their honeymoon they'd seen rattlesnakes dance. She had started to hurry away as fast as she could, but he grabbed her, held her tight, whispered, "Wait," stood behind her and put his cheek against hers. They watched the two snakes rise up, coil their bodies together, sometimes their heads touching just as their own were, and dance, weaving back and forth, they as hypnotized by it as if the snakes were the snake charmers. Even snakes, then, caught up in . . . just as they were: "ecstasy." A word she'd never thought about till then and never would say out loud, but that's what came to mind. Snakes, and she, and he holding her tight. Who would have thought, she of all people? And with this funny man, nothing to him but sinew and bones and those crooked teeth of his and a mustache. In spite of what the books said, how could it be wrong if all of nature . . . ? All!

> The health of the reproductive organs can only be maintained by a temperate life. . . . Lascivious thought should be displaced by cultivating a taste for liturature which is elevating in its nature.
>
> Excessive sexual indulgence not only prostrates the nervous system, enfeebles the body, drains the blood of its quickening elements, but is inconsistent with intellectual activity, morality, and spiritual development. . . . Hence the gratification of sexual instincts should always be moderate.
>
> *The People's Common Sense Medical Adviser*
> R. V. Pierce, 1883

They had not been moderate. Neither on their honeymoon nor before.

"Remember the rattlesnakes?"

Ah, there was the look in his eyes she liked to see, and a bit of that old down-turning grin. She'd thought maybe it was gone forever.

One sunset up there on the mountain, he'd lain with his head in her lap, his fingers smoothing back her pink-red hair, looking at her instead of the pink-red in the sky behind her. He said, "The sun's gone down, but you're still out and shining." That was on their honeymoon, too.

—•—

So Beal went and fetched Jacob. Even before he and Oriana left, Lotti was jabbering at Jacob in a way she seldom did anymore at home. And she was listening, too. She liked his tales of the olden days, of Indian fights and soldiers and such, right here on their land. Lotti was sorry the Paiutes weren't on the warpath anymore and sorry everything was so settled up now. Jacob said the Indians were much better off being civilized. He said everybody was better off civilized, but Lotti said she didn't think so because who would want to do other people's laundry or work in other people's fields and eat potatoes?

Before Beal had come, Lotti said she wished her mother would go ahead and marry Jacob. She said it after Beal had come, too. Sometimes Oriana thought that might have made everything a lot easier. But maybe it wouldn't have been easier because sooner or later, she'd have met Beal, and she had loved him almost at first sight. Except, knowing she was Jacob's wife, Beal wouldn't have looked at her as he did. Knowing she was Jacob's wife, he never would have come close. He almost hadn't anyway, with nothing in his way but himself.

—•—

They had horses now and two mules. Beal rode his big mule, Matou, and Oriana rode Lotti's little mustang. They took the pack mule and, just in case, the tent, but they didn't use it. They did lie looking up, at the stars and the moon and sometimes into the tops of trees. In the moonlight she was even more aware of how much gray hair he'd gotten just in the last few months. He was so streaked with silver in that light. So beautiful.

But she could see that Beal, looking up, wasn't seeing anything. He had said he was through with the stars, and that looked to be true. She said, "You're still staring at the ceiling, aren't you? Do you sleep at all?"

"It's better when I'm with you."

She thought, Well, why not stay here with me then? But she said, "I wish I knew what to do for you."

"I'm the one who did it."

"But you hardly knew what you were doing. You were in such a state. I never saw the like."

"If everybody went around saying they didn't know what they were doing, it would be a sorry world. It was a terrible thing I did, specially to you, specially since I know what you've been through. I wanted to be the one to help you and keep you safe, and all I've done is hurt you more." And he made one of those coughing noises.

"You're hurting me now, Beal. Besides, remember when I couldn't and I thought I'd never be able to, and when you tried, I hit you? I couldn't stop hitting. You were already so bruised from that fight. I've always felt bad about that. I'll forgive myself if you forgive yourself."

"What I did is different."

"You taught me love and now you're taking it away."

"Not love."

She was surprised he could bring himself to use the word at all.

He turned, took the pins from her hair as he always liked to do. He always said that was his job. Then his hands were all over like they used to be. The moon . . . it was so bright she could see his eyes were shut. And all that white hair! He started to, but he couldn't keep on. And then he cried and it didn't sound like coughing anymore. He said the same thing he'd said when he got drunk by mistake on their wedding night more from not eating than from drinking. *"J'ai tout gâté."* Tibo had told her what it meant: "I've spoiled everything."

— • —

She thought after he'd let himself cry himself out at last that he might be better, but he wasn't. It took her almost dying to bring him back in all the ways she wanted him. That was six months later when they lost that other baby that neither of them wanted. Stillborn. Dead, Aunt Jenny said, maybe days before her first labor pains.

She was so sick she hardly remembered anything of that birth but a fog of pain—much worse than with Fayette. Aunt Jenny didn't let her see the baby. She said it would be bad for her, and she wouldn't say its sex. Much later Beal said it was a boy, and when she wanted to know more, he finally said it looked all right, but he wouldn't say anything else.

Aunt Jenny was there for a long time after that, but Beal was always there, too. Every time she opened her eyes, there he was; sometimes he was holding her hand; sometimes he was asleep, leaning forward in the chair, resting his head on the edge of the bed; sometimes he was standing in the doorway, lost in thought, it seemed. She thought she remembered his whispering, "I love you," into her ear, and not just once, though it might have been a wishful dream. She wouldn't ask him about it. He wouldn't like her to. If he wanted to say it when she was awake, that was for him to decide. And maybe he hadn't said it anyway.

She didn't know he was there. He was by her bed most every minute, but Oriana thought he wasn't. She'd look right at him and say where was he? She called Aunt Jenny over and over to ask her, "Is he coming back?" and he'd be right there, holding her hand. Once she looked straight into his eyes and said, "Aunt Jenny, I can't bear to see him so unhappy." It was no use saying, "I'm here," and "I'll not leave you." He even said, "I'll be happy."

She would toss and turn and say how tired she was and yet not be able to lie quietly. "Everything's falling apart," she said.

"It's not. I'm holding it together."

"I knew he'd go someday."

"We'll have a hundred honeymoons."

"I'm scared."

—·—

He, like Oriana, turned to Aunt Jenny. "Have I really been gone so much?"

"When a person wants you here, a little bit of gone goes a long ways."

"She never says a word."

"Well, that's Oriana. She won't push."

—·—

It wasn't until he and Aunt Jenny put her into the big zinc bathtub of warm water that she finally came to herself, stopped her restlessness, held on to him, said, "I thought you weren't ever coming back."

For modesty's sake, in the bath, Aunt Jenny had partly covered her with wet towels. They clung to her body. She looked like the pictures in her fancy art book—like a Greek statue. A Diana. Even after these children . . . Hard to think three and only Fayette to show for it. (No, four. He forgot about Lotti.) And even at her age, still looking like a young girl.

Didn't matter what had happened to her. Didn't matter what he'd done to her himself, she always looked so innocent. And was.

As he held her and helped to bathe her, he said, "Aunt Jenny, without her I couldn't."

"I expect you'd do what we all do."

"No!"

"You have Fayette and Lotti to look after. You'd do what we do."

"Maybe."

"But she'll be all right now."

Lotti writes: I had not thought to set myself on fire and I'm not sure why I did it. I decided at the last minute when sparks had already burst onto my skirt. I didn't wear skirts that often, even back then. They were always in the way. I suppose, partly, I wanted to burn that skirt up. I only had one other. First I brushed the sparks off and then I took the little fireplace shovel and put them back on. I don't remember thinking much of anything. I was only ten and didn't think things out as I do now. I guess I wanted to change things—any way I could. I had to do something big and important. But really I didn't think at all.

Old You-Know-Who was just outside, and the little one (I always think of Fayette as the little one of him) was right there by the fireplace. I wanted Fay to see me do it. (He was three then.) I wanted to hear him scream, and he did scream. I didn't. I'm always braver than Fayette and I always will be. No matter how old he gets to be, I'll be braver. I suppose it was Fayette's screaming that saved me. Without him I'd have burned up for sure because the fire burned faster than I thought it would. It was as if my whole skirt was tinder. It went up all at the same time once it got started.

I'd like to do something sort of like that over again now—now that I have bosoms. I would have felt like a woman to him as he lay on top of me. Of course I couldn't do that exact same thing. And the pain lasted a long time. Much longer than I thought it would. A whole year. More in fact. I thought it would be like a kitchen burn—just last a few days. Old Him was in pain, too. Ma and Fay had to do up his buttons.

He was so quick, so strong. It all went so fast I hardly realized what was happening. I made no sound at all, Fayette screamed, and he was there before I knew it, tore off my burning dress (burnt cloth and buttons scattering away). He knocked me down, rolled on top, his jacket pulled around both of us. I felt his body against me. He seemed all ropes and knobs and knots and . . . so naked under his clothes. I felt—well, strange. Embarrassed, kind of. I didn't like it. I didn't think I'd feel that way.

Afterward I covered my bare breasts with my hands—or rather, where my breasts would have been if I'd had any. I covered them because they weren't there. If I'd had them, I'd not have been so quick to cover myself up.

She did that on purpose. He saw it in her face. Just let herself burn and not said a word or raised a hand to save herself. Jealous of Oriana—they knew that already, but so jealous of Christy, too, she would have died to be like her. Almost did. And out of her head with . . . hard to say what it was she felt for him, and he old enough to be her father. *Is* her father, for heaven's sake!

She didn't like it when he fell on her and rolled. She jumped away as soon as he let her go, as if being close to him was worse than burning up. He'd not forget the look on her face. Surprise and outrage and fear. As if he was about to hit her, though he'd never spanked her—except that one time when she shot arrows at him. She pushed him away like he was the fire. Ran off, naked, to her room. Bolted the door. Why had he let her put in that damn bolt? First thing she gets a real room of her own and that's what she does. Made it and nailed it up all by herself. Well, she'd have to make another. Trust Lotti to make a good strong one, too, but he managed to break through.

She lay on the floor, still silent. Skinny little stick figure, trying to cover up what wasn't even there. He wanted to help her, comfort her, though when had she ever let anybody do that? She was huddled by her bed, hugging herself and shaking. In shock most likely. She didn't want him near. He threw a blanket over her. He could see she wanted that. She must have been in pain but you couldn't tell. Maybe she wasn't feeling it yet. He didn't either until later. He'd rubbed the burned skin clean off his hands slamming at her door before he took his shoulder to it, and didn't even feel it. Oriana came. At first Lotti wouldn't let her near either, but finally she let herself be looked after. But no hugging. Of course with Lotti, no hugging allowed, even then. He ended up having to comfort Fayette instead. Or maybe it was Fay who was comforting him.

Echinacea, comfrey, sweet butter, marshmallow on the burns.

Meadowsweet, white willow, valerian, hot gooseberry wine for the inside. It made him sick, but Lotti kept it down and slept.

Couldn't hold reins, let alone saddle up. Couldn't milk a cow. Couldn't turn the pages of a book. Could just barely hold a cup, two-handed. Wedged a spoon into his bandage to feed himself. Stopped smoking so at least he wouldn't have to bother Oriana with that. She offered to help him do it, but he wouldn't let her. Couldn't touch her. Even her warmth near his hands hurt.

> Dr. H. C. F. Meyer used echinacea in his Meyer's Blood Purifier. He promoted the remedy as an absolute cure for rattlesnake bite, blood poisoning, and a host of other ills. Claims like Dr. Meyer's gave echinacea the name "snake oil." But the Indians had called it "snake oil" from the start.

Lotti writes: So now they want to send me east to school and after that to college. I guess I'm supposed to do all the things Ma didn't—at least the college part. She only went two years. Ma is sewing clothes I'd never wear anywhere. One dress is even pink! They haven't the tiniest idea of who I really am, and they don't even care. If they bothered to ask, I could tell them. Sometimes I try to tell Ma, but she always says I'll change when I'm older, but I won't let myself. Ma says she changed. I wonder if I'd have liked her better as she was before. But I don't think she really changed as much as she thinks. She always gives the exact same example: how her mother wanted her to play the piano and she didn't want to learn, but her mother made her and now she's glad she did. If she's so glad, how come she doesn't ever play on our organ anymore? That's not so much of a change, anyway.

More books than ever are coming into the house. I know they're meant for me. I don't read any of them. Instead, like I always do, I read his state and government bulletins. I've been reading them ever since I was able to read at all. In fact I learned how to read from them. They're always interesting.

> The second factor instrumental in producing loco-fiends among animals is that of suggestion. It is a matter of observation by many stockmen that loco-disease was unknown in a herd or flock until after the introduction of a locoed animal. This animal teaches the others to eat the plant. . . . After a few animals once have acquired the habit, it rapidly spreads through the whole herd.
>
> "Some Stock-Poisoning Plants"
> North Dakota Agricultural College Bulletin, no. 58, 1903

LOCO WEED.
Natural Size.

Oxytropis Lamberti Pursh.
(U. S. Dept. Agriculture.)

Ma wants to make me "nice" and a "lady" and "marriageable" and the mother of—*mother* of!—I hardly know what. Scholars, I suppose. Neither Ma nor him want any of us to be at all like they were. Ma would never have married without having met up with him, and he would still be a tramp without her. (Uncle T-Bone thinks he would be dead. Uncle T-Bone thinks he wasn't going to hold out much longer.)

But Old Snaggleteeth cares about book learning, too, though he hardly has any. I used to think he knew everything there was to know, but he only knows about hay and cows and coyotes and how to make water flow around and things the Indians know. By now I guess I know just about everything he does, and I don't think I need to know one thing more than I already know. If Ma had her way I'd never stop learning things. It would be *endless*.

Ma's been teaching me and Fay at home. She thinks she's better at it than any of the teachers around here, and I suppose she is. (Aunt Henriette does the French.) There was a roving teacher who used to pass through here on her way from one school to another. She taught me once a week for a little while. She didn't approve of me at all, and especially she didn't approve of Old Him. She wanted to save me from myself and from him, "while," she said, "there's still time." She always talked about "a woman of your class," by which she meant my so-called mother's class, not his. She said, "Drinking begets violence and depravity, and I have good reason to believe that your stepfather drinks." She said she also heard my stepfather say bad words when he thought nobody was around. She said it was a woman's nature to forgive and that was all well and good, but for one's family's sake, a woman shouldn't be too forgiving, which my mother was. She said she couldn't understand why a woman like my mother stayed with "that man" (she always called him "that man") or had married him in the first place. She kept wondering what could have possessed her. She said I should wear my hair the grown-up way and have a real hat so I'd have a hat pin in case some man . . . "*you* know," she said. I said I'd shoot any man who tried. She said I shouldn't cross my legs any way at all but especially not at the ankles. She said it had a meaning I didn't know about. I'd never heard of that before, but I said I already knew everything of that nature, and if she wanted details, I could supply them. I would have made some up on the spot. I don't really talk that way much, but she brought out my worst side.

She believed elocution would save me, as it had saved, she said, others like me who were teetering on the edge. She had me memorize uplifting things. (I still have one stuck in my head, worse luck: "What-will-become-of-the-West-if-her-prosperity-rushes-up-to-such-a-majesty-of-power-while-those-great-institutions-of-learning-and-religion-linger-which-are-necessary-to-form-the-mind-and-the-conscience . . ." With gestures, too. When it came to reciting it in front of everybody, she couldn't make me.)

I never said a word against her. I'm not like a girl in any way, and I never will be. (I want people to look at me and think, She's as good as a man in every way.) I just grit my teeth, but Ma saw things and that teacher stopped coming. Sometimes, in comparison with some people, Ma isn't as bad as she might be.

— • —

I've already had many and varied experiences and adventures, and I've been far from here, so it's not as if I don't know what it's like in the East. Ma and I and Fay went all the way to Cincinnati to visit a lady who'd helped Ma before she got ahold of me. Nobody says a word about it, but I think Ma got me after she came out West. I'm a western kind of person. But I think Aunt Hazel knows something. She and Ma have secrets. They whispered a lot and always stopped talking when I'd come in on them. I tried to trick Aunt Hazel into saying something about me, but she didn't get tricked. I said things like "I suppose Ma had to leave here where everything was so nice for her and go get me even though she didn't want to." Aunt Hazel just looked at me funny and said, "Mm-hmmm," which was a yes, but not like she meant it. Then she said, "It was what your ma wanted," and she looked at me as though that had some great meaning or other and I was supposed to puzzle it out.

That trip was after I set myself on fire. Ma never wants to be away from him. She thinks it's bad enough that he goes off to help Uncle T-Bone or Grandpa Jacob or anybody, and she feels even worse those other times when he goes off drinking. She's not the same when he's gone. I don't know how she could let herself go off to Aunt Hazel's.

Of course she wouldn't go anywhere without Fayette. I think she wanted to show him off to Aunt Hazel and to all the old ladies there, though what's to show? When we were there and on our way there, sometimes it seemed she used Fayette in place of Old Leather Head.

They decided on the trip because I was still hurting too much to be able to ride a horse and I was going crazy sitting around the house where all there was to do was lady's things. (Old Him said I was "barn sour.") They thought maybe if we stayed a month or so, I'd be able to ride when we came back. But I wonder if Ma went there partly so she could talk to Aunt Hazel about me. I'm a big problem.

One good thing: ice cream! That's the first I ever had it. They made lots of it for me. Pretty near all I and Fay wanted, though not quite.

I could see why Ma liked Aunt Hazel. She was easy to be around and funny when she wanted to be and never made a fuss when things went wrong. Sort of like Old Him in those ways. But when I think back over my life, I think it was Aunt Jenny who really, really knew who I was. When I was at Grandpa's while they were busy having their honeymoon, she got me some old thrown-away spurs and I went around jangling like a cowboy. She found an old rope that was still both stiff enough and soft enough so I could learn to throw with it. She made me chinks out of a piece of an old tarp. You could hardly tell they weren't leather. I didn't ask her to do any of this. Seems like she just looked at me and knew.

There was a little while when I thought he understood me just about as well as anybody, but now I don't think he understands *anything*, else why would he let Ma send me away from everything I care about? I just can't be who they want me to be, and too many things are being done "for my own good."

I couldn't hardly stand being in Cincinnati even for just a month. Everything was green and very, very wet. It rained almost every other day and it wasn't even winter. My hair frizzed up almost as bad as Ma's, but thank goodness, not quite. I missed my mountains and my mustang. If I'd known how it was going to be, I'd have brought some of my rocks and arrowheads along, even though Ma said not to. It was good I still had pain so it wasn't as hard to sit around as it might have been. I liked the train ride but I didn't let on, and I had a good book on how to be a farrier. At first I thought it was interesting seeing all that green, but then I got tired of it and tired of hills that were all the same rounded shape. I thought of them as girl hills, soft and all dressed up in fancy greenery. Sissy hills. I wanted black volcanic flows and red cinder cones and little volcanoes with obsidian centers, and pinnacles all around. And I wanted sage and the smell of sage. When we got there, I felt hemmed in, as if there wasn't any sky, and hemmed in by Ma and Aunt Hazel, too. They made me dress up and since I hardly knew where I was, I let them. (Ma didn't even let me bring one pair of trousers, though, of course, there wasn't anything to do there that I would have needed them for.) Aunt Hazel made sure we dressed up and went to church. (Ma is a hypocrite. She told me not to say a word about how we didn't go at home. I was going to say something anyway, but I never got around to it.)

I missed the sounds at night: cows and calves calling to each other, owls, the rooster, coyotes (sometimes a whole family of them will come yipping right into our yard—that drives the rooster and the dog crazy). When we separate the calves from the cows to wean them, you have to get used to a terrible racket for a lot of nights in a row. The city was too quiet. Thank goodness there was a donkey in an empty lot behind Aunt Hazel's place so there was a more normal sound to wake up to. I spent a lot of time out there talking to him. I needed some company that wasn't just ladies or Fayette. (All the boarders at Aunt Hazel's place were ladies. I wasn't used to that. No men around at all! I'm not ever going to live that way. With me, it's going to be either men or nobody.)

—•—

On that trip Fayette got everything. No sooner did we get to the first train station than the conductor took him up to visit the engine. He got to throw in some coal, too.

He *always* gets everything. Later on Uncle T-Bone taught us to swim *at the same time!* I guess I was already twelve or thirteen but Fayette was only five or six. That wasn't fair. Ma wanted us to learn to swim because of me almost drowning. Old You-Know-Who rescued me and he couldn't even swim, and still can't, and he almost drowned, too.

—•—

I don't think Fayette has ever thought to run away. These are his real parents and he likes them. I've told him how they aren't my parents, and he says, "That's easy enough to see," but he thinks I ought to like them anyway because they take good care of me. I say it depends on what you mean by "good." I don't starve. He says they *are so* good, and he puts his fingers in his ears so as not to hear any bad things about them. I keep right on talking because he's just pretending not to hear. (Fayette, if you're ever reading this, just go right ahead. You might learn a thing or two.) He does say he'll come with me to help me find my own parents, good as these parents are. To Fay they're both *absolutely perfect!* He says maybe I'm right about how everybody ought to find out about their real ma and pa. He says, "Except what if your folks are robbers?" Then he says I'd better not steal any of the special things he keeps in his lockbox, and I say, "Who would want any of those things?" (Old Horse Face gave Fayette that box and lock when he gave me this diary. I would have preferred a lockbox.) Fayette says maybe I'll steal horses and then I'll be hung, but I know my real folks are special. I can feel that inside me. They're strong and tall like me, and aren't afraid of anything. We'll probably recognize each other right off.

I couldn't think how to begin to find them except to write to Aunt Hazel, so I did that. There's not much time left.

That name Cochran is about all I know of anything, and I don't know if Cochran is my so-called ma's married name or not or if she ever married at all or if maybe she just picked that name out of nowhere just to have a name that's nothing like her real one. For all I know, her name might really be Schvinghummer. (There *is* somebody named that.) Since Ma ran away and never went back, she ought to understand what I'm going to do, but she won't. She likes everything cozy. She likes for the whole family to be together (not counting me), having picnics or sitting around the fireplace, all safe, maybe with a big storm going on outside and nobody—of us—out in it. (I'll bet nights like that are when they do you-know-what.) She doesn't want anybody to ever grow up and leave. Except for me.

Since Fayette isn't going to want to be leaving here forever, I'm not going to tell him anything until we're a long ways on our way, and of course I won't be telling him he's being kidnapped.

But I may not be leaving when I think I am nor to anywhere I know of. If there's a good answer from Aunt Hazel, I may just go to be with my real parents.

—•—

Dear Aunt Hazel,

I'm writing to you because I know Ma confides in you and I think you may know things about me. I need to find out about myself. I *beg* you, if you know *anything* at all about me, please write and tell me!!!

Everybody here is well. I hope you are, too. Your brother, Grandpa Jacob, is not well, but I suppose you know that already. We don't see him very often anymore, though Ma visits him whenever she can.

Very truly yours,

Charlotte (Lotti) "Ledoyt"

P.S. When you write to me, seal it up tight. If you have sealing wax, use that, *too.* Don't put a return address on the outside.

P.P.S. If you know my real last name, please include it.

My dear, dear Lotti,

What an unexpected pleasure to hear from you. The years have certainly flown by, and here you are, already a young lady. But, Lotti dear, I fear that if your poor dear mother hasn't seen fit to tell you anything about yourself, it is certainly not my place to do it. I have searched my conscience long and hard in this matter, and I believe you must not question certain unmentionable aspects pertaining to your birth. Be happy, dear child, that you are here in this world for your allotted time, considering all that transpired in regard to your birth and all that might have been, and do not question how or why.

However, dear Lotti, as I think of what dangers, trials, and griefs lie before us all, I have decided it is my duty to give you this address. Only the good Lord knows, but something might happen to your mother before she has a chance to give it to you. Promise me you will not try to contact these people. It is very important to your dear mother that they not know where she is and especially that they not know of your existence! Don't ever let on that I gave you this address, and do not use it now! It is for the future.

As to a certain person (who will remain nameless), don't

delude yourself with thoughts that he could ever be a father to you. He isn't worthy of a place in your or your dear mother's lives.

Your mother has told me Mr. Ledoyt has adopted you legally and that he is kind to you. Take my advice and forget about that other man who has caused only pain. Believe me, Lotti, I know what I'm talking about. Someday you'll understand.

Your letter brought to mind the happy times we had together and that all-too-fleeting month you and Fayette and your dear mother spent here.

Harry the donkey is still out in back and hee-hawing every morning so we don't need a rooster to wake us up. I'm sure he misses you.

I trust you in this matter, Lotti. Promise me you will be patient. Believe me, some things one is better off not knowing.

You and your mother are ever in my heart.

With love,

Aunt Hazel

That didn't sound much like Aunt Hazel to me. Some of it did, but most of it didn't. I know she never had much schooling. I'll bet one of the old lady boarders helped her with it.

Littlefield, Mass.

Dear Sir or Madam,

Perhaps you can help me find out who I am. Since I know nothing about myself, *anything* at all would help. My name now is Charlotte though I'm not sure it always was. They say I was born on May 4, 1896. The woman who has claimed all these years to be my mother calls herself Oriana Cochran. In June of 1902, she married a man named Beal (also know as Bill) Ledoyt.

I don't know how to describe myself to you. I don't have any characteristics that stick out. I don't have freckles or red hair as Oriana Cochran does. My teeth are not crooked. My face is round and a little on the plump side, my nose is straight. I have black, wavy hair. My eyes are brown though not as dark a brown as some. I'm rather tall and strong for a woman. Some people have called me handsome. Most likely I was born someplace out West. I only feel at home here, and my first memories are of a ranch belonging to Jacob Carswell.

I'll include this drawing I made of myself.

Do you know anything about me? If so, please write and tell me about myself.

Anxiously awaiting your reply,

Charlotte "Ledoyt"

It's been exactly fifty-three days since I sent that last letter, and still no answer. I got, or somebody went and got, our mail twenty-two times during that time. I kept a chart. I got it eighteen of those times myself. I picked it up so often they don't wonder anymore what's got into me, or I guess they still do, and I know they suspect something, but no matter *what* I do, they *always* suspect something.

The narrow gauge comes up through the long valley—*everything* comes up and down the valley. There's no place else for anything to go unless you go into the mountains, east or west. The train people toss the mail out. Sometimes they'll pick you up or drop you off even though it's the middle of nowhere, but you have to let them know ahead. It's only a couple of hours to go get the mail. Sometimes I go slowly on purpose so as to miss chores. Or sometimes it's just nice out there.

They've already notified the train to pick me up a week from Monday. I have to do something right now, even though I haven't yet heard from those people. At least I know a few things now. Number one: Aunt Hazel does know something about me. Number two: it sure sounds as if my father is alive. Number three: he's not an ordinary person. I knew that already, but it's nice to know for sure that he's special and different. Nobody understands him, just like nobody understands me either. And what does Aunt Hazel know of good or bad? What's bad to her is good to me. Lots of times people think *I'm* a bad lot.

I know I'd recognize my father anywhere. Even now, whenever anybody new comes around, I always take a good look. That man that beat up on him—we see him out somewhere now and then. He's the right size, but he doesn't look right. My father could beat up on Old You-Know-Who, too, and just as easily.

It might seem like I'll be heading in the wrong direction to be looking for my father. First of all, it's just for now, and second of all, everybody comes out here eventually. East is where everybody comes from. My father probably came here, too.

I'm going to bring along the little derringer Old Him got for Ma a long time ago that she keeps in her bureau drawer underneath her underthings. She won't even know it's gone. I'm the only one who checks on it now and then. Ma probably forgot all about it. He'll be angry if he finds out I took it, though it's always hard to tell if he's angry or not. He just gets quieter than usual and looks as if he's chewing something. If he could see me now, that would probably be happening because I cut my hair off, except I wouldn't put it past him to not even notice. Ma would be horrified. I horrify her a lot. He'd probably tell Ma, "Don't ride herd on her," even if he didn't like it. Maybe *now* he'll be sorry he didn't ride herd on me more. And at least when it comes to Fayette coming with me, I guess he'll ride herd all right.

I didn't do a very good job of cutting my hair. I didn't want Fay helping me (not that he could have done it any better), but I wanted to get used to how I looked before anybody saw me. I tried to cut my hair so it would look like You-Know-Who's, slanting sideways over my forehead, but it won't do that. (Fayette's hair does that no matter if it's cut that way or not.) My hair has always been a bother. Ma keeps saying how lucky I am to have this bit of natural wave. It's exactly that little bit of curl that keeps it from looking right no matter what I do. Since I chopped it off, it curled up even more, and the more I wet it to stick it down, the more it curls. I look less and less like him the more I try. Fayette will probably start calling me Curly. He'd better not unless he wants to be called Horse Face permanently.

We have to have new names anyway. Fayette will have to get used to calling me Lon. This isn't the first time I've had him call me that, so he's in practice. Nobody will know I'm not a boy except Fayette. And Fay never has liked his name. He always wants to be called Bill, but I don't want to have to keep saying the name they call Old Him half the time. (If anybody gets to be called Bill, it'll be me. I've told Fay that a hundred times.) Fay always says, "How about Will, then?" I can stand that and it won't be the first time. We'll be brothers just like he and Uncle T-Bone were, and I'm almost as old as he was when they came west.

I feel like I'm already on top of a mountain though we haven't even started out. I'm all dizzy as if I was looking far, far down on everything—as if everybody and everything here (except for Fay and me) aren't important anymore. They have nothing at all to do with us. They're not even real.

—•—

Sometimes the whole family, with Uncle Bone's whole family, too, and usually even Grandpa Jacob, will come over, or we'll go to their places, and we'll ride as high as we can, up to some pass or other. There won't be any trees up there, but somebody will have made some sort of tie-line or hitching post at the very top (if there isn't one, he and Uncle Bone will put one up themselves, so by now there always is one) and we'll tie up, and Ma and Aunt Henriette will get out the picnic things. There'll be icy snow in big patches and yet we won't need more than a sweater. We make ice balls and pour molasses on them. Fayette always freezes the roof of his mouth and hurts himself, and sometimes he eats so many so fast he makes himself sick. Grandpa Jacob will sit and smoke his pipe and look at Ma as if he's still in love with her. Most of the rest of us will climb whatever peak seems the hardest or highest. Aunt Henriette is the only one with fancy hiking boots from Monkey Ward's that lace up to her knees, but she never climbs. You-Know-Who wanted to get some like that for my so-called ma, but she said the money'd be better used for something else—besides, how often did she ever climb? *I* would have liked to have boots like that, but he never asked *me* and I *do* climb—every single time except for a while after I got burned. They didn't even think about how I might like boots like that.

Ma wouldn't let Fayette climb with us until last year because he's always slamming around not looking where he's going. Uncle T-Bone and a couple of his children will start up with us. (Henri still keeps clear of me as if he thinks I might suddenly decide to pound on him again. I wouldn't give him the satisfaction. I still scare him. I scare lots of kids, but not Fayette.) Uncle T-Bone is sort of plump and never likes to climb very far. All his children climb on down with their "papá." That leaves me alone at the top with Old Him almost every time. We're the tough ones. Two of a kind. If we decide to get to the top, then we do it, no matter what. We look down on them all from up there. Sometimes he says what I'm thinking only he reverses it: "We must look like a couple of gnats to them down there," but I always feel like I'm a giant and they're the gnats. And that's how I feel right this very minute.

Once, when we were at the top, he must have been feeling that dizzy, excited feeling I always get when I'm up there. That was on the first climb after I'd recovered from getting burned. (He had pretty much recovered, too.) He put his arm across my shoulders like we were pals—like he always does to Fayette. Maybe he forgot I was me. Or maybe it was just so pretty. He was looking off, down on our land, his, all tan and hilly with little dots of green that were the sagebrush and the rabbitbrush; and Ma's pastures, green all over and flat and with the shine of the ditches in the sun and the shine of the river, too, snaking through it. Sometimes when he puts his arm around Fay I think, Why doesn't he ever do that to me? But when he did it, I pulled away fast. I couldn't stand that, and it wasn't because he was all sweaty. I surprised myself. I surprised him, too. He took his arm away pretty quick. He didn't look at me even when he handed me the canteen. He kept looking down at our land and chewing on nothing like he does when he's angry. He looked like he wanted to give me a good talking to, but I didn't worry that he would do it. I doubt if he'll get around to saying anything. Besides, I'll be gone. I can't wait to get out of here and into my own real life.

—·—

I was so anxious to go I almost took off before he went out to get drunk. I knew that would be the best time to leave. Then last night I saw how he didn't look at Ma. It's as if he feels guilty even before he does it. I suppose he promised he wouldn't and then goes ahead and does it anyway. Ma did-n't look at him either, like she sure doesn't want him reading anything in her eyes. Briant and Gabby started being pals all of a sudden instead of Briant picking on the little one. When Briant is good to Gabby, that's one of the first signs that things aren't right around here. So I took all our trip things out to the barn to be ready to leave. The slowest was this morning, cutting my hair out there while Ma was busy baking.

I'm not bringing any rags for that that Ma says not to call the curse even though it is. (Besides, she never gave me any other words for it that *she* thought were all right.) I'm thinking that since hardships stop it, I'm going to see to it that I have lots of *them*. Maybe if I have enough for a long enough time, it will stop for good.

They're gathered around the fireplace, but he sits apart. Lotti sits apart, too, but then she always does. She has her special spot where she can write or draw with her back to the wall so nobody can see what she's doing. She doesn't use a table or desk, just a piece of board she cut and sanded for herself. It even has a lid so she can hide what she's working on quickly. She's got everyone trained not to peek, except Briant. When he tries it, she snaps the lid down on his fingers. He tries anyway.

He thinks Lotti's just pretending to draw. Well, he's pretending to sit here.

Usually he has the two little ones on his lap in the evenings, and usually Oriana comes when she's done with the dishes. She'll bring her darning or knitting and he'll offer her the big chair, and she'll say, no, she'd rather be on the stool by his knees. But she won't be finishing her work now. She'll go on and on with anything that needs doing. Later on he'll pretend to go to bed with her. He'll pretend to hold her. Give her that much. After all she's been through, she needs somebody strong and steady and he's never been that. Wasn't even on their wedding night. He remembers it only vaguely. What a fiasco! She was . . . Who'd have thought so much, so many—her whole front sopping with his tears? And it was exactly as he'd always feared, once he started, he couldn't stop.

Now those two littlest ones hunker down on the bearskin. They lean over the big bear head that everybody's always tripping on. (He'd like to get rid of that head except none of the children want him to.) Briant, the big little one, whispers to Gabby, the little little one, two fuzzy pink heads almost touching. He often wonders what it is a two-year-old can be telling, and so earnestly, to a one-year-old who listens carefully and answers in sensible-sounding nonsense. He would like to gather them up—even the two dead babies—even that one conceived in rage . . . or more like it, conceived in terror (by now he can feel for that black-headed boy he could hardly bear to look at)—gather them, all his children, into a bouquet of red heads and black heads. Save them. But he can't even save them from himself. It does seem, though, that he has been, after all, capable of . . . at least a kind of love—more than he'd thought.

He had tried to tell Oriana about himself before the wedding. She wouldn't listen. There's a lot of things she just won't hear. Henriette told her about him, too, and right in front of him, but she told them too much like jokes. They were all true.

Except it's true, too, though not rich, they are richer than they ever expected to be, and there's this house she loves, built mostly by his own hand and to her plan, this big kitchen where everybody sits now, and just as she wanted, she can be washing dishes and look out the window at the mountains at the same time. And he had been the one who'd put loving where fear and pain and rage had been. And then there's that time she stepped into his pond! He'd not seen the like, nor even thought to ever see such a sight as she was . . . in the sunlight with the shadows of the leaves across her body. Naked because he'd asked her to be. Looking like . . . no, much better than any painting he'd ever seen hanging over any bar. His pregnant wife. They already knew, though they'd only just married, that they were to have a child. She'd worried, would it live? And he'd worried, would she?

Now she's scrubbing at pots and pans more than need be. She never has believed in getting drunk, especially not the kind of drunk he gets. And he'd promised. He'd promised her everything he could think of to promise when she almost died, and he'd kept all those promises except this one. The one that really counts.

He'll put in a full day's worth of work—pretend to—well, he will, but he won't be back for supper.

How odd that, exactly now, there are only three pages left of the journal. It's as if *it's time.*

And here's another odd thing, besides only these three pages left, his tally book is brand new. He's only used, and *exactly,* three pages of it. I tore them out. It has a waterproof cover and a little pencil that fits right into it. He'll notice it's gone all right, probably before he even notices *we're* gone, because Ma gave it to him.

I will wrap this up in oilcloth and hide it in the very, very back of the cold cave just in case the house burns down. Years from now I'll come back. No matter where I roam or how old I get.

So now, this is how real life begins!

He's naked in the hot spring though he's still wearing his hat. He's down where the water has cooled some as it mixes with stream water. He's drunk, but not yet too drunk. It's about the time for the first star, the wishing one. It's been a long time since he believed in much of anything, let alone wishes, though as a boy he wished and wished. Mostly not to get whipped, but what good did that do? Still, he always does wish. "Star bright, star light . . ." Let me get myself together. A little bit. But then when has he ever had himself together? Not since Christianne. (Christy. He would have taught Christy the names of the stars and constellations the way Christianne had taught him. He would have told her to make wishes.) Is there any sense in doing anything at all? Or then again, is there any sense in *not* doing anything? The rotgut has begun to soothe him.

Wait long enough and every creature nearby will come to drink from the rusty water. If he sits still, they'll hardly notice him. Or they'll notice but they'll think he's harmless, which he is. The rattlesnake will come to swallow some small thirsty thing. He will let it be. There's tricks of the light and air: a dust devil could be anything or nothing. (There are times when a dust devil, with the whole desert to do its dance in, will come right to him, envelop him in its miniature tornado, leave him blinded, dustier than ever, things in his pockets from some entirely different part of the desert.) Magpie, Coyote, Great God Clown seem just out of sight. "In the beginning was the creosote bush, from which all things come"—so the Indians say. He wished it was true. Then maybe he would be a part of it all instead of arm's length from everything he cares about. He would be the father he pretends to be, and the house builder, the pond maker, the husband and lover of his beautiful woman. . . .

A dust devil does come. No, it's somebody off in the distance riding hard. He thinks, Not good for the horse, and how long will they keep that up? There's something flapping. Skirts it is, flapping on each side. A woman astride. As he usually does, he recognizes the horse first—that rangy, rough lope. It's Lockjaw. He was trying to straighten that horse up so he'd be good enough to sell. Then he sees it's his—he always thinks *his* —it's *my* Oriana. That must have been the only horse handy or she'd never have tried to ride him. He wonders where she got the courage even to saddle him up or to put the bit in his mouth. But when courage is needed, Oriana has it. By the time she gets up to him, he's mostly dressed and has chewed a couple of pinches of ground coffee.

Oriana can't stop that horse. He shouts for her to pull his head around so all he can do is circle. She does, and Lockjaw dances until he can grab the reins and give him a good jerk.

She can't talk right away. It's exactly like when he'd first decided it was all right for them to be in love. Or at least he'd given up fighting it. Then all she could say was "Oh, Mr. Ledoyt," over and over. Now all she can say is "Oh, Beal," only this time something bad has happened. It scares him to think of any more bad things.

She slides down into his arms and Lockjaw trots off, reins on the ground, holding his head sideways so as not to step on them, too ornery and too smart to be ground tied. He lets the horse go. Nothing he can do about it. No doubt Lockjaw will stay just far enough away to try and tempt him into chasing him, which he won't. Instead he holds her. He wants to stand strong for her, but the desert rocks around him, and with that unbrewed coffee he swallowed so fast, he feels queasy. She mustn't know. And she mustn't know how drunk he is. (After their wedding night, he'd resolved she'd not ever see him like that again. So far that's one thing he's stuck to.) He mustn't hang on to her to steady himself. Thinks, At least she's safe. Thinks, I will not let myself outlive her.

Before he'd met Oriana he'd thought to not let himself last much longer—to let it happen off someplace where T-Bone would never find out about it. T-Bone and Henriette could always be wondering if he might not turn up one of these springs, until he faded from their memories. Better than knowing for sure.

"They've gone," Oriana says when she can catch her breath.

And he says, "Who?" but he knows who. He'd seen it—or something —last night but he hadn't paid attention. He even knows what pass they took. Lotti'd be crossing by the highest, hardest one. She'd want to scare herself and especially scare Oriana—and Fayette, *pauv' gars*. He thought she'd maybe outgrown that crazy kind of . . . whatever it was she felt for him. She hadn't said a word about the trip east. That should have been a clue. Lotti, always on the verge of some crazy thing. Like that fire. She'd do anything she knew to do to make life harder for him and for Oriana. She'd picked a day when he'd gone off. She'd chased off all the horses except for Lockjaw. And of course Fayette. Those two were always together, but it's a sure guess Fay didn't want to go. There's the same seven years' difference between those two, yet they're nothing at all like he and Christianne used to be. Even so, they're just as close.

What will Oriana do while he goes after them? He'll have to ride on up to T-Bone's first and send back one of the girls. Maybe Henri, too.

"Damnation!" (He never wanted Oriana to hear him say such things. Usually he could switch to "dag nab" or "pshaw" or some such just in time.) He throws the still-half-full bottle of whiskey up onto the rocks behind them as far as he can. Feels satisfaction hearing it shatter, even though a couple of good drunks gone forever. "We'll walk on back," he says. "It's too late to go after them tonight. They'll be all right. Lotti knows how to take care of herself." She does, too, you could count on it, except when she's trying to prove something—which is just about all the time. But Lord knows what the weather is up there.

Here the stars are just about all the way out. It's almost as bright as moonlight. The only clouds circle the mountaintops.

"She left her hair. She cut off all her hair and left it on our bureau."

Has Oriana noticed the night?

They're so seldom alone anymore. How long has it been since they've done something just for the two of them? The night reminds him of their honeymoon and before, too, when they did what they shouldn't have been doing. Partly because of nights like this one.

He never wanted Oriana to see him drunk, but he *is* drunk—and amorous. For sure this is the wrong time, but he wants to kiss her. And more. For sure he smells of whiskey. She's up pretty close, anyway, hanging on to his elbow. He helps her over rough spots and she lets herself be helped. He knows, and he knows she knows, she doesn't need help. She stumbles, but that's because she's looking at the stars. He stumbles, but he only sees the stars on the horizon as a backdrop for her face, the Teapot rising behind her profile. She stops. "When the Seven Sisters get up there this time of year," she says, "it will be midnight. You taught me that."

For a few minutes it's as if she feels exactly as he does. It's as if she doesn't care to notice the smell of cheap rotgut, but then when they've dropped to their knees and he's thinking to take off his shirt for under her, and thinking he will hold his hand under her head to keep her from the sand, she pulls away and says, "How can you! At a time like this!" And he's kneeling there without her and she's half running in the direction of home. Yet she had felt what he felt. She'd wanted to. She shouts back, "The little ones. Alone. How could you forget!" Yet she'd forgotten. "And poor little Fayette . . ."

Ah, Fayette. She won't be mentioning Lotti. Not in the same way. He can hardly blame her.

She *must* go with him and he *must* let her. Though he won't. He'll say he can go faster without her, and that he won't need sleep or food. That's just the trouble, he keeps forgetting or won't admit—even to himself—that he's not a young man anymore. (Sometimes she wonders if—though he can be so childlike and playful—if he ever was, deep inside, a young man.) "And," he'll say, "in your condition."

"But this is *always* my condition."

Where will she find the energy? She used to have plenty back when she only had Lotti and Fayette. She would bounce from one task to the next, happy because Beal was just around the corner. But then Christy. And the way Beal was afterward. Something went out of her. Him, too. They never talk about it. What is there to say? She doesn't dare remind him of it, anyway. When it comes to that baby, she's still afraid of him, and for him. Back then, even Fayette, not yet three, knew to keep out of his way. Not that Beal would ever do anything that would hurt the children, but he looked scary. Even Lotti tiptoed instead of stomping around with her usual unladylike striding. (Sometimes they call her "Elephant.") And then that next baby. She always felt it died because it had been conceived in a kind of hopeless rage. And then these two little ones, one after another, and now, *again* . . .

They've mentioned abstaining, though not in so many words. And they *have* abstained. And they've heard that there's a way, but they don't know how to find out about it. Neither one would feel like discussing such a thing, even with a doctor. They do get along for a while without loving in that way—quite a while sometimes, before each child is weaned. And sometimes they work so hard and are so tired it hardly feels like a deprivation at all. She will ask nothing more of life, then, except that she be able to sleep in this bony man's bony arms, except that she rest her head on his bony chest, except that she thread her knees in with his knobby ones. And he, also, it seems to her, would ask nothing more except that he sleep with his head on her breast. But then something will happen and they will need again, something extra nice or something scary that reminds them of how they will someday lose each other: Beal, kicked in the head by a horse, and not the first time; trampled by steers, and not the first time. . . . Almost always it's something happening to him. Nothing much happens to her except pregnancies.

Then, early this spring, not so long ago, he had plowed her kitchen garden as he always did and helped her plant it. They rarely worked all day side by side like that. It was iris time. Her irrigated meadows seemed nothing but one gigantic iris patch, killdeer nests, it seemed, in almost every other clump—meadowlarks, swallows. . . . The coyotes yipping sounding more like birds than coyotes. (When she'd first come west they'd laughed at her at Jacob's because she thought they *were* birds. Not when they howled. That she could tell.) They had eaten a late supper of left-overs, sitting out on the porch steps watching the clouds streaming, flaglike, south out of every notch in the mountains. They'd watched until the sun left even the tops of the peaks in the dark and the mountains seemed to huddle in close, small and black. The little ones went to sleep early. Fayette fed the orphaned foal, which he loved to do, and asked as he always did, "Will he really take the bit all by himself and never have to be called?" And Beal had said, "Mmm-hmm," and "Mmm-hmm," and moved her plate so he could sit close to her. There was something soft and quiet in the air. She could tell what Beal was thinking. She was thinking it, too. They had meant not to, but it had been such a long time.

———•———

She says, "I'm going with you or else I'm following after you, whichever way you choose to have it. Some things you can't do anything about." She said it the way she'd told him she was going to be in love with him whether he'd let her be or not. But she doesn't get her way this time.

She has to go through a whole day waiting while Beal goes to fetch somebody to be with her. She cooks chicken and makes more jerky (Lotti took it all). She puts a harness bell on each baby to keep track of them now that Lotti and Fayette aren't there to help. She plays with them. When they nap, she starts sewing on a shirt for Fayette, a warm woolly one. He'll say it itches, and she'll say he has to wear it anyway.

She still has half a mind to find some way of going with him, but when Beal comes back with Henri and Henriette, he and Henriette talk her out of going. And then Oriana says what she promised herself she wouldn't: "You're too old. You can't go off like this any more than I can, going without food and sleep. Remember how your hip feels whenever the weather gets damp?"

She's wondering why she's going on and on with it. He won't even let himself know that she's hurting him, but he is hurt. She can tell because he's looking thoughtful and chewing on nothing.

Henriette goes outside to give them a chance to be alone. There's a lot of shrieking going on out there where Henri is on all fours bucking the two little ones off his back.

"Don't you think I know it? You're not saying anything I don't already know. I was already too old when you married me." He reaches for her. "I warned you, back when I thought you were hardly nineteen. But I'm still—"

"I know. Just like Henriette always says, you're still all gristle and aggravation. But I want you safe. I want everybody safe."

"There's no such thing."

"Shouldn't you have somebody with you? Henri's right here."

"I'll go faster without."

He takes his favorite big gray mule. He thinks it's odd that Lotti didn't take him. He'd have preferred it if she had. They'd be a lot better off on those mountain trails. You could count on that mule. He wouldn't do anything it wasn't safe to do. He'd just stop. And he'd never lose his head, which is more than you can say about most horses.

Average (not maximum) loads and distance traveled per day. Contrast of horse and mule.		
	Load	Miles per day
HORSE	200 lbs.	30
MULE	260 lbs.	60
	Price in 1900	Price in 1909
HORSE	$45	$80
MULE	$55	$100

The eastern side of the mountains is the high, steep side, but it starts slowly, up from flat desert, first a long sloping alluvial fan, then low hills covered with rounded well-worn boulders and sagebrush, and then quite suddenly, the cracked and splintered mountains and the pines begin. For a while the trees are tall and the ground covered with lupine and mule ears and penstemon. (This is where they come every year to pick currants. This is where they meet Paiute families doing the same.) Then the trees spread out to few and far between, become twisted and gnarled (lupine growing up there is so tiny it looks like an entirely different plant). In some places the underbrush is in impenetrable patches of manzanita. You have to keep to the trails. Switchbacks begin and it's so steep the horses must be rested often. Finally the stunted trees end, and there's just jagged boulders and talus and scree. Though the trail is fairly well used—by miners, hunters, fishermen, sometimes artists and photographers—in some spots it has slid away or been covered over by landslides.

> As early as the 1850s fishermen had stocked the streams with trout where no trout had ever been simply by carrying a few up in buckets.

P a always brought a spade in case of landslides. Pa is always ready for anything, but Lotti didn't bring one. Pa said if you stand real still and keep real quiet, you can hear the whole mountain trickling down.

Lotti leads the horses across these slides by blindfolding them. She says she's going to blindfold him, and it's not a joke. He's not afraid of heights, but this sliding gravel is different. He doesn't care if she calls him lily-livered, just as long as she lets him hang on to the end of her lariat when he crosses.

It's cold and getting colder. The sun has already set in the valley, but not up here at the top of the pass. They are right at one of the picnic spots they go to. There's the hitching post and the patches of old snow. (Every year the exact same patches. It's been melted and refrozen and melted and refrozen and wind dried until it's halfway between crushed ice and snow and is exactly the best there is for putting molasses on.) Even though it's the windiest spot of all, and even though there's a sheltered place just a little bit lower, this is where Lotti decides they should eat supper. He knows that as always, Lotti's trying to make things hard—sometimes, it seems, just to see what he'll do about it and sometimes, it seems, to see if she can pass whatever test it is she's made up for herself. She always passes, at least according to her rules.

She stole a whole apple pie. ("I helped peel the apples, didn't I? So it's half mine, anyway.") She gets it out as if it's a special present just for him. And she's proud that she's gotten it this far and only a little bit squashed, and Ma's fancy glass pie plate still all in one piece.

"After this there'll be nothing to eat but jerky and jackass rabbits," she says. "So enjoy it." But it's too windy to enjoy it. He wolfs it down. He wants to be done quickly so they can get on over the top and maybe get out of the wind a little bit. It's pretty up here, spires like churches and pinnacles like castles and glaciers below them. It goes on as far as you can see, all directions except toward home. That way you can see all the way to the

Fay by Lotti

valley. If you think hard, you can think you see the poplars that make their house look like a sailing ship in the middle of a pasture sea. But the wind makes his eyes water and his nose run. He'd like to look, but it's too hard.

And he'd like to be asking Lotti where they're going and when are they going home, but what would be the use? She'll lie. And then when that lie gets to be not true, she'll lie another lie. If he thinks about how to ask her in a very special way, maybe he can get a halfways truthful answer, but he isn't going to give her the satisfaction of him asking any questions yet. He doesn't want to be called a worried old lady or a quitter. If he says, Why do we have to stop and eat way up here in the wind? she'll call him a yellow-bellied goony. And since she seems to think having nothing but a whole pie for supper is so wonderful, if he told her he didn't feel like having a meal of just that, she'd be angry and call him Horse Face. (It's his secret, but he doesn't mind getting called that because he looks just like Pa. Everybody says so. She can't hurt him with that, but he'll not let on to her. He only pretends he doesn't like it.) But she's right about him. He does want to quit, and he is just a little old girl because he still likes leaning up against Pa, though he doesn't sit on his lap anymore. If it wasn't for Lotti, he'd probably still be doing that. Pa's lap is bony, but he'd like to be there anyway. Lotti says she never did things like sit on laps and never ever would. She jerks away whenever anybody gets too close, but he's seen her hug and kiss horses a lot, even Lockjaw, though Lockjaw bit her a couple of times and Ma said would she please stay away from that animal.

Pa isn't like other men in lots of ways. He hugs. Grandpa Jacob likes them a lot, but he doesn't do that. Uncle T-Bone kind of does it, and Aunt Henriette is terrible. She ups and grabs you from behind when you aren't expecting it and kisses and hugs and it's over before you hardly know what happened, but he likes the way Pa puts his arm around him and calls him *"mon vieux"* and *"vieux copain."* Lotti doesn't get to be called those, and she doesn't ever want anybody's arm around her.

So he admits it, he *is* like a girl. He always kind of knew it from the start. He wants to go home and he wants Ma and Pa. If they go much farther he won't know the way back. If they go really, really far, maybe even the horses won't know. And anyway, who's going to feed his foal? That has got to be done. Ma won't have time and she won't remember. Except it's important. She's always thinking about other things, as if clean clothes were the most important. That's what she worries about, clothes and what's for supper. He'd named Goldy Goldy even though Pa said you never could tell for sure what color he'd be when he grew up. Lotti said it was just like him to pick such a silly name, but Pa told her she didn't always have to say everything that came into her head, and maybe she should try just saying half. And what about his pet hen? And anyway, it's getting dark so Lotti should be stopping, though they'd have a hard time right here finding a level spot to sleep in or one without stones since it's all stones. But he's half asleep already and sometimes dozes off completely. Last time he went to sleep on a horse was at Grandpa Jacob's when he and Pa worked together. Pa knew. Pa knew everything. Pa said many's the time he'd done that himself, and it was all right. The horse knew what to do and if there was trouble, the horse would know that, too, and wake him up soon enough.

As he dozes, Crazy Colt takes a false trail and he finds himself on a dead end a dozen yards below Lotti. She says, "Try, just for once, to be a little bit smarter than the horse," and he says, "Pa says it's not easy to be smarter than a horse."

"Don't tell me what he says. I know all about it, and besides, I don't care what he says."

Tears come out, but it's dark and Lotti can't see so it doesn't matter. Anyway, he isn't *really* crying. From now on he won't be saying a single word to Lotti. Anyway, he doesn't want to get her to telling scary stories about mountain lions or rattlesnakes or bears. Pa said climb a *thin* tree, but it's too dark to see, and up here the trees are too gnarled and not very many. He can see their scary outlines against the sky. Lotti calls them tree ghosts and says they used to be bad people and they don't like people that are good and they come after them. When he told Pa, Pa said, "Hogwash." If Pa were here he wouldn't be scared. Not even if bears came. Pa said, "Whatever you do, don't run," but without Pa there he might run by mistake. He might not be able to make himself stand still and move slowly. Pa would be talking to that bear like he talks to a scared horse, but then Pa's voice is kind of rumbly. The bear would think it was another bear. His own voice would be squeaky and probably get him in worse trouble. "Talking a lot of nothin'," Pa calls it. He's never heard Pa talk to a bear, though he's heard him talk to everything else. Pa is magic. Even Ma says so.

But a long time ago he promised Lotti he'd help her find her real parents. Maybe that's what she's doing now. Maybe she's on her way to join up with the Paiutes and find her mother and be a Paiute queen. She would be lonely going off to find them all by herself. Maybe be lonely even *after* she finds them. He should stick by her like he said he would—stick to his word like Pa would do—stay at least until she settles in and gets to know her people a little bit. She needs him. One way or another, she always seems to be needing him.

A storm is coming. He can't see the silhouettes of the trees anymore, except now and then when there's lightning. Lotti says, "Way up here, for sure it won't be just rain." She always thinks the worst just to worry him, but she turns out to be right, it's hail. It will ruin his new hat that Ma and Pa gave him for his birthday—his one and only present, but just what he wanted. It isn't as if it's a really waterproof beaver hat. Probably not even a little bit beaver like Pa's is.

They're far enough down to find shelter in among scrub oak, though not very good shelter. Lotti rigs up a piece of tarp she brought just for this. They huddle under it. Crazy and Strawberry have to be out in it. They stand with their tails to the wind and look miserable. The hail makes such a racket on the tarp and all around, too, they can hardly hear each other. Lotti sits (knees apart like Ma never wants her to) and rolls a cigarette. She's good at it. She must have been practicing. He's smelled tobacco on her a few times before. She won't share it with him. Not even one puff. She says, damned if she'll be a party to corrupting a child. He says he's not a child—not if he earned five dollars working at Grandpa's. But he doesn't really care. He leans against Lotti and Lotti lets him. Sometimes she does do nice things, but you never know when.

Lotti has been telling Fayette that her mother is an Indian so often she partly believes it, yet sitting here smoking, tired, she knows it probably isn't true. What she knows about herself, once you get right down to it, wouldn't be half as big as one of these hailstones, and really, once you get right down to it, she looks to be about as Indian as any black-haired white person. Well, at least she comes from tall, brave people so Ma can't be her ma. Though maybe she can't be completely sure of that either, because to look at Fayette, you'd think Ma had nothing whatsoever to do with it.

All of a sudden she's glad to have Fay leaning up against her so warm and floppy. His hat is halfway off, and now and then in the lightning, she can see tear streaks in the dirt on his face. Maybe she won't mention that. Still, she might be able to use it later on. For sure he's been crying. He's a lot more like a girl than she ever was. Well, she won't mention the crying unless he says something dumb, but chances are, he will.

She thought maybe she'd keep an all-night watch, but with Fayette curled up next to her . . . (She might, after all, like to have him for her real half-brother, which everybody thinks he is.)

She throws the cigarette butt off into the hail and curls up around him. She pushes his hat all the way off and rests her cheek on his head—he'll never know—and falls asleep in spite of herself.

He will not come back without his son. He realizes that, just like Oriana two nights before, he's hardly thinking of Lotti. Not in terms of rescuing. By God, she knows exactly what she's doing. She wants him just exactly as angry as he is. Rescue! Let her go on off and do what she has to do someplace far away from him and his. Rescued her from fire. Rescued her from flood and he couldn't even swim. He went in anyway, hardly thinking about it. Almost killed himself, but never gave a second thought. If he'd had his rope he'd have lassoed her instead. He should have waited for T-Bone to catch up. T-Bone can swim. But then it would have been too late. Thank God it wasn't a big one, though big enough. They'd only just twenty minutes earlier told the children to stay away from the creek. (They should have known better than to tell Lotti not to do something—especially not in front of Henri.) It was the flash-flood season. Henri came running, yelling that he hadn't dared her. They couldn't understand what he was talking about. (Both those children must have been about twelve or so—old enough to have a little horse sense.) They ran back with Henri. "She dared *me*. I *didn't* dare her. I really didn't. She went and did it anyway."

There was a boulder in the middle of the creek. The children played there in the dry season. Not a good habit to be in. Now Lotti had told Henri the water wouldn't cover it—dared him to sit there. Henri said they could even hear the flood coming. He said she'd said, "You're just a yellow-bellied girl," and then she'd gone right out on it herself.

He heard Oriana shouting, "No! Don't!" as he waded in. He worried she'd jump in right behind him just to be following after him—share whatever would be happening to him. T-Bone would stop her. He got to Lotti just before the worst part hit and threw them off the rock. After that he doesn't know what happened or how he got them on shore finally, two miles downstream—or if he had anything to do with it. Hit stones, got into a shallow spot—everything happened too fast and afterward seemed swept right out of his head. Suddenly there they were, half drowned but beached, choking and coughing. He dragged her out and held her, top half upside down, even before he could catch his own breath. Pounded her back. Then they collapsed facedown, side by side, until he realized they ought to get out from under the willows so the others could find them. His boots had filled with sand and pebbles, which maybe had helped him get his footing. While they lay there, Lotti rolled over and held on to his arm with both hands, and when he carried her away from the shore, she held him around the neck as if she was an ordinary child and he an ordinary father.

God knows he's tried and tried and is about to do for her again. He does understand—up to a point—though in some ways she's completely beyond his ken. But if anything happens to that boy! Poor Fay, pushed and pulled every which way. He'll be homesick and scared. Like as not, missing him. Thinks he's about the best thing on two legs, birds included. Nice, but it won't last more'n a few more years. He'll be missing his foal, too. He should have told him before that that'll be his horse. It would be something nice for him to think about. Lotti will be scared, too, though she won't admit it even to herself. He ought to keep that in mind.

He keeps waiting for the day when she'll learn. She will, too. There's a softness in her she won't let on to, though maybe it won't ever come to anything except, as it already has, with horses.

He left before dawn. He doesn't need any light for trotting across their meadows. He knows where the gopher holes aren't. And the hornet's nests. In his saddlebags the chicken and jerky Oriana made the day before. She'd packed his bedroll, too, before he got back with Henriette and Henri. Rolled it almost as tight and neat as he'd have done himself, but it's plump. No doubt it's full of socks and sweaters. He can't ever look at it without remembering their times together—on it or in it. He's still been, even so, if he thinks about *all* of it, a lucky man. Even so. Though sometimes it doesn't feel like it. Just so his luck, what there is left of it, holds now. Just a little while longer.

He's up on the last of his stony hills when dawn begins. All this drama (Lotti does like drama) going on around him and still these clouds piling up on top of each other, worrisome but beautiful. Too bad they don't do enough for Lotti but that she has to make more scenes. The mountains start out dark purple, then orange stripes their tops. He stops to watch the orange wash down them, little bit by little bit but faster than you'd expect, and rests the mule. He'll get off and walk him for a while. He turns to look down on their home, still in the dark. He can just barely make it out. Before he hardly realizes what he's doing, he thinks, Great God Clown, let us be. For a little while. Then he laughs out loud at himself. It shocks him. It sounds more like Great God Clown's kind of laugh. More like a laugh he might have laughed before he'd met Oriana. A laugh that doesn't believe or hope or trust. Something cold and crazy in it.

Lotti is in Lotti heaven. She's cold and wet but she hasn't put on her sweater or jacket. She takes wide steps. In her imagination she's wearing men's riding boots instead of these lace-ups that barely cover her ankles. She *is* wearing a man's hat. It's become a tradition that whenever Ledoyt gets a new hat, Lotti gets the old one—except he hardly ever gets a new one. Oriana has never let Lotti buy a new man's hat (she seems to think that any minute Lotti will get over wanting one, even though it's been years), and yet they bought Fayette a new hat and he's only eight. The hailstorm has made his hat look about as old as Lotti's secondhand one. She's glad it did. If it hadn't, she'd have helped age it some when Fay wasn't looking.

She has built a tiny fire. Though all the wood on the ground is wet, Lotti knows to gather the dry dead branches that are still on the lower trunks of trees where they've been sheltered by live branches above them. She's shot a brace of quail, silently, with bow and arrows. (It was the "tick-tick-tick, tobacco, tobacco" of the quail that woke her.) She's recovered her arrowheads. In her saddlebags she has the makings for biscuits and beans, but in Lotti heaven, that's too easy. The quail will hardly be enough for the two of them, but being hungry is part of her heaven, too.

Half hidden in this early morning mist, she feels herself to be, after all, really and truly part Indian. Every move she makes shows it. The mist is rising. That's a sign of good weather. Maybe it's an omen of how things will be from now on.

As she hunted and then went for wood, she scouted out the trail ahead. (Fayette still sleeps. Lotti prefers he stay that way so she can pretend she's out in the wilds alone.) The trail forks up ahead, a main part heading west and another one, a steep, little-used trail, heading south. At the fork there's a handmade sign reading: SAN FRANCISCO CHIPPIES 200 MILES DUE WEST. Lotti wonders what chippies are. Some kind of chickens, sounds like.

Old Him will think they'd be crossing the mountains to San Francisco toward the chickens. He'll think if they were going south, they wouldn't be so foolish as to do it right in the middle of the mountains. They'd have started out the logical way, straight down through the long valley. But careful as she's been, she knows You-Know-Who will probably be able to follow them. He always seems to know things you'd think he wouldn't. She thinks, Clever bastard, just so she can think words Ma wouldn't like her to and words Old Him would say when he thought nobody was around.

In her mind he has become the villain—an outlaw, a horse thief, a white man chasing Indians, or he's the Indian chasing white people. Swarthy, unshaven—he has become to her the scary, stony man he was when Christy died and she didn't dare look at him. Even his name seems sinister. It's not the first time she's made him out as villain. She's stalked him as rustler, as mountain lion, as grizzly, but now *he* is stalking *her*. Goose bumps pop out all over when she thinks of being found and found out. What might he do now that she's kidnapped the apple of his eye? She's never known him to lose control, but she senses anger in him she's never seen expressed. She wonders if that's why he needs to be getting drunk, and if someday he'll burst. It'll probably be all her fault. But even Christy hadn't done that to him. Or maybe he went off and burst some-place else. Winnemucca it was.

She can handle it. She's a grown-up, after all. (Hitting somebody in the Adam's apple can kill just like that. He told her that and not to do it.) She's the hero. (Not heroine. Even the word makes her cringe.) And she looks like a hero, tall and strong and square-jawed—scars at her neck from when she burned herself, rope burns across her hands, nicks all over them she hardly knows from what. Ma's pistol in her pocket and she's not afraid to use it. She squints and frowns. Anyone seeing her now would know not to mess with her.

Oriana thinks she should have noticed. She should have been paying attention. Lotti was too calm and too well behaved. And she was writing and writing and writing as though it was her last chance ever. She was even wearing the big apron and she hates aprons—it seemed just so she could keep her journal in the front pocket. Where is that book? It might have some clue about where Lotti is going and why, though Lotti never seemed to need a reason for doing anything. Maybe Henri can help look for it. Except Lotti might have taken it with her just to keep it secret.

Lotti had never said one single word against the trip east. Of course everybody knew she didn't relish it, but she seemed resigned, though when was Lotti ever resigned to anything? But it was an adventure. Lotti always liked adventures.

This hair. It means something beyond just insult and anger. She hardly knows what to think. It's like a little death. Things won't ever be the same. Or Lotti won't be, not even when—even *if* she lets her hair grow out.

Oriana ties the hair together carefully at the cut ends and wraps it in an embroidered towel. She's often wished she had hair like this, so heavy and wavy and thick—black with reddish glints. (Those reddish glints Lotti got from her. She got the best of the red, just a sort of coppery overlay. About the only thing Lotti seems to have inherited from her side.) This hair is exactly like what every woman (except for Lotti) yearns for. What a difficult child! And it's likely Oriana's own fault. Even after Hazel told her she had to be a real mother . . . Well, she'd tried—gone through the motions—but she hadn't wanted to be a mother, not at all until Fayette. Fayette is exactly what she wants, a tiny Beal, who is now a little bit bigger Beal, and she'd wanted to name him Beal, but Beal didn't want him "saddled," as he said, with that. "Anything but Beal," he'd said, and she said, "If not Beal, then anything," so here he is, saddled with Fayette. At first she thought that was a pretty name, but she's heard Fay, as he plays, pretending to be Bill. Both those children want to be Bill. They argue about it so much she wonders sometimes if there's ever any time left over for playing.

But what if . . . ? Lotti used to draw landslides as well as fires. Who would think of drawing people with boulders falling on them and half covered with debris? Fayette does draw wars. (First people shooting at each other, and then explosions, until the whole drawing is black. She's managed to rescue a few before they got completely covered up.) Somehow that seems all right for a boy to do. And Fay is such a gentle child. But fire and landslides seem so shocking for a girl to draw. Beal always says, "Let be." If she lost him! And it so often seems as if she has—or is about to. She should have let him . . . on the sand, night before last. Out under the stars. It would have been like it used to be, and the little ones were fine after all. He should have been angry with her. He should have insisted, but he never does.

Henriette is leaving her by herself in the big kitchen. Henriette always seems to know what to do. The kitchen/living room is exactly the way she told Beal she wanted it, with the sink right under a big window that looks out on their sandy front yard and the mountains. She can watch the children and cook or wash dishes as she watches. Now she just stands pretending to do the dishes, watching them outside. That skinny Henri looks six inches taller and even thinner than when she saw him hardly more than a month ago. There's a downy fuzz on his upper lip. Fayette will look like that one day. If nothing happens. Beal must have been like that, too. Sometimes there's still that same boyish shyness in Beal even now. Without Lotti here, Henri will speak up more. She's glad he's here. He's always nice to her two little pink-headed ones. The Ledoyt knack with little ones? Is that *"dans le sang,"* as Henriette would say? Henri has so much the Ledoyt look she loves—coarse black hair always falling into his eyes, the long sad face that's usually grinning, the Ledoyt buckteeth (Beal's are the worst of any of them). . . . Sometimes she thinks, Half-starving farmer faces. Sometimes she thinks, Brooding poets who do nothing but joke.

With Beal around, life seems fun and funny. Even most of the disasters. He can joke when he's sick or hurt. (The only time she ever saw him not joking was . . . But then she didn't want to hear any jokes either.)

When he's not here she can't imagine what there is to laugh about. With Henriette here it will be a little bit the same. Even under these circumstances, Henriette will be making outrageous remarks. (Though she didn't that time when Christy. Henriette's was the hand to cling to then. Tibo's, too.) Now they'll be laughing in spite of worrying. Or laughing all the harder because they're worried. Henriette will be saying, as she always does, "It takes a tough lady to live with a Ledoyt and Beal is the worst of the lot," and Oriana will defend him. That will make her feel better.

He said not to worry. He said, "It isn't as bad as it looks to be." Maybe not, but what about this hair? Lotti must look—well, exactly as she's always wanted to look. How can she go east like that? What kind of a mother will Oriana look like with a shorn child? Maybe she can go anyway. Maybe Beal will get them back in a hurry. And it's true, what he'd said, Lotti can look after herself. And—and she has to keep reminding herself—nobody is, as far as she knows, hurt.

Waiting is hard. First she works on the shirt for Fayette. She's always wanted a sewing machine, but now she's glad she doesn't have one. It would make too much noise and go too fast. The shirt would be finished in a day. Whatever would she do when it's done?

Time goes by. All by itself. There's noon dinner. Henriette and Henri prepare it. Gabby and Briant sit on her lap, patting her hair and her cheeks and eating from her plate. That's a good thing because she's not eating. Henri does talk for a change, but she's not listening. She talks. She's not listening to herself either. Even in the middle of talking she wonders what there is to talk about. Afterward she wants to clean up the dishes just to be doing something, and they let her.

She hardly gets started when the hail comes. Everybody's safely inside. It sounds as if their roof is tin. Gabby and Briant jump around like crazies, Henri just as wild as they are. They rush from window to window, and then Henri opens the door so as to see better. The hail, big as grouse eggs, hits and then bounces up eight inches. The whole yard is dancing, shining, silvery. Her most precious people might be out in the same kind of storm. The weather will be different in the mountains, but it's usually worse. Lots of hail up there and this is the season for it. (They all have their slickers. She checked that first thing night before last. She hopes they have the sense to put them on.) She pushes the little ones off her lap and steps out the door before anyone can stop her. She wants to feel what they might be feeling. But she's driven back and has bruises to show for it. Henriette says, *"Mais tu es folle."*

That's the end of her kitchen garden. End of her flowers, too. She doesn't have to look to know the hay is all knocked flat. It's not the first time and it won't be the last. At least Gabby and Briant enjoy the storm. If Beal were here, he would be making some joke about how they'll have to eat a lot of broken-up squash fast before it spoils. If he were here she might already be starting on the pie crust for squash pie. They'd be laughing, but he'd be worried even so. It was hard to tell, but she thought he suffered more than she when things like this happened. As if it was all his fault. She never cares as long as everybody is safe. But they're not safe. He said not to worry. Now they'll have to buy hay. He'll worry, though he won't admit it. He'll think, as he always does, that he's failing her. He always thinks she should have more than other people have and that he should be the one giving everything to her, but if he really wanted to do something for her, he should have let her come along with him. She has half a mind to take off right now by herself. (The hail's already over with. It didn't take more than five minutes for it to do its damage.) There's no way of following them, but she'd take off in any old direction rather than just sit here and wait. She'd be out in the weather along with them—suffer what they suffer. He should have known things can happen any time. They always do. She had been ready to enjoy Henriette, or try to, but everything is going wrong. She feels nauseous. And now cramps. She wishes Henriette wasn't here. She wouldn't have to be folding up Fay's shirt so carefully and sticking the needle through it. She wouldn't have to stand up so straight getting to her room.

She can do this by herself. She's hardly four months pregnant. Henriette calls her a tough lady—*"petit souris, forte comme un Turc"*— though she never feels that way inside herself.

She locks her door and then hunches over. She ought to change out of this dress, but she's not up to that yet. Is this even worse than having the babies? But that can't be. Now she's down on her hands and knees. The floor will be the best place, but not on the rug. She pulls the chamber pot out from under the bed.

Perhaps it's for the best. It's a relief in a way. She'll be able to go anywhere. Follow after. But what if this baby was to have been another little black-headed Ledoyt? And what if things happen to them out there? At least she would have had this one. Now the pain stops. Maybe everything is all right after all.

She should have thought to bring in Beal's whiskey while he was out getting Henriette and Henri. She knows where it's hidden in the tool and buggy barn, hanging high so the children don't get at it, but they do. She's seen Lotti reaching it down on the end of a clawed hoe. She didn't tell Beal. She no more dares to speak about his liquor than she dares to speak about . . . men and women embracing. Anyway, what's the use? Lotti can get into anything and always has. Beal knows that already.

She always thought there was something immoral—well, but Beal is never immoral (besides, he doesn't drink that often, not like a lot of men), but there's something not right at all with alcohol. She never wanted to have anything to do with the smelly stuff. Even when the doctor said she should have beer, she could hardly get down half a bottle a day. (Beal had made it for her out of mountain gooseberries.) Decent people don't get drunk. Except for Beal. Maybe some do. Now she knows how they feel. But she didn't do it even after Christy, though she thought about it. And Beal. He never drank a drop in front of her except at the wedding. It's all about the thoughts, they keep going round and round, not the pain. If she was with him it would be different. He's never there when she needs him the most. Except she wouldn't want him to see her now. But she might want him outside the door trying to get in. He'd break it down. Come right in on her . . . all this repulsiveness. But she's failed him from the start. She hasn't been the kind of woman that he needs. No wonder he's never been able to bring himself to say he loves her.

Cramps come again. She leans her head on the edge of the bed. For a few minutes the pain takes over. Is it worse than a regular birth? It's so easy to forget physical pain. Not the other kind. If only, just one single time, he'd told her he loved her, she could be thinking about that now.

Look at all this . . . clumps of blood and— Unclean. She is . . . still that. She was soiled and he knew it and married her anyway. She'd overheard things. Even at Jacob's where everybody was so nice, people said things, made jokes, "damaged goods, grass widow." Beal had probably married her because he was sorry for her—that would be just like him. Marry her to be nice. And because they'd done *that*. He's duty-bound, just like her father. Not stern and humorless about it, but like her father anyway. It's a wonder she hadn't noticed before how similar they are. And Beal hadn't even really ever asked her to marry him. How had all this come about? And there they were, married. She'd pushed him into it. Even pushed him into doing *that*. She had ruined his life, on purpose, for her own selfish reasons. But how could she have thought a man like him would stay put? Though she never *had* thought it. She knew one day he'd leave. She's been preparing herself for it ever since he walked in that very first time. How could she have fooled herself into believing she was happy? This poor little one is the smart one, to not let itself get born—not properly born—at all. She will lose, as she always knew, everybody. But he could have said he loved her just once even if he didn't believe it. Is that too much to ask?

The pain subsides. She *will* run away. *He* always does. But in a minute. Even Henriette had said she ought to go off someday. The pain starts up again, worse than ever. Suddenly she fears for herself. This can't be right. Even for what's happening. She groans without meaning to—meaning not to. Henriette is at the door calling and knocking. She wishes she'd go away. She doesn't want to hear for the hundredth time how he really does love her. How Henriette can see it in his face. She thinks of the two of them, her and Beal, in the pond . . . that first time she'd seen a completely naked man. How could she have thought—herself so skimpy, exposed there—to ever hang on to such a steel spring of a man? Oh, even then—especially then—she knew one day he'd leave her.

In a minute she'll go herself, out the window. Escape. But *they* are at the window. Henri is breaking one of the panes. They can't afford that—to buy hay *and* a window. And how can Henriette be letting that boy see her like this? It's outrageous. Henriette is the crazy one.

He can't ever be what Oriana needs. He won't even say the words she most wants to hear. Gives up before he starts. And then drinking—even though he doesn't drink all that often, when he does it's exactly the kind of dead drunk she hates. She never says a word. That's a wonder to him, that quietness. He liked that about her from the start— anxious and nervous, frightened even, and yet quiet. And he loves her for it, but even so, he can't love her enough to keep his promises. If he really cared about her he'd have managed to leave her before it all began. But it was as if his body . . . all by itself. Except he doesn't believe in that. He could have not. Even with her wanting him to, he didn't have to. He ought to have left that very first afternoon, turned around and walked away the minute he saw her hair all coming down and how she tried to straighten it as he came up, how hot and flushed and blushing she was. He'd wanted to take over clothes washing right then and there. He'd wanted to make her happy before he even knew who she was.

What Oriana said was right as usual: he's too old, for most every-thing. Aches all over. Christy . . . That's what made him old. He's ached all over ever since.

Everything is working out fine, just as Lotti expected it to. Jays watch from the tops of trees, warning them away with their "shack-shack-shack." Woodpeckers peck in staccato bursts that resonate all through the mountains. A chickadee says chickadee. Ma could tell whether it was a titmouse or a chickadee just by listening. She could imitate any bird so fine you couldn't tell the difference between a real bird and Ma. Lotti would have rathered that Ma wasn't that good at it. She wanted to be the one who could do all those things. But at least it was lady stuff. And at least she was the one up here listening to the birds and seeing the flowers. Their horses walk through fields of lupine and paintbrush in almost every valley. Ma would like that, but she's down where she belongs.

They top a rise and circle a cliff of broken rocks—broken off straight into cubes and squares, all sizes. As they round this corner, Lotti almost shouts at the view: a whole row of snowcapped peaks with glaciers hanging in the hollows just below the tops. She stops herself just in time. She wouldn't ever want Fayette to hear her do that. And it's a good thing she didn't, because in a little mountain meadow about a mile below them, there's smoke curling up. Sounds carry in a different way on the mountain. For sure they'd have heard her. Even now, as she and Fayette stop and listen, they can hear voices, though they can't catch the words. Whoever it is down there hasn't heard them. They're just going right on talking. Fay hasn't said a word but Lotti says, "Shut up, Fay."

She makes sure Ma's pistol is loaded and handy. She tells Fay to stay back and mind the horses while she creeps up to investigate. He says he thinks they ought to circle around or go back and find some other way or just plain go back. Lotti says, "It could be my father, you know, or somebody who knows about him." Of course that's ridiculous, she knows perfectly well, though sometimes stranger things than that do happen. The nice thing about having Fayette around is, mostly anyway, he believes her.

He says, "You forgot."

"What?"

"You called me Fay. That's the second time."

"Well, damn it, Fay you'll have to stay and that's all there is to it, even if it is a girl's name. They'll think I'm the boy and you're the girl. Will is too much like Bill anyway."

He won't argue. He almost always gives up, though it isn't exactly giving up. It's more as if he's doing what Old Leather Face does when he says, "Let be." Fayette says, "Let be," almost as often as Old Him says it. She's getting tired of "Let be." Why doesn't somebody *do* something instead of always letting things be?

——•——

Down in the meadow, the two pack mules know before the horses that Lotti is creeping up on them. Men call out, "Come on in and show yourself. The coffee's still hot."

Two men—both big enough to be her father. One has a round face just like hers, but he's chubby all over and too blond. He has a handlebar mustache just as big and fancy as You-Know-Who's, full in the middle and curling down each side, but it doesn't look as if he has anything to hide. The other man is thin and hunched over and has a funny little devil's beard. It's easy to see they're rich. Their clothes are different from any she's ever seen. They look even fancier than Aunt Henriette's. They have light-colored vests and no stains on them, their hats are black and floppy, and they have *everything:* folding chairs and a folding table, a tent with an awning. . . . She came in past their horses first. One is a little gray Arab and the other a big rangy bay. She isn't sure exactly what kind, nose as straight as a racehorse, slim neck, seventeen hands at least. Their pack mules are a matched pair.

"What are you doing out here all by yourself, son?" (They're sitting on their chairs beside their table, smoking cigars and drinking.)

That's the first time she's ever been called son. It's as if the truth of herself has finally come about, but it frightens her. As if the real truth of herself might be better after all, simply because it's the truth no matter how bad that is. Except if nobody ever knows from now on except herself and Fay, why can't it become a kind of truth of its own? And she will live up to it. She's always tried to. She will not let men down by ever becoming womanish.

"I'm looking for my pa." That word pa makes her feel good, too. She really does have one somewhere. All she has to do is find him.

"We haven't seen a soul since Soda City."

She's been studying the men and their horses, but suddenly she sees the paintings, four of them, two propped against pine trees and two on easels. They're so lifelike, for a minute she doesn't know what they are. She's never seen anything like them. Never thought such things existed. Even looking at Ma's big book of *Famous Paintings of the World,* hand colored, she hadn't thought the paintings pictured in it might be like this or could be so large. And the main thing is, they're of her mountains. One of them, the biggest, is of that same scene she'd just come upon as they'd topped the rise, the one that had almost made her shout without meaning to.

She can't stop looking. She forgets about Fayette. They hand her a cup of coffee, but she hardly notices. She just stares. It comes to her that she can't live without possessing one of these paintings. The way it would look in her little room! Except of course she's never going back.

There are other paintings there, a dozen maybe, all rolled up and bound together. At first she hadn't realized they were paintings, too. They have so many. All she wants is just one. But they must be worth a lot. A lot! They're mostly all huge. In her little room they would take up a whole wall. Expecially that big one of five peaks in a row. Even so, that's the one she wants. If she owned it, just thinking it was hers would make her happy. She'd be happy even if it was all rolled up. Then, no matter where she was, she'd have the mountains with her. Even if it ever did come about that she had to go east to school—though she can't imagine herself letting such a thing happen—she'd have something to remember the West by so it wouldn't hurt quite so much to leave it. She would bring it with her on the train. All the Cincinnati kind of people who only knew about rain and round green hills would look at it and wonder and know that she had come from there. It would show everybody who she really was. That might almost make going east worthwhile.

"I see you like them."

She sits on the ground in front of them and doesn't stop looking and doesn't answer. They're almost better than the real thing. Or different. Why hadn't she ever really tried to draw just the mountains by themselves? But it wouldn't be the same as painting them, even if it came out pretty good.

"How much does one of these cost?"

"We paint for millionaires, you know."

Her father could have been a painter. Everybody always says how well she draws. Or maybe he's a millionaire and buys paintings.

The other man says, "We might let a little one go for a hundred dollars."

"I mean the big ones."

"Oh, a thousand or so. The one you're staring at, maybe more. Last year Teddy Roosevelt bought one of his."

Even if she'd been saving all the money she ever got from working for Grandpa Jacob and Uncle T-Bone, she wouldn't have had half enough.

They serve her biscuits and bacon and bacon gravy. She eats, hardly noticing she does. She can tell they're laughing at her—especially the devilish-looking one. She doesn't like it. She could threaten them with her pistol. Then they wouldn't laugh. She'd grab the painting and ride off. It would be very awkward. If she could hold on to it at all, it'd blow out of her arms in the first wind. She should wait until dark to steal it. Roll it up first.

It isn't until she hears Fayette riding in, leading her horse, that she remembers him. She feels ashamed of their half-breed horses, ashamed of their homemade hackamores and reins and ropes and of the old army saddles that Old Him bought, two for five dollars, and fixed up with homemade fenders—and it isn't as if you couldn't tell. She should steal a saddle and a horse, too. Probably get hanged as much for stealing a painting as for stealing a horse anyway.

Fayette seems as fascinated by the paintings as she is. He doesn't even dismount. He rides right into the middle of their campground, horse apples or not, and just sits there staring. She hopes he won't be saying all the wrong things.

"Well, bless me, here's another art critic. Hungry, son?"

"Yessir."

"Looking for your pa, I guess."

"No, sir."

"That's . . . Well, that's Will. We already know where his pa is." She thinks, More than likely chasing after us.

But this is very, very important. She must write it down and soon. All about how this was the start of how she got to be a famous artist. She'll write, I first saw painting as it really is, there in the forest in the mountains, under the Jeffrey pines—towering Jeffrey pines, and I knew these paintings were just as grand and glorious as the scenes that were being painted, and I knew instantly that art would fill my life from then on. In those early days I couldn't guess with what, though now I can see it has fulfilled all my wildest expectations. Even then I thought, I *can* do this; I'd never tried nor had the stuff to do it with, but I could do it. I knew I would be traveling off into the world alone, my life forever changed, and I knew one of these masterpieces would be in my possession. I would never be without it, and I haven't been, all this long, long time.

"I can draw. Everybody says if they didn't see me doing it right in front of them, they wouldn't believe it was me who drew it. I'm really good." Something has come over her. She doesn't usually talk this way about herself. She's embarrassing herself, but . . . she's . . . frantic. She wants right then and there to say something or draw something that will prove how good at it she is, but all she has for paper is Old His vest-pocket tally book and not a single picture in it. Yet "could I learn this? I *can* learn this." What she really wants to ask is, is there a place where they'd let girls learn it? Except if she asks that they'll know she's not a boy. But maybe she could keep on pretending to be a boy all the way through art school. "I draw all the time, but I don't have any with me."

"Sounds like you're halfway there already, but paint is tricky. Look at all these bottles and tubes." (That's the chubby blond one. He's the nicest.) "And these can't get rolled up until they're good and dry. We're stuck with hanging them out like this for the next few days, and if we paint more we'll just be stuck here longer, so we have to sit and smoke. Down in the desert they'd be dry in no time."

(Drink, too, it looks like.)

Fayette slides off his horse and lands on his rump. She knew he would. She especially knew he would when she saw the chubby man getting up to go help him. Fay wouldn't want that. Old You-Know-Who always let him do it by himself, and Fay just about always fell. As soon as he dusts his back end off, Fay says, "Could I do this, too?" Compared to her, Fay can't draw worth chicken feed, but the man says, "You betcha," anyway, as though she and Fayette were the same. Well, they'll be sorry when she gets to be famous.

What she'll do is not sleep at all. She'll leave Fay behind. These are good enough people, and then Old Him will be coming along pretty soon. Maybe if he gets Fay back he won't bother going after her. Except he probably will. She doesn't much like the idea of leaving Fayette, except he won't like what she's going to do. He might tell everything first off, or try to stop her, though maybe she can get the painting packed up and wake him afterward so he won't know anything about it. But he guesses things. And he always seems to know what's the right thing to do no matter how she explains it to him. Seems like he was born knowing right from wrong, and what's worse, he always has to act the right thing. She knows all that, too, but doesn't much bother with it—now she will steal without a backward thought. In fact it will make her very, very happy.

"So you boys aren't brothers?"

"Do we look like brothers? Are *you* brothers?"

"Come to think of it, we're not." And then they slap each other on the back and joke about how they wouldn't have each other for a brother if they were the last two brothers on the face of the earth, but she's off studying how the paintings are tacked to the frames, and how it won't do any good knocking out the little wedges. She'll have to cut. She won't lose much, and it's already so big. But then when she stretches it out again she'll lose another few inches on all sides tacking it back up. That's a lot of inches all together, and it's too bad, but not as bad as not having the painting at all. It'll fit all the better in her room–*if* she ever goes back home.

She goes out to help with gathering firewood so she can check the trail beyond. After that she'll make friends with the horses. The Arab will be a nasty little bitch. "Nasty bitch of an Arab," they usually say, though Aunt Henriette has a pretty nice one. Lotti can understand nasty. She knows exactly how that horse feels. But she'll most likely take the big one anyway. He looks so sleek and fast, and she likes the arch of his neck.

That old hope chest is all Oriana's mother has of Oriana. Heavy—
with silverware, silver platters, Rosenthal china, lacy tablecloths;
embroidered towels and pillow slips that she and Oriana had worked on
side by side (she talking and Oriana silent)—crocheted edges, backstitch-
ing all over them. She had loved working on those things with her daughter. Truth to tell, she had thought more about them than she had about
Oriana. When she thought of her at all, it was always about how she was
already twenty-five and that she'd finally managed to attract a suitable
man, exactly the right sort. Even the judge was pleased or seemed so. It
wasn't as though Oriana wasn't pretty in a freckled sort of way, but she was
too shy and absentminded, even in front of the best of men—always looking out the window or at the floor. Or fiddling with her handkerchief no
matter how often she told her to please keep her hands still and that "a
man never trusts a nervous woman."

She hadn't ever wondered if her daughter was happy or would be.
Nobody wondered things like that. She hadn't ever wondered if she herself was happy. Happiness didn't pertain to much of anything, and it was
immoral to think about it. Life was but a veil of tears, after all. But she
thought of happiness now only because since the judge had died three
years ago, she had actually been rather happy and would have been more
so if she'd known where and how Oriana was and why she'd run away
without a single word.

Now she guessed. The drawing showed it all. She had it framed in a
little silver frame and carried it with her everywhere. She never showed it
to anyone. That would have been too revealing to anyone who knew the
man, but she kept it wrapped in lace in her reticule, which she always
hung from her wrist.

Perhaps Oriana had been wondering about her, too. Maybe even
needing her but hadn't had the courage to write. And certainly she'd want
this hope chest and all the good things it contained. Who in the world

wouldn't need extra sheets and blankets and lacy nightgowns and silk underwear?

The almost-finished wedding dress she will bring to her granddaughter. Already fourteen years old! That was exactly the time it would have taken. Whose fault was it? Not Oriana's. Not if she had to run away afterward and not leave a trace. There was nothing else for her to do. She'd have done the same herself. They never could have talked about it, and even if they could have, neither of them could have said a word to the judge.

She had stuffed that wedding dress into the top of the hope chest as soon as she understood that Oriana wasn't coming back. She didn't want to see it ever again. The judge never said a single word, but she thought he'd burst. He was always either too pale or too flushed. She herself hardly knew what to feel. Sometimes she was angry and sometimes sad, but mostly she wondered what in the world had happened.

Of course there was all that work to be done undoing the wedding preparations. For a while she told people the wedding was just postponed (she'd hoped that's all it was), and she tried to keep it a secret that Oriana had gone, but in no time everybody knew. Oriana had been a secretive, shy girl, with few friends, but people noticed right away. How could she have thought they wouldn't? Still, she'd hoped. And hoped that maybe she'd be back before anybody knew. Then she made up a story that Oriana had gone to her aunt's in Boston, but, as years and years went by, that sounded more and more foolish. Even so, she kept on saying it. Right to their faces. (Odd, the groom had gone off shortly after Oriana had, but only for a few days.)

West. Who would have thought it? She can't imagine her Oriana—or herself for that matter—out there in the wilds with Indians and cowboys and God knows what. And what was this husband her grandchild had mentioned? Certainly not Scottish. He sounded French. Could Oriana really have married one of them? Well, the French could be . . . Some of them, anyway . . . But those around New England certainly weren't. They were all dirt poor with missing teeth and starving faces. That is, those who weren't too fat. They hardly ate anything but bread. Oriana never seemed to be attracted to the proper people.

She studied. She made plans. There was a stop on the railroad line called Ledoyt. Right along with Jawbone, Soda City, and Knuckle Under. That must be the place. Odd to have a railroad station of your own. Perhaps Oriana's husband was a rich or famous man.

He wakes when Lotti's rolling up her bedroll, which is right next to his. She'd slept (if she'd even slept at all) almost as close to him as Pa does when they camp out when they go hunting, just the two of them —which they hardly ever do, but those times are the best. Better even than when they work at Grandpa Jacob's and he and Pa sleep in the bunkhouse, which they don't let Lotti do.

He doesn't let on that he's awake. Just watches her get ready to go— without him. How come she's doing that? The fire makes enough light for him to see a little bit, even though they'd slept a ways from it so as not to be near the men. He sees she has a painting, rolled up real tight, and she's rolling her bedroll around it. She'll have to tie it on sideways like a rifle, and even then it will stick way out the back.

He feels really, really tired, but Pa would want him to keep an eye on her, and he always does try to. When she'd started to burn up, Pa said he'd saved her by yelling. Pa said if it wasn't for him, who knows what would have happened? No more Lotti most likely, and maybe no more house either. After that burning he'd been Pa's hands for a long time (Ma helped some, too). He was pretty little then, but Pa didn't know what he'd do without him. He got really good at buttons, though he hadn't been before. Pa said he was his right-hand man *and* his left-hand man. Even peeing— he'd undone and done up Pa's pants buttons. He rode in front and held the reins for him. Pa's hands hurt so much he had to stand on the mounting rock to get himself up on a horse. He's good at looking after things, so now he has to get up and look after Lotti. Pa said that was his job. Pa said if it was really, really dangerous he had to tell right away even if it was tattling.

He waits a little bit, and then he goes to get his pony. Strawberry is still there. He can guess which horse she's taken without even looking. He's getting kind of upset now that she's turned into a horse thief. He doesn't saddle up or bring his bedroll or even the canteen, just jumps on

Crazy Colt and takes off, quiet and fast, *metata* in one hand and a bunch of mane in the other. Bareback is slippery.

He doesn't have to be so quiet. The fire is still crackling some, and the horses and mules talk to each other every now and then but don't give any warnings. (Last night there was a horse fight because Lotti tied Strawberry too close to their Arab. She did that on purpose just to see what would happen. He could have told them even before that she would do that.) And then the men had been drinking. They'd even offered some to them. Said it was good rum, the best, and they ought to at least taste it. He didn't want any and Lotti didn't either, which was strange for her. (He never once called her Lotti by mistake, but she called him Fay a lot and then she called him Jimmy, which she never had before. It wasn't a mistake. After that they couldn't stop giggling.)

He's tired and thirsty, but Lotti is getting herself in trouble. Anyway, there might be a landslide right in front of her. Or right *on* her. Anyway, even though she stole a horse, the family should stick together. She could say she just borrowed it for a couple of hours. Nobody could hang her for that. But maybe they would, and they might hang him along with her just because he'd be with her. Then he'd jump on the best horse there was around and make a run for it. If he catches up with her before daylight, he could give her some good advice. She could take the horse back before anybody knew about it, because those men drank such a lot they won't wake up for a long time. They'll be like Pa is afterward. Only just once Pa told him he hoped he wouldn't do that when he grew up, but he isn't sure if he will or not.

He keeps Crazy Colt at a trot whenever the trail is level. He knows not to lope her. She'll get too tired as it is. She's breathing hard up the hills. He keeps resting her. At this rate maybe he'll never catch up with Lotti.

He doesn't like riding in the dark, but he does like the feel of riding bareback—the warmth of the horse's body, especially nice on this cold morning; the moving of her muscles against his legs. How strong she is! He likes the feeling of being so close to her. She's a good friend. But he hopes they're not going past many steep places in the dark. If he falls at all, he'll fall off right where it's steepest for sure. And anyway, maybe *he'll* be the one caught in a landslide. Or there'll be an earthquake and he'll be right under a big rock. Sometimes hanging lakes break through their boundaries and water comes down in one huge, huge, huge rush that sweeps away everything, even wider and longer than a landslide. Except like Pa says, "You'll be just as dead in the one as t'other, though maybe just a little bit deader in the hanging-lake ones." And what about bears? There won't be any above the tree line because no food, but maybe he's the food. They don't usually eat people, but they might eat him. He's little. They might not even know he's a person.

After it gets light he feels better, but Crazy is tired. It might be bad for her to keep on going. She's too old for this. Just a good old safe horse and he wants to be good to her, but he keeps on anyway. He'd like to give her some grain, but he hasn't brought any and not even any water. There are streams, but they can't get down to them.

Then, as they climb a steep rise, he slips gently off over Crazy's haunches. He grabs her tail on the way down, but he can't keep a grip on it. She stops and looks at him, shakes herself all over. She's too tired to give any crow hops of freedom as she usually does. She just turns around and heads for home.

The getaway is easy. She herself is the clever bastard. She's riding the big bay gelding. She was sorry to leave the nasty little Arab, but the bay is like no horse she's ever seen, or ridden. He's a willing horse. No meanness in him. He tries even when he doesn't understand. Might have been a house-pet horse like Goldy. Old You-Know-Who always said (and more often than she wanted to hear it), "When you're on a horse he should be paying attention to you, and you should see to it by keeping him busy with something or other." But with this horse she sure doesn't have to. This horse keeps twitching his ears every other minute, asking her, What's the next move?

The horse has a running walk she's never ridden. Old Him could get Matou to do that, but she never could. She's as good a horseman as Old Him any day, but she couldn't do that. This horse does it naturally. By the time the others wake up, she'll be long gone and way ahead of Old Saddle Face, too. The horse is strong. She often leans over and puts her hand on his breast, but he never feels too hot, even with all this climbing. She rests him every now and then anyway, and feeds him a little grain. She only brought food for him, so it's good she ate a big supper last night. It should last her a long time. She's going to let herself get good and hungry. Maybe if she doesn't eat much, her breasts won't get any bigger—than they already are, which is too big already.

She's been up above the tree line for a long time, but now with the coming of dawn she's down among the pines. Since seeing those paintings yesterday, everything looks different—mountains, clouds, the gnarled trees. . . . Why hadn't she ever thought to draw them? They have shapes she hadn't noticed. Well, she *had* noticed—the jagged outlines of the cliffs, the stripy shadows down their sides, gray on gray—but she'd not thought, This, then this, then this, and these lines going on down behind those other lines and rocks in front. And you could end the picture here, with a tree in front on one side and there, with the cliff on the other. And how purple the snow, and the green of these pine trees is as if especially made to go against the blue of this sky. She and Old Him had talked about how dark the sky looked sometimes next to the snow when they were way high up and and they'd wondered, was it a trick of the dazzled eye or a true thing? Those men had painted that: the snow silvery with blue shadows and the almost black sky. They could see better than she could, except now she could, too. Everything seems to be sitting there waiting for her to learn to paint, and the more beautiful things are, the more in a hurry they are for her to get to it. She would stop right now, if she dared, and draw.

She hasn't any idea where she's going or where this trail might end up. She wasn't sure where she was going before, but at least she knew who she was and what she was up to. Now all she knows is wherever she goes or whatever she does, it has to have something to do with this painting. She'll do whatever the painting needs. What the horse needs, too.

She keeps thinking, I'm in love, I'm in love, I love you, hardly knowing what she means by that. In love with herself because she will paint, and in love with the mountains because she will paint them, in love with the horse and in love with the painting she stole and in love with the man who painted it, even though he's even chubbier than Uncle T-Bone. If it turns out she can't be a painter herself, why then she'll marry one. She could see to it that his life ran smoothly. She would be like Ma is with Old Him, telling everybody not to bother him with this and that.

Does Ma know about paintings like these? Has she seen some before? This big? Why hadn't she said anything about them? There she was, teaching her all about art and never said one single word. She should have said. Or Aunt Henriette—she must have known. She'd been to Paris. Why hadn't anybody said?

Henriette sends Henri out to fill the hot water bottle from the kettle that's always at the back of the stove. "And see," she says, "the water's good and hot, but not too much hot, and bring a *cuvette*—what you call it?—of warm water and *serviettes*." So at least Henri is gone, though he must have seen everything there was to see. Henriette helps her undress and takes her bloodied clothes away. That's embarrassing, too, and Oriana tells her she wants to take care of those herself. She insists. She must! But Henriette says, "I'm the big chief here for now. You have to be busy being unwell. I've had the same thing you know. And no more too much thinking. It never does any good."

She is, after all, glad Henriette is here, and maybe she does, after all, want to hear her say over again how she'd never seen Beal in love, even the slightest bit, until she saw him with her. Even soiled as she is, he must have loved her. And Oriana can answer, "But lots of times I'm not as good to him as I should be. I criticize," and Henriette will say, "You're the best that ever happen to him. I told you that *déjà* a hundred times."

Henriette asks if there's any of Beal's rotgut around so she can make a medicinal drink, but when Henri goes out to the barn to get it down, it isn't there. At first Oriana thinks Beal must have taken it with him, and she thinks, How could he do that at a time like this? Then she remembers he'd thrown the bottle away—shattered it on the rocks and she'd been glad of it—glad that he wasn't going to have what he needs—maybe needs the way she needs it now, for some sort of pain, maybe not just for thoughts but maybe for some of those old broken bones. And of course he wouldn't be taking it along. That wouldn't be at all like him. Much more likely that Lotti would have taken it, if it had been there for her to take.

Henriette puts up some cider and honey to make apple mead or applejack. That won't be ready for days, but she'll have it for later. Henriette says Beal won't have to know anything about it, though why on earth not? That was Henriette's way, not hers.

She had gotten up with Beal at two in the morning to make him coffee and to make sure he ate and to see him off, and she hadn't slept much the night before either, so what with the hot water bottle and the goldenseal and shepherd's purse tea . . . And now everything is taken care of and she can have her pain in peace without the little ones crawling all over her.

—•—

She wakes to the sound of trotting and wheels on the gravelly sand outside. It sounds like Tibo's fancy fast trap. What would he be doing coming over here again? Is it good news or bad? If bad, she hardly has the energy to wake up for it. She should get up and see, but let the others worry for a change. They'll let her know.

But then her door is open already and there's Henriette and behind her, Tibo, and behind him . . . It can't be. It mustn't be. A dressed-up lady who comes right straight on in and takes her hand and looks at her with pity. Exactly what she never wanted—not from her—and now no way of avoiding her, maybe never ever anymore. Mother had always seemed to like it best when Oriana was in trouble.

First thing she says is "I brought your hope chest. Look." She's holding a silk nightgown. Oriana recognizes it right away even after all this time. She had embroidered the violets herself.

Cramps come again as though brought in by her mother. Oriana pulls her hand away and puts her arms around herself, hugging her threadbare nightgown close around her stomach. That nightgown, too, she'd sewn every stitch.

Henriette, and in a nice way, takes her mother's arm, says, "It must be a shock. Let her habituate herself. Come. Take coffee."

Henriette, at least, is well dressed as usual and looks as wealthy as she really is, but she herself . . . And their house is so small compared to the houses her mother is used to. She had been thinking it was getting nicer and nicer, and all those flowers—though of course they're gone now after the hail. Even the landscape. But you have to get used to it before you can love it. And when they all come back they'll not have had a bath for days. Beal will be halfway to a full beard by then. And he never looks clean shaven anyway. But—and really—she doesn't want him any other way. And Fayette. Just about perfect. It makes her laugh sometimes just to look at that boy. Sometimes she thinks she must have found him under a mushroom instead of giving birth to him. Having him made her understand Beal all the better, too. Tibo had told her how Beal had been beaten by their father all his growing up, and how their father never beat the other boys except maybe once or twice a year, but Beal, all the time. How Beal had never cried even when he was little. Who would do a thing like that to such a child—or any child? And Beal had grown up never wanting even to slap a child. She didn't think he ever had. Not that she knew of.

Just as she'd daydreamed before, Mother will have to sleep in Lotti's room, and just as it is probably, arrowheads and geodes, moth-eaten army blankets, drawings of people falling off bucking horses or cowboys with bandaged arms and or legs tacked up all over the walls, practically on top of each other. Lots of those now that Lotti didn't burn them up so much. It was when she got a room of her own that she started to save them.

But how had this come about? Whose fault is it? Henriette's! It would be just like her, and the proof that she's in on it is that Tibo had brought her mother over. That's where Mother went first. How could Henriette do such a thing and not say a single word? And why now? After all these years? It's the worst time of any.

But something else is happening. There's a lot of scurrying around. She hears Henriette say, "Don't let Oriana see her." Her who? She'd already seen her. But something in Henriette's voice makes Oriana get up and go to the window and pull away the cardboard they'd put in the pane Henri had broken. Crazy Colt is out there, limping badly, head hanging, looking as draggled as any horse she's ever seen. How had Crazy gotten past Beal? It was just like Crazy to come on home. Matou would never leave Beal. Beal could be lying there dead, and Matou would stay beside him. He *could* be dead—they all could be—Matou standing there beside them.

There's no horse that she knows of that can keep up with this one, except maybe Matou, but he's a mule and, as they say, tough as boiled owl. She'd like to know this horse's name. Why hadn't she thought to ask? It's not like her to forget such an important thing. She wasn't herself—and isn't now—and never will be again—and doesn't even want to be.

She can hardly wait to get another look at the painting. She'd studied it the night before but not at all as much as she wanted to. From the start she'd had the thought she shouldn't seem too interested in front of them, though it was probably too late for that practically from the start. Now she'll ride on into the night, especially if the ground isn't too rough, but the next day she'll have to give the horse a real rest. Find a grassy patch and let him graze. Then she'll unroll the painting and look at it all she wants.

First she calls the horse Magic and then she calls him Racer, and Magic Racer, and Racer Magic. She wants to show him off to somebody. Henri or Fayette. *My* horse. It would do Fay good to see what a real horse is like for once. Maybe a time would come when she would even let Fay ride him. Just for a little bit.

Real life. She was sure right about that. Another little bit of things like these and she'll be able to say she really has lived. She'd thought she was beginning to get some bits of real life when Aunt Jenny died. That was the first death of anybody she knew fairly well and liked, not counting babies. She didn't care much for babies anyway. Up to now just Aunt Jenny and old dog Dewey were the only little bits of real life she'd ever known, and they were all bad bits.

She's singing a song the cowboys always sing: "I married another, the devil's grandmother, and I wish I was single again, again." At Grandpa Jacob's those boys sang all sort of songs like that to make her angry, but she never did get angry. What did any of those songs have to do with her? First of all, she isn't ever going to get married, and second of all, even if she did, she would never be the "devil's grandmother" kind of wife. Whoever she married could go right on doing whatever he always did and she'd be doing it right along with him, drinking and smoking and swearing and everything.

The trail is steep and rocky, first steeply down for a long ways, far below the tree line. The horse hates all this going down. In that way he's just like any other horse. Then the trail levels off for a bit, with trees and bushes, mostly scrub oak and manzanita. The only thing that slows her down some is she has to nail up a loose shoe. But she's still way ahead anyway.

Then they start steeply up again and round a sharp corner, boulders on each side, and suddenly there's a man standing in the middle of the trail, rifle at the ready, or at least ready to shoot from the hip. Magic Racer shies, as surprised as she is. She keeps her seat just fine. Too bad Fay isn't there to see. They could have gone right over the side, though it wouldn't have turned out as bad as it might have in some places. There's plenty of underbrush to catch them.

"Well, now, there's a horse if I ever saw one."

He's the dirtiest man she ever saw and she's seen lots. Not this kind of dirt, though—as if he *never* washed. And the ugliest, though it's hard to tell what he looks like under all that dirt. She can smell him from where she sits, and she wonders why she and Magic didn't smell him a long time ago. They're downwind for sure. He's chewing tobacco (his beard is all yellow from it), and he spits off down toward the cliff. She's always hated that spitting. At least nobody close to her does it except, now and then, Grandpa Jacob, though "more then than now," as Old Him would put it.

"What you doin' out here, girlie?"

Is he calling her girlie as an insult, like the men at Grandpa's call each other, or does he really know she's a girl? Except how? For now she'll just go on being a boy and see what happens, though maybe she should say, Don't call me girlie. Well, she will if he says it a second time.

"What in hell you doing out here all by yourself? Didn't your Ma ever learn you? You could fall off a cliff right this very minute, you and your horse, too, and nobody would ever know but me. There's all kinds of people out here. Crazy as you, bein' out here by themselves."

She doesn't like the look of that rifle. It's the kind they call a buffalo gun, even though there aren't any more buffalo.

Fayette. He wouldn't be much help, but at least the man would have to keep an eye on both of them, and he couldn't push them both off the side at the same time.

"Get down."

"Where's *your* horse?"

He doesn't answer.

"And don't call me girlie."

"Get on down, and we'll see for sure."

She once heard of a horse that would trample people if you gave the signal—rear up and squash them flat.

The best thing would be for her to turn around and hightail it out of there, but that would be the end of all this real life. First thing she would meet up with Old Him and the men and have to get back on an ordinary horse and give back the painting and have to get punished in ways she can't even guess at because she's never done things as bad as these before. The sheriff would have to be in on it most likely. They couldn't hang a fourteen-year-old girl, could they? And the painting is worth maybe a thousand dollars. It's like she robbed the bank. What do people do with somebody like her? She'll have to take her chances here. And even this man—he's real life, too, though she'd like not to think so.

"Get down, I said."

"No, Goddamn it!" That should help to make him think she's a boy.

The horse is dancing all over the place. Maybe he *will* kick out. But the man puts down the rifle, grabs the horse's nostrils with one fist and an ear with the other, and shakes the horse's head hard. She's seen that done before when horses misbehave, but she doubts anybody ever did that to this one. Then the man keeps on twisting the horse's nose with one hand and grabs her leg with the other. "You getting off or am I pulling you off?"

She kicks out at him with the *tapadero,* but that makes it all the easier for him to get a good grip on her ankle and pull her down, against him. Those big breasts of hers smack-dab right on him, and then she slides on down till she's on her back on the ground and he's still got a grip on her leg. She's helpless with her leg in the air like that. With his other hand he flips the reins to the side and lets them hang beside Magic's hooves. Then he picks her up by her shirtfront. She's wearing two shirts. He grabs them at the neck and pulls so hard most of the buttons fly off and the old one, that used to belong to Old Him, rips half to pieces. Underneath she's bound her breasts as tightly as she could bear. She'd thought they wouldn't grow so much if they were always tied up a little bit too tight.

"You *are* crazy. Girl out here alone. I can't even remember when I last saw a filly."

"They're right behind me. You'll be sorry."

"S'not true. I been watching you from up top."

Had she even peed in front of him?

He doesn't bother undoing the safty pins of the bindings of her breasts, just yanks the pins apart. They scratch but she hardly feels it.

"Damn! Damn nice! But got yourself burned some, didn't ya."

. . . And then, and tobacco juice all over her, and his hands, and he smells worse than any really dirty stable or pigpen. She might throw up. He so dirty he probably wouldn't even care if she did, right in his face. She spits at him and he laughs and spits back. He has good aim, too. She fights. She always thought if she used all her strength, she could beat off any man, but there's nothing she can do. She tries to punch him in the throat, but he blocks it easily. He's pulled her down flat on the rocks, all his weight—and he's a big man, big enough to be one of the men she might have looked at hard, though now she realizes she had only searched for her father among men on the cleaner side—all his weight on top of her. He's fumbling at his pants. She can feel him . . . right exactly there. When he puts his face just inches from hers and whispers for her to stay put or she'll be sorry, she sees his eyes (bloodshot and red rimmed) are the exact same brown as her own. It's not a usual color, that goldenish brown, and there's little flecks of green and tan just like in hers. She's inside there, too, a minuscule person reflected in his pupils. (There's a woodpecker's hollow-log tapping not far off. There's the rustling, trickle-down sounds of the slow landslides. There's an angry jay. . . .)

Her pants are down around her ankles. That's where the pistol is, way down there in her pocket. There's no way she can get at it now. He's forcing her knees apart. Ma! Did Ma? But she's always . . . *always* known it and didn't want it to be true. She herself . . . born out of this exact same thing.

Now the man is hitting her face and banging her head back against the rocks, but she keeps fighting. She's so angry. She's never been this angry. In a minute it'll be too late.

But all of a sudden he's fighting something that's not her. Something on his back. He reaches over his shoulder and grabs at it, and Fayette comes somersaulting forward, pulled right over the man's head, landing on top of her, and now the man is beating on him instead of her. How can a full-grown man beat up this way on a little boy? Who's not even big as most eight-year-olds. People don't do that. And the man is hitting him in bad places. There's already blood.

She manages to crawl out from under them, her pants around her ankles like hobbles. Her pistol down there somewhere. She'll have to be careful not to hit Fay by mistake. She'll have to move in real close. Shoot right into the man's head. The gun is so small. It won't kill unless she shoots just right.

She shoots and shoots and shoots. There's only five shots in this little gun, but she's clicking on the empty chambers. The man falls on top of Fayette and still she can't stop pulling the trigger. When she finally does, everything is quiet: woodpeckers, jays, marmots, pikas—nothing squeaks or scurries, just that trickling-down sound left. It seems very loud.

It takes a while before she thinks to pull her pants back up. Then it's as if someone else is telling her what to do, someone else telling her to pull the man off Fayette. Do it now. Finally she does, though she doesn't want to touch him even though his smell and goo are all over her. First she tries to kick him away, but she has to use her hands. Put her arms around him, actually. She pulls him to the side of the trail and then kneels beside Fay.

His eyes are open. She can see he's concious. It's not like when he has a nightmare and you can tell he's not seeing anything. There's dirt and bruises all over his face and blood—from his nose and from his mouth, too. She can't tell if it's coming from way inside or just from his lips and nose. She says, "You saved me." He just lies there and looks, blinking now and then. She says, "Where does it hurt?" but he won't answer. She goes to get her canteen. (That's a good horse. Even after all this, he's still there.) She wipes Fayette's face with his kerchief. It's dirty, but so is everything else. Then she wets his cracked and swollen lips. She tries to give him a tiny sip, but it just drips out. She should put something soft under his head.

That's when she realizes she's still half-naked, her two shirts thrown aside on the rocks. First she rolls up one and puts it under Fayette's head, carefully in case his neck is hurt—"Can't you move? Can't you talk?"—but he just keeps on staring and, every now and then, blinking at her. She's getting scared. If he'd just make some kind of sound. It's as if he's some-place beyond her, beyond pain. She says, "Don't move," like they always say when somebody falls off a horse, but he's not moving anyway.

There doesn't seem to be anything she can do. She puts on her other shirt and knots it in front to hold it together. There's only one button left on it, and it's not in the right place. She unsaddles Magic and gives him a drink in her hat. Then she sits beside Fayette. "I'm sorry I ever called you Horse Face. You don't even have a horse face."

She waits. As if suspended someplace where there is no time. Seems like it's the same place where Fayette looks to be. She wipes his face again, says, "You have a nice face." (It's hard to tell which are bruises and which is dirt.) She tries again to give him a drink, and then again. Just a tiny sip each time. She sits and sits. What if there is another man out there? Or three or four? But she's got the buffalo gun now. Maybe she could smell them coming. "Pa will come," she says. "You know he will. Everything will be all right then." But there could be slides that close off the trail. It hap-pens all the time. "He'll get through," she says. "You know him." He will, too, even if he has to climb straight up to the top of the mountain to do it. For Fayette. But for her sake, too. He always has. Even for her.

There's Lotti and beyond her all those tops of trees. He's floating around, inside himself. It's as if he could fly if he really wanted to. Every single top of every single tree leans way over to the side. That's the prevailing winds. Pa said it. He will come. Everything will be all right then. Lotti didn't have to tell him that. There's pain, but he hardly knows where. All over. Pa can fix that. All he has to do is get through the now—the right now. It might take a while. There's a hawk way, way, way up behind Lotti's head, going round and round. That means there's not much wind. That's the thermals. He could be up there. Pa could, too. They'd be kites. Pa makes great big ones. It takes both of them hanging on tight so as not to go right on into the sky. Lotti should be looking up, too. There's a lot of things behind her head but not a single cloud. It's very, very blue, and Lotti is being very, very nice. He saved her. She said so. He was scared to do it, but Pa would have done it if he'd been here. Except Pa would have smashed that bad man to smithereens. He's just like Pa except too small, and now even more like him. Pa gets hurt and doesn't say a word. Pa got kicked in the head, but Crazy never did that. This is exactly what it feels like. He heard Pa groan some. You could do that if you needed to, but he's not going to. He doesn't even feel like it. He's just going to float around.

Finally she hears them. They're on a switchback way below. All of them are coming, him and the two men. The men are talking and shouting out to each other as if it was a lark. Old Him is usually the first to start everybody horsing around. Ma always says to him, "If you weren't here there'd be three less children," but she likes it anyway. He won't be doing that now. But how can those two men be cutting up so much when she just stole their painting and their special horse? Maybe they think she's just a joke. Maybe it's just as well if they do.

He's the one to round the curve first. She hardly dares look at him and yet she must. This is all her fault. She backs away from Fayette while he gets off Matou. He gets off in an odd way, stiff, hangs on to the saddle to steady himself for a moment, limps worse than ever.

She sees how he takes everything in, the buffalo gun and Ma's pistol beside it, and the dead man at the edge of the trail. Till now she'd been thinking so much about Fay she'd forgotten about being all slimy with tobacco juice and smelly and her shirt torn and with no buttons, and then he's never seen her with her hair cut off and all curly. He touches her shoulder as if to comfort and as if he knows she never wants his touch or anybody's, and it does comfort. Then he squats down next to Fayette.

She sees how he hardly dares touch Fay either. He puts his hand on him so lightly it must feel like a butterfly kiss—on Fayette's cheek and then neck and then chest. He says, "Vieux copain." Fayette just looks. He says, "Pauv' ti' bonhomme."

She thought Fay would be all right when Old Him got there, but he's the same. She feels tears on her cheeks (it was that so light touch that started her off), but being like a girl doesn't seem to matter much anymore.

"Tell me."

She kneels beside them and tells. The men are quiet now, listening. Then they go to unpack their painting.

"Are you all right then? I mean, really?"

"Well. Mostly. It didn't happen. Not exactly. Fayette saved me."

"You're pretty bruised up, too."

That's the first she realizes she hurts—all over and down there, too. He didn't quite, but it hurts, anyway. She needs to talk to Ma, or just be with her. Tears come again, but they hardly feel like hers. It's like a part of herself is standing back and watching. Old Him touches her cheek as lightly as he'd touched Fayette's, and again, as if he thought she might jerk away at anything stronger, but she wouldn't have. For a moment he seems reluctant to turn from her, then he says, "I have to see to Fay."

That same touch, then, that hardly seems like touching at all, all over Fayette. And then he does touch. "Son" (he hardly ever calls him that), "try to let me know what hurts." But Fay doesn't. Then he does move him. Straightens him out little by little.

She watches. (All that gray hair he has now, and the three or four days' growth of beard, mustache ends all mussed up . . .) She watches as he leans back on his heels, shuts his eyes, and takes a big quivering breath. He's lost other children. He's lost people she doesn't even know. She's heard—not from him, from Uncle T-Bone.

She whispers, "Pa," but he doesn't hear. Surely if he'd heard . . . It's hard to say. She's not sure she'll be able to manage it a second time.

—•—

The men come up with the rum. (Lotti'd seen them kicking the body down through the brush and over the cliff. She was wondering if that was all right to do when maybe the sheriff should be in on it. When she thinks about that man, she feels angry all over again. She isn't sorry for what she's done.) The men hand the rum to Old Him. "For the boy," they say, "and for you, too." He says, "No," and then, "Maybe later." That's a worry to her. It hardly takes any. Maybe she should tell them not to let him. He sees how she looks at him, says, "Not that much," but she's heard Uncle T-Bone say how all he has to do is smell the cork.

With Fayette, the rum drips out just like when she tried to give him sips of water.

One of the men, the skinny one, tells her, "You're going to need a stiff drink yourself, boy." The other one, the chubby one she likes the best and who had painted the big painting says, "She's a girl, Jack, but you're right about she needs a drink." At least he'd noticed who she was and how she felt, but she mustn't drink if Old Him might.

The thin one says, "I guess you'll want a drink in a minute."

They take her to where they've spread out the painting. She'd rolled it too tight and creased the canvas, and she'd rolled it before it was dry, so it smeared. It doesn't look like mountains anymore. More like a rainstorm.

"We need a couple of stiff drinks, too."

The chubby man takes his nice white handkerchief and begins to wipe the smeared paint off. Only a little is dry enough to stay. What's left hardly makes any sense at all. He says, "I guess this is done for."

She'd never, even for a minute, had the painting. She'd spoiled it first thing. The way she spoils everything—especially everything she cares about. She can't even tell them she's sorry. This is much too big a thing for "sorry." Like with Fayette, no words can fix any of it. If they didn't need her now, she'd leave this very minute with no horse or food or anything, but if he drinks, she might be the only one.

If he took just a little bit of rum it would help his hip. Help a lot of other things, too, but he mustn't. He won't.

Can't do much of anything about anything tonight. The men are going back to their camp where there's food and water and shelter and they want them all to come, but it would be dark well before they'd get there and he doesn't want to risk moving Fayette yet. Fay might be some bit better in the morning, or if he's worse, maybe he could tell what was wrong by then. It'll be a cold night. He'll put his bedroll down and he'll lie on it and put Fay on top and then have Lotti pile all the blankets and slickers on top of Fay. He himself will likely sleep, no matter that he'll be lying on a lot of lumpy boulders. He hasn't slept for—he can't remember how many nights gone by. Hasn't eaten much either. Should eat. He'd promised Oriana. Sometimes eating helps even when he doesn't feel like it. But he can't face any more jerky.

The men say Lotti should go back with them where she can wash up and they'll give her a clean shirt and then they'll all come back in the morning and bring dinner. He's glad she doesn't want to go, even though for her sake, it would be best. He needs her help. She's already built a fire nearby and gathered enough wood for half the night. She's making broth out of jerky. That's a good idea.

But they'll have to get back home sometime, no matter what's wrong with Fay. A horse will be bumpy, especially downhill. He'll have to mostly carry him. At least Lotti managed to kill the man. Probably saved both children. So far he's never killed anybody, but he would have killed the man who'd raped Oriana. He always thought of himself as somebody who wouldn't kill anybody, but that's not true.

He's numb. It's not the first time.

She keeps watching Old Him. The bottle of rum looks exactly as full as it was when the men left it for them and yet he seems . . . kind of odd—shaky and trying to hide it. She sees it most when he finds himself a rock and lets himself down on it—carefully, sideways as usual because of his hip—and sits and rolls a cigarette. He almost can't do it. She could do it for him but she doesn't want him to find out she knows how. He wouldn't want help, anyway. And she feels shaky, too. But he looks . . . kind of collapsed, even though he's sitting up. Was this what she'd always wanted to do to him? All this time—reduce him to this? Well, here it is.

They sit. She'd like to say something. She needs to. Or do something. A nice thing.

"Here. Your tally book. I'm sorry I tore out the first pages. I knew you cared about it because Ma gave it to you, but I took it anyway."

All he says is "Yes," but seeing it seems to perk him up some. He starts to take it but then gives it back. "You might need to write."

"I don't think I'll be writing anymore."

"Keep it for now. Write in it if you want. There's nothing I'm going to keep tally of out here."

"Ma's pistol. I took that, too. You gave it to her. That's what I killed him with."

"You did right."

He looks just as greenish as he usually does after a drinking binge, and yet he hasn't drunk anything that she can tell.

Before the men headed back, the chubby man had said for her to take good care of everybody and herself, too, as if she really was the one in charge. You'd think after what she'd done, he wouldn't have said that, but it looks as if maybe it's true. The one called Jack had called the chubby one L. D., and the evening before she'd seen his name signed on the bottom of the painting: Lindell D. Root. Yesterday she'd thought, Well, he's just a big load for a little horse. That was still true, but he was nice anyway. He was so nice, in fact, he might forgive her for stealing and spoiling his painting, but she didn't want him to. She wouldn't let him.

But now it's to Old Him that she asks the question. "What are you going to do with me?"

"I don't know. Nothing. Seems like there's more than enough been done to you already." (That old "Let be" again. Sometimes she hates it and sometimes she likes it, but she doesn't like it now.)

He throws away the half-smoked cigarette, though usually he doesn't waste any bit of them but the paper. He always puts the tobacco back in the tin even if there's nothing but a nubbin left. He says, "I'll need your help getting Fayette set for the night," but he doesn't look as if he wants to get up and go do it. Still, in a minute, he does.

First they try to feed Fay some jerky broth and after that water. Maybe he gets some down, but it's hard to tell. Then she gets Old Him to have some broth, too. She says the same things Ma says: "You have to keep your strength up" and "It won't do Fay any good for you to let yourself starve." Ma would have said, "I don't know how you ever stayed alive before you met me." She won't be saying that.

Fayette has black eyes by now. They make him look sick and fragile and sad. Old His eyes look almost as bad. When she helps to roll Fay on top of him, Fay shuts his eyes finally and seems to cuddle up. She doesn't like the look of either of them. Fay seems a little more comfortable than before, but there's something wrong with Old Him, too. She covers them up and tucks them in, her tarp on top. Old Him says for her to come in with them and keep warm (all the blankets are on them), but she says she needs to sit up a little while and she wants to watch the fire and think some.

She's never in her life seen somebody go to sleep as fast as Old Him does. It's sure enough he didn't hear her answer. She could have said "Pa" a dozen times and he'd never have noticed a single one.

She reloads the pistol and brings the buffalo gun to where it'll be handy. His deer rifle is still in its scabbard on the saddle. For once he didn't do what he always did and always told everybody else to do first thing: unsaddle or loosen the cinch. She takes the deer rifle out and then unsaddles. She gives Matou a bit of a brushing where the saddle and cinch have been. Old Him would want her to do that. All she has to brush him with is her bandanna. She gives him grain and a little water. In her hat again. Then she sits. She thinks of rolling herself a smoke, but that doesn't seem right anymore.

That man obviously picked this place carefully. She wonders how long he'd been watching her. And what about other men who might be out there? All like him. Matou will give warning and she will fight—shoot and shoot and shoot to the death.

They—Ma and . . . him . . . Pa. . . . They didn't believe in God that she could tell, but maybe she ought to, a little bit anyway, just to make sure and not leave anything important out. When she was about eleven she had mostly believed—all kinds of things. Now she ought to see every side even if all at the same time. Pray. To everything. But not to Coyote. Best not to attract his attention. Ma once said an odd thing. They were on a picnic and she was looking up at the mountains and there was a little cloud around the top of each one like there so often is. She said—to him, "If I were to worship anything, you'd be first and this would be second, but not a close second." Sometimes Ma said things about as odd as what Aunt Henriette would say. She'd like to paint a scene like that and give it to Ma. But then she isn't going to paint anymore. She won't let herself. Maybe she shouldn't write either. She should just make things up to people. Help out. Be a nurse.

She'll not be able to sleep. She's too sore and dirty and smells too much of that man.

— • —

She wakes to a soft rain on her face and the fire spitting and hissing. They'll get wet, him and Fay. Their heads anyway. She goes to check on them. First she leans close to Fayette to see if he's breathing, and he is. She rigs up a lean-to using sticks from her woodpile to prop her slicker over their heads. She's cold, but they're nice and warm. He'd said for her to come in with them. She's awfully dirty, but does anyway. *He* smells good, of tobacco and man sweat and horse sweat and hay. He knows she's there because he puts his arm around her and pulls her up close with them. Maybe he thinks she's Ma. They're a nice bundle—a nice, nice family bundle. She begins to shake. A lot. It isn't from the cold because she's not that cold. She'll be bothering them. She shouldn't have come in so close. She moves away a little bit, but she's shaking so much she doesn't think she can stand up—maybe hardly sit up. He's waking. She whispers, "Pa." Right in his ear. It comes out all wobbly. Like a lamb.

First he says, "Fayette?" and then he says, "Lotti? Is it you?"

She's full of things she'd like to tell him, but all she says is "It's me, Pa."

"Honey. Come on in closer. *Ça ira, tu sais.* We'll get through it."

Henriette will handle Mother. She'll say exactly what she thinks and yet it won't come out mean-spirited. And it's been a long time. Maybe Mother has changed. Her hair's gone completely white. She had hardly recognized her. She'd known who it was in other ways than what could exactly be called recognizing. The light blue dress. She always liked to wear that color to match her eyes. And she was wearing a corset. You didn't see corsets much out here on the farms and in this heat. She'll have heatstroke. Henriette should warn her. She herself doesn't need one. Even after all these children, she's still skimpy. Beal doesn't seem to mind. Children . . . and this child . . . She hardly knows whether to be sorry or glad to have lost it. She doesn't know what Beal might feel. It's always hard to read him.

She might have wanted to get up and walk around a bit, but now all she wants to do is sleep—to avoid Mother. She doesn't want to think. She just wants to lie still and wait for Beal. Everything will be all right when he gets back. Cramps won't feel so bad with him here. He'd been there when Briant was born. He'd only been there twice for a live birth (too many spring babies when there was too much work to do). She'd been braver than ever when she knew he was just outside the bedroom door. She could imagine him holding her, and he wanted to, but Aunt Jenny wouldn't let him in. As if he hadn't seen and helped out with hundreds of births of all sorts of creatures. With Briant, she'd been imagining his arms around her and that he was whispering all sorts of nonsense, making her laugh even in the middle of it. It was easier to imagine with him right outside. He never said, but she thought he'd been hoping for a girl after Christy (it always seemed to her the French liked girls more than most—well, at least more than the Scots), but he seemed happy enough with his little bald boy baby. (Those bald ones—Christy, too—always turned out to be the redheads.)

—•—

Mother has left the silk nightgown lying at the foot of the bed. Has Beal ever seen or touched the like? His hands will snag it.

But that hope chest! Beal mustn't know about it. She has to get it out of sight right away. Out in the tool and buggy barn. Behind things. She must get up and tell Henriette. Or Tibo should take it back to their place. Right now.

"Henriette! Come quickly."

"*Mon dieu,* is that all? I thought you were in big pain. *Mais c'est ridicule.* Don't be *ridicule.* It's full of things you need. Your mother showed me. You said yourself you need sheets and towels—and all those lacy things are good for you."

"But, Henriette, Beal always wanted to give me things like that. And there's a big silver platter—I mean *big*—and matching bowls. There's a hot chocolate set with eight cups—with gold leaf, for heaven's sake! Who would need that?"

All these years she's hidden where she came from. She couldn't hide that she'd been educated or had grown up with money, but she's hidden how much. If Beal sees . . . And the silverware!

"Did you do that? Did you ask her to come here?"

"What you think? How would I know to find your mother? And why should you be having a mother when I don't have? It was Lotti, *tu sais.* Your mother has a letter, and she wears a drawing Lotti sent her in a frame like a locket."

"Henriette, I'll get up and move that hope chest myself if Tibo doesn't do it."

"All right. *Sois tranquille.*"

—•—

One look at Beal and Mother will think she had been desperate for any man that came along, but she hadn't been. First she hated everything male. (Jacob was the sweetest old man, but for a long time she hadn't trusted him. He was like a father to her—in fact, better than her father had ever been to her—for a whole year before she noticed how kind he was.) Mother would think marrying Beal was a last resort. She herself— and even though she'd loved him from the start—had sometimes, at least at first, looked at him as though through her mother's eyes. She'd thought, How thin, unshaven, limping, grinning—and sad. And he was—he really had been a vagrant. And Fayette. Mother would think, One more little

French farmer, good for raising beef and potatoes for his betters. She doesn't want them ever to meet. Things won't be at all right when they get back. If they do get back.

———•———

She rests, listening to the sounds from the kitchen just outside her door. Briant is already calling Mother "Grandma." Mother is saying, "Would you like to have a real rocking horse?" and he's saying, "Mine *is* real," and she's saying, "I mean, just like a horse and with real horsehair?" Oriana thinks, Please, Mother, and goes back to sleep in self-defense. Beal had made that rocking horse a while ago for Fayette.

———•———

She wakes to all sorts of things happening outside. She runs to the window so fast she feels dizzy and has to sit back down on the bed for a minute. There's a stranger out there, a tall man with a little devilish Vandyke beard and a floppy black hat. He's talking to Tibo, and Henri is hitching Tibo's team to the wagon. Why would they need the wagon, if not . . . ? Somebody is hurt. And now Henri is trotting off on his pony in the direction of town. He's going for the doctor.

She runs out barefoot and in her old torn nightgown. Henriette grabs her before she gets far.

"Fayette's all right. Someone beat him up, but he's all right. Henri's going for the doctor."

"Who would do that? How did Beal let it happen?"

"I think he got there afterward."

"Is he bad then? That they need the wagon? Maybe they shouldn't be moving him at all. Beal knows that. I should go to him."

"There's something else."

"It's Beal."

"He collapsed. They say he's half out of his head. They don't know what's wrong, but he has a fever. T-Bone is taking the wagon as far into the foothills as they can take it. They'll be down to it in a few hours."

"I knew this would happen. I always knew it. I told him so. I'm going with them. I can ride in the wagon."

"I've got a good grip on you, and you're not going if I have to hold you down all afternoon."

Lotti writes: I've started another journal. I promised myself I'd never write again, but here I am doing it. No matter how hard I try, I never seem to keep one single one of my resolutions. Not only that, I've started it in one of Fayette's copybooks. I even tore out his used pages. But I don't think he'll mind. I'll give him all my arrowheads and my little Paiute bow that looks as if it's a toy but it's the size they really do use. And I'll be the one looking after his foal and his chicken. I guess I have to, anyway. Nobody else will. I keep wondering how that poor foal survived. Henri must have noticed and fed him. I should thank him, except since I beat him up, we've never talked much. That foal thought Fay was his mother. Followed him all over. Sucked at his fingers. When we left I didn't even think about poor Goldy and how Ma maybe wouldn't think to feed him. He might have died. Then I'd have been to blame for that, too. It's good Fluff Buff was in with the other chickens and got fed with them. If Aunt Henriette had boiled her up for supper, that would have been my fault.

There's a lot to do. All those chores of Fayette's, and then I seem to have turned into the chief milker and separator, not to mention just about everything else, but even with all this work, it's lonely. I'm used to having Fay around. He's been hanging around me ever since he could hardly crawl. I thought I didn't like it, but I guess I did. And then everybody's busy with everybody else. I wanted to talk to Ma, but there isn't a chance, and I guess there isn't anything to say anyway. I'm not sure she would want to talk to me. If she didn't *ever* want to speak to me again, I wouldn't blame her. It's a wonder she's been talking to me all these years as it is. I want to make up to her for who I am—all the trouble I've caused just from getting born, and then all the stuff I've done on purpose. She looks as if this is the last straw. Aunt Henriette said she lost the baby. That's got to be my fault, too. I didn't even know she was going to have another one.

She looks like she hardly sees me when we pass each other. As if she's wiped me right out of her head. I guess I'd want to wipe me out of my head, too, if I was in her shoes. That man out there was big, and Ma's not even up to my size. She couldn't do anything. Even less than I could. And afterward there was me. I'd take off, too, and forget everybody I ever knew. Of course, with me it's different. Everything . . . all of it is my fault, so all the more reason to go. That's what I'm going to do. Go off forever as soon as they don't need me here anymore. I should have done that a long time ago. But now I have to see if he and Fayette are going to be all right. I'll go off after, then, like he did when Christy died. I'll send money back, too, if I can, only I'll never come back. *He* always gets work wherever he goes. People like him because he's funny, and then he never cares what sort of job he gets (I wouldn't either) and he already knows how to do just about everything there is to do. It would be just like me to have to steal for food and get myself in trouble. It's a lot easier for boys, but I don't seem to make a very good one. I've got bigger bosoms than Ma already, and who knows where they'll go from here? But I don't make a very good girl either, my hands all rough and ground-in dirt and my hair all cut off and I've been clumping around so much pretending I'm wearing boots that I can't stop. But I oughtn't to live here anymore. Except right now I'm the only one around who does the everyday chores.

But I wonder what I'll *really* do? I just can't keep track of myself. Here I am not only writing but drawing, too. I *had* to, first for L. D. (I just couldn't get out of it) and then for Fayette. He needed for me to.

—•—

They carried them in, Old Him and Fayette, to the double bed in his and Ma's room. Uncle T-Bone and Aunt Henriette stripped all his dirty clothes off right in front of everybody, even me and that grandma. They're very French that way. I was embarrassed for him, not so much because he was stark naked for a couple of minutes but because he's so hairy. I was used to it, but that grandma wasn't. I didn't want her to think badly of him. (You can tell from the way she dresses and what she says how she probably feels about things, like not enough hair on *my* head and too much all over *him*.)

So many people in their little bedroom, and everybody rushing around and basins of warm water and towels and the doctor in there, too, and Ma not doing much of anything but kneeling by the bed with her feet sticking out for everybody to trip over, and he, you could tell, not caring if she was there or not. Ma could tell, too, and she could tell he didn't want to be touched. It was as if he couldn't think about anything except being uncomfortable. He turned his head away when she tried to push his hair out of his eyes—it was all plastered down with sweat—and he pulled his hand away when she went to hold it, so she held the edge of the pillow or the folds of the blanket beside his hand. If he and Fayette needed rest, they certainly weren't getting any, but after they got washed and wrapped up good, and after the doctor said Fay had a bit of a concussion and Old . . . Old Pa . . . (It's even hard to write it. Is this the first time I ever have?) Pa. He had a pretty bad case of pneumonia and was suffering from exhaustion on top of it, so they left them there to sleep, except for Ma. She sat on the floor and leaned her head against the side of the bed. She looked sick, too. I guess she was, what with losing the baby just a little while ago. Aunt Henriette covered her with a quilt. I needed to be with Ma and to be in with them, but Aunt Henriette made me come out. I felt as if I belonged with them, but I needed to wash. I had to get my bath ready by myself. I was so tired I went to sleep in the tub, but I woke up when the water got cold and then I had another bout of shakes right after. I stayed in there until I could stop them. Nobody wondered where I was.

—•—

I brought him home. Practically all by myself. L. D. had to bring Fayette. I never thought Old Him would ever, ever collapse. Even when I knew, the night before, that there was something wrong, I still didn't think it. When he fell, I was right behind, leading Matou for him. He was carry-ing Fayette—piggyback so he could see his feet on the trail ahead. He was pretty unsteady, but I knew, I just *knew* he'd hold up no matter what. He was coughing some, but it didn't seem too bad. (I had lots worse when I had whooping cough.) Maybe he was even coughing the night before, but I was too sleepy to notice.

Then he just gave way all over but sort of slowly, and he turned to the side as if to protect Fayette. I thought he'd gone down on purpose, but he was completely out when I got up to him. I don't know for how long, but it felt long, like fifteen or twenty minutes. After he came to, he didn't seem to care about anything, whether we ever got home or not or whether we ever got anywhere. L. D. lifted him up on Matou and I got behind and held him in the saddle. (I told L. D. it should be me doing that.) I held him all the way. He was awfully clammy. Sometimes he almost fell off and sometimes he tried to get off. That was the worst. I kept telling him, "Ma needs for you to get on home," but he didn't care, not even about her.

I always wanted to test myself. Well, I guess I got tested and I guess I passed because we got home. Maybe real life is just one big test. Like right now. I'd have liked to have somebody get my bath and make me hot broth and tuck me in like they did for them. Except all this happened because of me so I guess it's only fair nobody looked after me.

We only took a couple of rests on the way down. One was when we got back to Jack and L. D.'s camping spot. (I should call them Mr. Sanderson and Mr. Root. But I call L. D. "Uncle L. D." He doesn't mind.) I had a chance to wash a bit in the stream. It comes right down from a glacier, but I *needed* that the water be so cold it hurt. L. D. lent me a fancy white shirt with little black stripes. I'd like to keep it, even though it's much too big—I'd buy it, I wouldn't steal it—but I'd probably spoil it first thing.

Funny, even though it was L. D.'s horse I ran off with and L. D.'s painting I stole and ruined, it was Mr. Sanderson who seemed to be angry with me. I heard him tell L. D., and more than once, that this was a waste of time and money, too, since they had to go home in a couple of weeks, but L. D. said there was no other way to do.

The more I saw of L. D., the more it seemed as if he'd never be angry with anybody. Old Him . . . Old Pa didn't get angry either, or never showed it, but even so, he was nothing but a bunch of nerves. Like Ma said, tight wound. L. D. hardly seems wound up at all. He just sits back and smokes those big cigars and drinks his special rum. He talks to me as if I'm a friend or maybe already an artist. I don't know what to say to him. I wish he would get angry. I told him I wanted to make everything up to him but that I didn't know how to do it, and he said he didn't know how either. I said I'd pay him back if it took me thirty years. He said he didn't want me to do that. His voice and everything about about him is like his body—kind of soft. He said he and Jack—Mr. Sanderson—they were going back to their camp after things got settled down here, and he said he'd paint more or less the same painting over again and, who knows, it might come out even better, but I said that didn't matter, I'd still ruined a beautiful thing.

He saw my drawings. (But that was after we'd had a good night's sleep and a big breakfast. I wore a skirt and I felt uncomfortable. I always do in a skirt, but why should I be comfortable? Ever anymore? Besides, a *lot* of other things were making me uncomfortable—I still felt filthy and still couldn't get that smell off me. But I wore the skirt because I wanted people to see I'd changed and that I was sorry and that I would do everything they said for me to do and more. In fact that's what I did do—secret good deeds nobody knew about, or at least they didn't suspect it was me who'd done them.)

L. D. said I should paint. I pretended I was going to. I couldn't tell him I wasn't going to let myself—that better I should become a nurse. He talked about places I might study. He said he'd like to see a woman out there in the mountains with her easel and her pack mules and her hiking boots. That made me want to do it all the more, like I could combine all the things I love the most. Used to love—and do still—but it didn't change my mind about what I have to do with my life. He wanted to talk to Ma about me, but she wasn't in a state where she could hear anything and he knew that. And she was always either in with him or with Fayette. (By then they'd put Fay in the parlor where it would be quieter.) That grandma had been staying in my room and I was supposed to sleep in with the babies, but that grandma said she'd go in there—that she even wanted to—and let me have my room back. She said I looked exhausted. She noticed.

Sleeping alone: Certain bodily effluvia are thrown off from our persons, and when two individuals sleep together each inhales from the other more or less of these emanations. There is no doubt but that consumption, and many other diseases, not considered contageous, are communicated in this manner.

Numerous cases have occurred where healthy robust children, have *"dwindled away"* and died within a few months from sleeping with old people.

The Care and Feeding of Children
L. Emmett Holt, M.D.
Appleton and Co., 1894, 1897, 1904

She certainly wasn't what I expected my letter to bring. I think I must have expected my father. That grandma looks just like a chubby version of Ma, and she's hard all around her middle because of her corset. I hope I don't ever grow up to be so old I have to wear one of those things and garters.

Since Ma was never there, L. D. wanted to talk to Aunt Henriette, but she was hurrying around even more than she usually does and saying "Oh-la-la-la-la" about everything, so then he talked to Uncle T-Bone a little bit, but Uncle Bone was in with Old Him a lot, too. So then he talked to that grandma. All she wanted to do was talk about me anyway. She seemed to think I was the absolute best of everybody, even though she'd hardly met me and most of that time I'd been sleeping. She thought I was beautiful. She thought I was sweet and kind and that my drawings were as good as they could ever get already.

Uncle L. D. (when I talk to him to his face I always call him Uncle), he asked me to come sit on the porch with him the evening after the evening we got back. He sat and smoked and looked out at our view. He said someday I should paint it and that he would do it except he was saving it for me. He had called me a brave girl as we were getting back down, and he called me that again, and then he said, "Who's looking after you?" and "Did you tell your mother or your aunt what happened to you?" I said I didn't need for them to know, and then he said, "It's always like this, isn't it?"

But then I realized it wasn't, even though I'd always thought it was. If Old Him hadn't been sick, he'd have seen to it Ma knew. He'd have taken special care of me. He always had, I just hadn't *wanted* to realize it.

I said, "No. It isn't. Not with him around. With him sick, it looks more that way than usual."

L. D. said, "Maybe."

I said, "No, it's true. He's . . . My pa is . . . He's always been good to me." I said, "But you have to know that all of this, from the very start, is all my fault. Even what happened to me. It was because I wanted to keep your painting and your horse that I didn't turn around when I should have."

He didn't answer. He just looked out and smoked, and after a bit he talked more about me being an artist. I went ahead and said "Mm-hmm" to everything because that way there wouldn't be any arguments. Then he told me things to try, like drawing full face and three-quarters face, which I hadn't done much. They're harder, but he said I should do it anyway. He said, from what he'd seen of me, I was good at doing hard things. He said I should try drawing a leg pretty much pointing straight at me, though not quite. Then he drew for me. First just pieces of things, like a leg the way he'd said to do. It was a naked lady's leg. I wondered what Ma or that grandma would say if they saw it, but it wasn't done in a bad sort of way. Just a this-is-how-it-is way. Then he drew horses' hooves and pasterns and hocks, and then people's ears. He said lots of artists were careless about ears but that I hadn't been. He drew a big ear all by itself and showed me how to shade it with the light coming from the left. Then he drew me—and it was wonderful! Who would think, even with my hair all gone! While he was drawing it, he said he was proud to have met me and that even though I'd begun it all, I should be proud of myself for the things I'd done after. I know it's because he doesn't know me very well, same as that grandma. I didn't know what to say. I felt like running off and hiding before he got to know me any better and changed his mind, but I was in the middle of posing for him, and besides, I didn't know how to run off right in front of him. Then he said, "I'm embarrassing you," and we laughed, and I felt better. "Now you do me," he said, "three-quarters view." There was no way I could say no. (I got a lot better even in just that hour or so he was teaching me.) And then later, I drew for Fayette.

I never thought I'd ever like a fattish man. He's not *that* fat, but he sure doesn't look like a rancher or a cowboy. He's pretty bald, and with his hair all tannish, he looks kind of bland. Even his eyes are bland, but I don't care. Not anymore. I guess I mostly got used to the looks of Old Him, even though I thought he was a criminal when I first saw him. I remember how Ma brought him right into the house with us the very first day and I thought he'd murder us both, he was that dark and hairy and bony and rumbly and snaggletoothed, and with his dirty old hat so low over his eyes, but pretty soon he got to be, to me, exactly what a cowboy ought to look like—or anybody, for that matter. I used to limp around just to be like him.

L. D. talks just like Ma. He comes from New England, too. He has the cleanest hands I ever saw.

—.—

I go in to Fayette when Ma isn't there. (I wonder where she sleeps. She's mostly in with Old Him, but I know she doesn't get in bed with him. I don't think she sleeps anywhere.) Fay isn't supposed to be too badly off, according to the doctor, but he's all purple and green and yellow with bruises and he still won't say anything. Most of the time he has a beefsteak on his face or an ice pack. We've used up just about the last of the ice. Usually by now Pa and Uncle T-Bone would have taken the pack mules to bring more down from the mountains, but they haven't had a chance. I wonder if they'll ever do that again. Maybe I should do it before I leave. But I couldn't lift big chunks.

I talk to Fay. I tell him about his foal. I brought Fluff Buff in to him. (I wanted to bring Goldy, too. I thought it was important, but Aunt Henriette wouldn't let me, especially since it was the parlor. And she only let Fluff Buff be in there for about fifteen minutes.) In the evenings I make shadow pictures on the ceiling. I make Fay the hero of all the stories I tell. (I used to make myself the hero in our games, and I always tried to make Fay be the villain, but he never would.) I draw him as Indian and cowboy and soldier, and I prop the drawings up by the bed. I wish he'd talk. Nobody knows why he won't. It's as if he got younger all of a sudden —and in other ways than just starting to wet his bed, which he'd never done much before. (I was the one who used to do that. Ma always made me wash out my own sheets and nightgowns. That wasn't so bad when I was bigger, but she made me do it when I was really little. I don't even remember the first time, but I remember I could hardly lift those wet sheets. She said the harder it was to do, the more it would teach me not to wet, but even though it was hard and even though I hated it, it never did teach me. It just stopped last year, by itself.)

The doctor has already come around again. I guess he must think things aren't going very well with Old Him.

Aunt Henriette sometimes comes in and stares at—well, at first I thought she was staring at Fayette, but now I know she's staring at me. Last evening she came in and practically picked me up out of the chair and brought me in to supper.

Sometimes, when he's sleeping on his back, Oriana can sneak her arm under the covers—lightly so he doesn't push her away. She puts her fingertips on his stomach just below his breastbone. If she finds the exact right spot, she can feel his heart: still beating. She can rest some then, leaning her head against the side of the bed and keeping her hand there as long as he lets it be, no matter how stiff and sore she gets. Sometimes she thinks it's her fingers that keep his heart beating—as if some magic flows from her body into his. She knows it isn't true, but what if it was? She doesn't believe in things like that, but she feels panic when he turns away from her touch.

—·—

He must think he's dying because he's told her he loves her. He may have told her before. She remembers how she thought he said it when she was sick after the born-dead baby. Back then she wasn't sure if she'd heard it or dreamed it. Now it's he who's out of his head half the time, but doesn't that make what he says all the truer—if, even in delirium, he thinks it and thinks to say it?

—·—

If she sleeps or when she sleeps, or if she eats or when, she hardly knows. She leaves that up to Henriette.

H e *could* talk. If he wanted to. *Maybe* he could. He hasn't tried for so long he's not sure. And what's the sense to it anyway? Horses don't. Goldy never needs to. And he always knows when Crazy Colt is mad at him or bored. He especially knows when Crazy's happy. Mostly that's when they're headed toward home or when he's being put out to pasture. That's what Crazy likes best of all, though he always waits for Strawberry to come before he goes off. If Strawberry doesn't come, he just waits and waits. They're good buddies. He and Lotti are good buddies, too. She feeds him first and then she feeds Goldy. When she feeds him, he pretends to be a horse. Not one like Goldy. He'd rather be a big black horse named Midnight.

The doctor said he should get out of bed by now, at least for part of each day, but he's not going to until Pa does. If Pa dies, he'll never get out of bed again. It isn't that being in bed is so nice—it isn't—but it's necessary. What he doesn't like the most about it is if he lies a certain way, he can hear his heart beating. What if he hears it stop all of a sudden? He wishes people didn't have hearts. It wouldn't be so scary. He knows hearts make the blood go round, but he doesn't know *why* blood has to go round. He'd rather it didn't.

Ma comes in sometimes. She's all trembly and her hair flies around even more than ever. (Pa likes her hair any old way. Pa likes to take it all the way apart.) When she comes in here, Ma always says everything will be all right and that he mustn't worry, but it's like she's talking to herself. She says, "Are you in pain? I wish you'd tell me," or she says, "Just make one little move. Anything, no matter how tiny. Just your little finger. Can you do that?" He wants to do it for her, but he can only do it after she goes—just his little finger. It wiggles all by itself. Maybe it isn't him doing it. Maybe it's just a twitch. Of course he does move some when nobody is there, and when Lotti's there he sometimes forgets and moves. The thing about Ma is, she isn't really looking at him, anyway. She's thinking about Pa.

Grandma comes in, too. She calls him a fine young man, but by her voice, you can tell she's just trying to be nice. When she says how lovely— she always says lovely, it must be her favorite word—how lovely Lotti's drawings are, she sounds a little bit more real. Sometimes Grandma says, "You'll talk when you're good and ready," or "You'll talk when you have something to say." She says, "I know you and I know you will." She doesn't know him at all. Even if he had things to say—which he doesn't—he wouldn't say them. He doesn't want to try because what if nothing comes out?

Lotti only asks him yes or no questions. She said tap one for no and two for yes. If she'd had a tap for maybe, he might have tapped that.

He thinks a lot about Pa falling down. He never thought Pa would fall like that, for hardly any reason. He didn't let go of Pa even when they tried to pull him away. It was important to hang on, but they pulled him off anyway. That Mr. Root—he wasn't being mean. He kept saying, "Give your dad some air." Letting go didn't seem like a way of giving any air. That was the very last thing he really and truly did: hang on to Pa.

Lotti writes: Last night it got terrible! I thought he was already dead and that I hadn't had a chance to see him even once since I'd brought him home four days ago. And I thought how Ma probably didn't want me to be there even with him completely dead. Only he wasn't.

The whole house woke up. The babies cried. Gabby just screamed and screamed. I don't know why she did. There wasn't that much noise at first. It was more as if there was something in the air. We all felt it, and then after that there was the hustling around. That grandma took care of the babies. I would have helped her, but Fayette was crying, too, and she said I should go in with him. I couldn't tell him things would be all right because I was pretty sure they weren't and wouldn't be.

Fay had wet his bed again so I cleaned him up. I was glad to have something to do that needed doing right away. I was glad he cried, too. He's been so still and silent all the time. At least this was something, even though he wasn't making much noise with it. After I cleaned him up, I sat in Ma's platform rocker and put him in my lap (that's the first time I ever did that), and we rocked and he sucked his thumb, which he hadn't done since he was three, and we listened while everybody ran around like crazy.

The parlor is right next to the kitchen/sitting room so we could hear everything. They were getting hot water and cold water and mustard plasters—for his feet! which I'd never heard of—and all sorts of tisanes. You could smell especially valerian. I don't know how they kept everything straight. Then when things calmed down some, we heard him shout out that they should leave him alone—it was more like croak out—and I thought they should, if he wanted that, and I wondered, when I got to be a nurse, what I would do if a person told me that. Even if—or especially if —he was dying. Why couldn't they leave him to do it in peace?

But I felt an awful dread that I wouldn't get to see him one more time and call him Pa once more while he still breathed and maybe could hear me. I didn't dare ask right then, and anyway, Fayette had gone to sleep on my lap.

Then things got completely quiet for a while, and I put Fay back in bed and went out to our kitchen/sitting room. Uncle T-Bone was lying on a quilt on the floor, snoring lightly. Aunt Henriette was sitting by the fireplace with her eyes shut, but she looked up at me as soon as I closed the parlor door. I told her I needed to see Pa. I said, "Just once is all. Before anything happens. Unless it's already too late." She said, "You have the right," and she went in to speak to Ma. It took some time, I guess, for her to convince Ma, but after a while Aunt Henriette came back and said I should go on in. She came with me.

It smelled of herbs and sweat and sickness. They had rigged up a kind of half-tent over him and had a kettle steaming on our little coal-oil stove. Ma was at the far side of the bed, looking as if she was afraid of me. She was kneeling on the floor and had hold of his foot. She looked like a wild animal and as sick as he did. She had crazy eyes, and I remembered how crazy she got after she gave birth to that dead baby. I'd been kept away from her then (I guess I was about nine), but I'd peeked in at her a couple of times. In those days I went right ahead and did just about everything I had a mind to.

Now Ma looked as if she'd attack me if I made any sort of move toward him, but Aunt Henriette hugged my shoulders and pushed me close. She said, "He's awake," though it didn't look like it.

He was all beard and eyebrows and plastered-down hair, and where it wasn't plastered down, it stuck straight up and made me think of how Fay's hair was when he was a tiny newborn. His big mustache had gotten lost in with his beard. He hardly looked like himself at all, except for that sharp nose—and his eyes, but at first they were shut. They had him up on pillows, though I knew he hated to sleep propped up that way. I'd heard somewhere that it could help you breathe.

I said, "Pa." He opened his eyes and looked at me and raised his hand a little bit. He said, "Good." I didn't know what he meant, but it made me feel better. I wanted to say more, but seeing him made everything fly right out of my head. Then he shut his eyes again, and I just stood there watching him breathe. Aunt Henriette was behind me holding on to my shoulders the whole time. I don't know how long we stood there—I didn't want to leave—but after a while Aunt Henriette pulled me away from the bedside. I said, "Thank you," to Ma. She gave a little flinch of her head, neither yes nor no nor anything, and then Aunt Henriette turned me around and brought me out.

Outside the door she hugged me. She said, "You know it's not your fault," and I said, "It is. *Everything* is," and she said, "He could have gotten sick anyway. He could have been sick before he started. You know him. He wouldn't have said a word."

"But he wouldn't have gotten *this* sick. The doctor said he was exhausted. And what about Fayette?"

She said I mustn't think that way. She called me *"ma chérie"* and said I was a wonderful help and they couldn't have gotten along without me and that Ma couldn't have, even before all this happened. She said I'd always looked after Fayette. She said I shouldn't forget it. She said Ma had always counted on me to keep him safe. That was funny. I'd thought it was just the opposite, but the minute she said it I knew it was—mostly anyway—true. Even from the beginning I'd kept him from all sorts of things: falling off the porch, climbing up the bookcase, reaching into the fireplace, putting dumb things in his mouth. . . .

"And the animals," she said. "You always looked after them. You were no bigger than a chick, *p'tit poussin*," she said, "but you never forgot."

It was true. I wondered, did Ma know?

It's morning. She's slept. Right straight out on the floor. She hadn't meant to. What if? Last night was the worst. Now of all the times, she should have stayed awake. They said sometimes you could see life leave the body. First you'd see the death when the breathing stopped, and then like a second death a little later, something left the body. She wouldn't call it soul. He wouldn't either. They'd been alike in that. He might have needed her to be there. Hold him. See the end and then the very end. He shouldn't have had to do it alone.

She will wear black from now on. She mustn't hope anything. She's already had more good things than she had expected. All those dark days when she thought life wouldn't amount to anything. Even before that bad thing happened to her, she hadn't thought life would amount to much. She'd thought, This is the way it is. When had hope begun? When Beal came. That was the start of the idea that life could be fun—every single day, fun. They'd laughed from the start. Even the very first day. She'd asked, "Mr. Ledoyt?" and he'd said, "'Fraid so." What she knew of life before that must have come from her father. Everything she knew of life now came from Beal.

She doesn't dare sit up and look at him. She doesn't want to know anything for sure.

She can see his hand: poor scarred, nicked, dirty fingernails. . . . He can't get them clean. But that was her mother's way of thinking. His hand isn't poor at all. It's strong and skilled. Can do most anything, and that's good farm dirt ground in.

She'll wait until it moves. Or just wait. While it doesn't.

A Nourishing Beverage for Invalids Recovering from Fever

Break into pieces three or four hard crackers that are baked quite brown, and let them boil fifteen minutes in one quart of water; then remove from the fire, let them stand three or four minutes, strain off the liquor through a fine wire sieve, and season it with sugar.

White House Cook Book
L. P. Miller and Co., 1887, 1891, 1909

otti writes: Once he started getting better, I thought everything would be all right. I thought we'd have this beautiful, wonderful family, which it was, and that it would stay that way for a long, long time. And then when things settled down and I wouldn't be needed so much, I would run away and get to be a nurse and not cause any more disasters. Just the opposite, in fact—I'd save people. Maybe I could even get to be a doctor. There is a lady doctor I've heard of.

At least he didn't die from anything I did. He died from being himself—doing what he always does. Maybe trying to be younger than he was or, more than likely, forgetting he wasn't young. (Ma said that lots of times.) Or trying to take care of everything all by himself. (Ma said that, too.) Ma was always trying to stop him from doing dangerous things. I know she tried to keep herself from doing that, but she couldn't help herself. He always said, "When you're raising wild beeves, you have to take the risks of it," and Ma would say, "Well, let's stop." Then right away she'd say, "No, don't. I know this is what you want to do." She said that even though she knew—and she told me sometimes—how all he *really* wanted to do was just roam around and sleep under the stars.

—•—

The day he got up and Uncle T-Bone shaved him seemed like a milestone. They sat him in our big kitchen and everybody watched. Even that grandma. It seemed as if it was a ceremony, and I guess it was. That grandma probably didn't really know yet who was under all that hair.

Fayette sat on his lap, both of them covered up with towels. (Fay still wasn't talking, but he did move around some—sort of as if he thought he might hurt himself if he didn't move carefully.) Part of the time Uncle T-Bone pretend-shaved Fay while he was doing Old Him. There was shaving cream all over. There was a lot of joking, like who would they find under all that hair? And maybe it wouldn't be Beal at all and they'd been taking care of the wrong man all this time and Beal was out, in town most likely, having himself a time. He, Pa, kept saying, "You know I can do this myself," and Uncle Bone said, "This is much too big a job for you to handle," and "Somebody better start raking up all this alfalfa."

Ma laughed—too loud. I laughed too loud, too. I could hear myself doing it, but I couldn't stop.

Uncle T-Bone waxed Old His mustache and turned it up at the sides just like his own and just like it used to be. Then he put his head down next to his as if to show them both off—like for a photograph—and as if they looked the same, but they didn't—much—except for the mustaches. Uncle Bone still hasn't any gray hair but he's getting more and more bald. (He always says it's because of his fancy beaver hat.) Even bald, you could say Uncle T-Bone is a lot better looking, but then you'd take a look at Old Pa's eyes. It's as if his eyes could blow you away. *Now* who else will ever have a look like that? I don't think Fayette. He's so open and sweet. Pa was sweet in a way, too, but there was something that grabbed at you—that startled. When I was a child it scared me.

Then—and I think maybe it was because of that look of his—but after we got him all shaved up, that grandma said something that really surprised Ma, and me, too. I could tell Ma didn't believe her for two seconds. That grandma is always on her good behavior, and you can't believe but a tiny bit of what she says. Everything is "just fine" at the very *least,* but mostly everything is a lot better than just fine. I mean *everything.*

What she said to Ma was "What an aristocratic-looking man!" I guess maybe if you could forget about the teeth—among other things . . . And he *was* very pale, and then all that gray hair, but I think what it was, was that that grandma had looked him in the eyes and, like everybody else, got to thinking of him as seeing right through things and knowing secrets. Or maybe it was what Ma always said about him: "Tight wound inside." Maybe that's what grabbed at you so.

—•—

Nobody could figure what to do about Fayette back then, and now that Pa's dead they can't figure what to do even more. He still won't talk and you never know where you're going to find him. As soon as you find one hiding place, he finds another, but I can usually figure out where he'll be. There aren't any places I haven't hid in myself.

The minute Uncle T-Bone came to tell us Pa was dead, I thought right away, What about Fay? I wasn't ready to think about myself or Ma. Mostly I just prickled all over. I could feel the hair rising on the back of my neck. But I didn't exactly believe it—except for the way Uncle Bone looked. Then he handed me Old Pa's hat. He said, "Beal . . ." He said, "Your pa . . . wanted for you to . . . ," but he couldn't go on. Then I began to believe him because for sure, Old Pa would never be without his hat.

I said, "So then he must have known—so did he?—that he was going to die."

Uncle T-Bone said, "Oh, *he* knew. *I* didn't. I thought . . ." Then Uncle T-Bone kind of fell into a chair and started to cry right in front of all of us. I didn't know what to do, like should I pretend I didn't see? But he wasn't trying to hide it. He got out his big blue bandanna, but he didn't try to hide his face.

That was the first of the times Ma fainted. Uncle Bone had to stop crying and pick her up. He held her as if he was in love with her and then, holding her, he cried all the harder. Fay made a funny kind of animal sound—at first I didn't know what it was—and then he ran out.

I said I'd get Ma some water, but Uncle T-Bone said to let her stay this way and that I should go get Fayette.

At first I couldn't find him, but then I did. I had to carry him back. He was all loose and floppy just like he was for such a long time after that man beat him up. I was wishing he would cry but I knew he wouldn't. He hadn't really cried since that man beat on him. That night when everybody thought Pa was a goner, he mostly just whimpered. I wished I'd never teased him about crying. I said, "Oh, please cry," but I knew that wouldn't do any good. Maybe he felt like I did sometimes, sort of floating up above everything. I wanted to say, "Come down here with us." He wouldn't have known what I meant, but maybe he would have. Fay knows things like that. But I couldn't say *I* was really down here either. All I could think about was that now I'd have to write, When my father died . . . When my stepfather died . . .

Uncle T-Bone took us all to his house, not even asking did Ma want to go. He and I packed us up while Ma was still out. When she came to, she just lay there anyway.

Then, over at Uncle T-Bone's there were those middle-of-the-night sounds again. This time it was Uncle T-Bone making the coffin.

Old Pa was the only one beginning to get Fay back to how he used to be. Fay spent a lot of time on his lap. Ma said that kept them both out of trouble. They ate every single meal like that. And when Pa would do some work around the house, he would get Fay to help hold things. Then Pa started Fay off braiding horsehair for hatbands and stampede strings, but mostly bracelets for Ma, which they tried to keep secret. When Fay got to working on those things, there were times you could see he was just about to say something, but then he'd look up and smile instead. I wonder if he's ever going to talk or move around like a regular person instead of so slow and jerky.

That grandma said we ought to give Fayette a good spanking—that we hadn't yet tried that and since the doctor said he was fine, it might be just what he needed. Fay was sitting right there on Old Him's lap listening. Old Him just got right up and went outside carrying Fay, even though it was just about Fay's bedtime. First Ma said, "That's not our way," and then after they'd gone out, she told that grandma how Old Him had been whipped as a boy and how he never wanted that done to any of his children and that he didn't even like to hear any talk about it. That grandma apologized—more than she needed to, as usual—but then she said why didn't Oriana try it secretly when Beal was away because it might work and how would they know if they didn't try it? Ma said, "Mother!" in the way I've sometimes kind of overheard myself say "Maaa" to Ma. These days just about every time I turn around I get a whole different idea about Ma.

—•—

She's having another baby. She told *me* first of anybody! She kept saying, "He doesn't know, he doesn't even know," as if he was alive somewhere not knowing. I figure that baby must have happened when they took those two nights camping out at their special place. Ma didn't think he was well enough to go anywhere, but he wanted to take her someplace where they'd be off alone, since he knew Uncle T-Bone was going to need him in a few days and he was going to go help out no matter what Ma said and no matter that Uncle Bone hadn't asked him to. Ma was right. He probably shouldn't have gone back to hard work so soon. Maybe he wasn't up to doing the things he usually could have done.

Me and that grandma had a chance to talk while they were gone. We were both to watch over things, but that grandma doesn't know chicken feed. She can't milk. She won't even try. She can't even talk about it without looking disgusted. She can just barely do the dishes. She can't cook, except she can bake cakes, that's about all. I wouldn't say she knows anything about children, though she thinks she does. Mostly she tells the little ones they're wonderful, but only after she gives them all sorts of moral lessons, even Gabby. Gabby doesn't understand a single word she says, but Gabby can look as if she's taking everything in (I suppose, in a way, she is), and Gabby says yes as if she knows everything that's said, and that grandma believes she does. But we did get along that time Ma and Pa were gone, though I did all the work and that grandma got in the way a lot trying to help out.

The first night we talked past midnight. We sat on the porch near the babies' window but we listened for Fay, too. His nightmares were tapering off, but he still had them. (He didn't even really cry in his nightmares. Just always sounded like some sort of little animal.) You could see the mountains just as plain as could be in the moonlight. I was glad that grandma could see them at their best, even though they always look littler at night. I was glad, too, that Ma and Old Pa were up there alone together on a night like this. It was just the right sort. I don't suppose anything like that will ever happen to me.

I had a whole different reason now for needing to know about my real father. I was so afraid he might be like that man—that I killed and that I'd kill again without a second thought if I had to do it. (I get angry every time I think about him—what he did to Fay, too.) I hardly dared ask in case that was what he was like, but I had to know. I knew he couldn't be the greatest person in the world, but I had to know just how bad he was so I could plan my life and know what I was up against inside myself. I needed to know even more than I'd wanted to know before when I thought he must be better than anybody around here.

At first that grandma said she couldn't hardly bear to speak of him and that scared me. I asked her, did she know him? Did she know anything about him at all?

"Oh, my, yes, I knew him very well indeed, but I never ever thought . . . Not until you sent me your drawing of yourself. You're the spitting image, though I shouldn't use that phrase."

So if she knew him and never thought, he couldn't have been like that man, so dirty and smelly. "How did you come to know somebody like that?"

"He was a friend of your grandfather's, a lawyer friend. Handsome. Like you. Now why do you want to distress yourself with him? He's best forgotten. Your mother knows that. And she's done it."

"I'm one-half him whether I want to be or not. Grandma, I *need* to know. Lots of things. Like, did he paint?"

"He might have. He was considered very artistic. He liked music, I know that, and poetry. I do believe he wrote sonnets. I suppose he must have liked painting, too." Then she said, "Maybe he actually thought what he did to your mother was all right since they were engaged and the wedding was to be in just a couple of weeks, but," she said, "it wasn't right anyway and I do believe he must have forced her. He *must* have. I don't suppose she would have run away if she'd consented. I should say I had a hard time of it myself, what with Oriana going off right in the middle of all our preparations. My goodness, I had to send back all those gifts. . . . But, poor thing . . . she must have been frightened. She might not have known what to do. I suppose . . ." But then she just looked off at the mountains.

It was odd to think "poor thing" about Ma. I wasn't used to thinking of her that way—not until recently. But she had been "poor thing," no doubt about it, what with that and then with me coming along and all. And not even counting how much it must have hurt, and it didn't even really happen with me. I said, "Ma couldn't have loved that person, then, because with Pa, they weren't even engaged, and it wasn't just once."

"Well, that wasn't right either. Not at all. I hope you remember that, young lady."

"But it turned out all right, so it was the right thing." Tears came to my eyes when I said it. (I was glad it was dark.) That was happening a lot these days. Just exactly when I thought things were getting wonderful, I kept crying.

"It doesn't matter at all how right it turned out to be in the long run, they shouldn't have, and especially not so that a child would know about it. What were they thinking? *If* they were thinking at all. Six years old, for heaven's sake." Then she muttered things I couldn't hear.

"Grandma, *I* was the bad one. I did everything I could to make them unhappy. The burn scars on his hands. That's from me."

"That's hard to believe when I see you helping out the way you do. I'm just not going to believe it."

"But it's true, and I made Fayette unhappy, too."

"I don't believe it. Look at yourself. Look what you did—just today. You're a wonderful young woman," she said, "beautiful and wonderful."

That was nice, but I wanted her to see me—to really know me—and I wanted her to tell me real things about my father. I wanted to shake her up. Out of how she always, always, always is.

"Grandma, listen, what happened to Ma almost happened to me out there. Did Aunt Henriette tell you? Ma doesn't know. He was the most awful man I ever saw in my life. He was hitting Fay, and I killed him. I was so afraid he might be just like my father. I was afraid he *was* my father."

"Oh, my poor dear Charlotte. Don't think about it. Never ever again. When it comes into your mind unbidden, think of something cheerful like flowers and sunsets. If you set your mind to it, you can do it. There are so many beautiful things in this world. Think of hummingbirds, how they feed right there by your window."

"But, Grandma, I can't help it and I can't help my dreams."

"Best yet, think of all the paintings you'll do. Think of how you draw. Think how one of these days you'll paint just like Mr. Root. Even he said so. Think of all the pleasure you'll give to others through your art."

I didn't say it, but I was thinking that if I ever do get to be a painter, I know it will give *me* a lot more pleasure than any other person. In fact I can't think of anything nicer to do—except I'm not going to do it.

—•—

No matter how hard I begged and begged that night, Grandma wouldn't tell me my father's name, which is my real name. She just wouldn't. She said my mind would dwell "in realms that were unhealthy" and best I not know. For my own good, she said, she wouldn't say. She wanted nothing but the best for me, and did I understand that? Did I understand that I deserved the best? So I guess I'll never know. I can't ask Ma.

—•—

Ma came back from those three days out with him looking like she used to, pink and sunburned and dimply even though she doesn't have any dimples. Even more than ever, I thought how things would be wonderful from now on, what with Fayette almost talking again.

They had circled home through town and he had bought her another ring. This one had a greenish blue stone. I knew right away he bought it because it was the color of her eyes. It was small and delicate. A lot nicer than the things he usually got for her. For sure she'd picked it out herself. He got her cloth for a dress, too, and a little apricot tree that already had one apricot on it. I knew everything he got had a special meaning. She didn't plant the tree—she never would have—I did, but not where she can see it all the time. I thought she might burn up the cloth, so I took it and hid it. For now. She does keep the ring on. She holds it to her lips a lot. Not so much like kissing—more like thinking. Except I don't think she is thinking.

I don't know what we're going to do. He was the one putting everything back together. I guess I'm the one to try and keep things going now, but I hardly even know who I am anymore. One thing, though, Ma really does want this baby. As if it's the last thing she'll ever have of him, and I guess it is. I wonder if she wishes now that she'd let him buy her some big, heavy ring that was more like what he would have picked out if he'd been by himself.

—•—

Henri said they were laughing. That's all he'll say. He won't talk about it. Uncle T-Bone *can't* talk about it because every time he tries he starts to cry. He doesn't care who sees him, but sometimes he turns around and leaves for someplace private. (I can't believe all the important things in my life that I'll probably never know anything about.)

—•—

I can't stop drawing and writing. I might as well give up trying to stop for now. It keeps me from thinking too much. The drawing does. The writing helps in a different way. Kind of gets things off my chest and sometimes clears up my thoughts when I feel all muddled. Clears me up a *little* bit. I just always feel muddled.

—•—

Yesterday I drew him—Pa—three-quarter view and it came out so good, I jumped up to go show him. I knew he'd be surprised. And then I remembered. I didn't want Ma or Fay to see it, so I hid it in my bottom drawer. Maybe I'll show it to Grandma—except she likes everything equally. Or when L. D. passes back through here, maybe I'll get to show it to him. But even if I wanted to, which I don't, I couldn't go to art school now. I have to help out here, and I worry about what Ma will do once the baby comes. She really did go kind of crazy while he was sick. I think that baby is all that's holding her together now. (I see her hugging her stomach all the time like she needs to hug something.) Aunt Henriette always said he was driving Ma crazy, but it was just the opposite.

I think Uncle T-Bone wants that baby as much as Ma does. I think they all think it'll be Old Him all over again. Of course we already do have Fayette.

He watches them put Pa deep down and then start to cover him up with dirt. It makes a big thump and thump, thump and thump, every time the two men shovel the dirt on top. It goes thump and thump another time, and then Ma faints again. It's Grandpa Jacob who catches her. He'd have caught her himself if he was a little bit bigger—maybe ten. But maybe not, because he's moving slowly and not very much. That's necessary. Grandpa Jacob falls down on his knees trying to hold Ma up. He's old. If somebody had to die, Grandpa Jacob should have done it. Grandpa is nice, but that's the way it's supposed to be, and not Pa. Lotti says Grandpa Jacob is in love with Ma. She says if Ma had married Grandpa Jacob like he wanted her to, then Lotti would still be here, but there wouldn't be any Fayette at all—ever—and nobody would even know he wasn't here. Even he wouldn't know he wasn't here. He felt bad when she told him that and he tried to feel what it would be like not to be here, but it was too hard. Now he doesn't care. He isn't really here anyway.

They carry Ma in to Uncle T-Bone's house, and Aunt Henriette goes in there with her. He wanted to go with Ma, but Uncle T-Bone wouldn't let him. He kicked and bit, but Uncle T-Bone didn't hardly notice. He held him really tight and made him stay and see the dirt go thunking down.

There isn't anybody to be like anymore. And they won't be able to say he looks just like Pa without Pa somewhere around.

Ma wanted Pa to be put right alongside where Christy is. She's deep in the ground, too, and dirt on top of her, too. There's a little circle of red and white stones all around where Christy is. Ma didn't do that. Aunt Henriette's big, big girls did it. They picked flowers. If those girls put stones around where Pa is, they'll have to make a great big long circle.

He doesn't even remember Christy.

They said we all die. Not stones (they wear away and turn into all this sand), and not iron, and not even gold. What they *exactly* said was, everything alive dies. He doesn't like it like that. He's seen dead things just about every day. (The bones and skin are all that's left and pretty soon the skin gets gone, too.) But he didn't think we all had to do it. Even Pa. It seems like something he himself might do, but not Pa.

Anything can happen. And to Ma, too. And even to Lotti. Lotti says Pa was being the kind of man he always was. Now he'll never be able to do the kinds of things Pa did, even if he grows up. Who would show him how? Pa showed him how to make a hatband. He was making one for Pa. It couldn't be a surprise because Pa was right there all the time and knew it was for him. Pa even picked out the colors: dark from Strawberry's tail and lighter from Crazy's and lightest from Matou's. He could have got some reddish over here at Uncle Bone's. That would have been a surprise. But he's not going to finish it. He locked it up in his lockbox. Pa gave him that box. Pa only gave real things. They didn't have much money, not like Uncle T-Bone, so they had to be careful. He was always careful. He didn't even ask for things he really, really wanted a lot. That helped out. But he wouldn't want anything anymore. When Christmas comes, he won't say one single word. That will help out, too. Pa would want him not to want things.

Henri said they were laughing because Uncle T-Bone tried to climb the tiniest little tree and it started leaning way over. It kept Uncle T-Bone safe from the bull, though. It was not a laughing matter. Pa would say that, even right in the middle of laughing. Henri said Pa was laughing right exactly *then*. They shouldn't have laughed.

Henri told him things he didn't tell anybody else. That was because he just looked and listened and didn't answer back. Henri said Uncle Bill had saved his life. Henri said Fay shouldn't worry about anything because Henri would help any time he needed help. Henri said he owed him. He said, "You just call on me even if it's the middle of the night and I'll come," but he can't imagine wanting or needing anything ever anymore.

You had to go on listening to the thunking. You couldn't hold your ears because Uncle T-Bone had hold of your arms. And you couldn't run away.

otti writes: He looked as if asleep and a lot better than he looked when he almost died from pneumonia. Uncle T-Bone—Ma, too—looked worse than he did. Uncle T-Bone leaned over the coffin and kissed him on the cheeks and on the forehead. I never knew a man would do that to another man even if they were brothers and even if one of them was dead. But then again, they're French. Uncle T-Bone said, *"Sans toi je n'aurai pas pu m'en débrouiller,"* and then he couldn't go on. Then he said, *"Jamais . . . ,"* and then he said, *"On n'en a jamais parlé. Et maintenant tu m'as donné mon Henri—mon seul fils.* I never thanked you for any of it." He hung over the coffin for a while. I could see his tears dropping down on Old Him. He's been crying so much lately I wondered how come the tears never got all used up.

Uncle T-Bone was acting more the way I thought Ma would act, but Ma was keeping very still. When her turn came to say good-bye, she didn't kiss him. She just brushed at his hair as if she was pushing it off his forehead like she always did, except he was neatly combed already. She smoothed out his eyebrows as she usually did, and his mustache. She moved her lips. A little bit after that she fainted again. I suppose that kept happening partly because of the baby.

—•—

Afterward I did a bad thing. Another bad thing. I guess I'm still who I always was. I stole a bottle from Aunt Henriette and Uncle T-Bone and it wasn't just rotgut either, and I walked out the way he did to the hot spring. Actually, when I got there I didn't feel like getting drunk. Just the opposite, in fact. It was too beautiful. I could see why he chose that place. I wondered why, out there, he needed to get so drunk. It always happened out in some special spot—beautiful like this one. But with him, it was as if beauty wasn't enough.

I knew they'd worry like they did when he went off, but I didn't tell anybody. Especially they'd worry now when I'd been helping out so much. They need me. That's the way he was—needed, too. Every single day and all day long, we needed him and not just for work either—we needed him for jokes and we needed to be teased and to be noticed.

I took off all my clothes except I left his hat on and I climbed down into the spring. The stones were still warm from the sun. I moved along the spring to the perfect spot where the river, mixing with it, makes it cool enough to bathe in.

I hadn't thought about my body in a long time. In fact I'd always tried to forget it, especially when it got breasts. There it was. A woman's body. No pretending it wasn't. Not a bit like Ma's. More like a woman's body than lots of women. Why did *I* have to have a body like this? I look like I'm twenty-five already. What was the sense, all this time, of me limping around in pants and wearing his old hats? What did that change? As it got darker, the whiteness of my body stood out even more against my brown hands. It was the whitest thing around. It just about glowed. That was the only nice thing about it.

The rattler came. His rattler. It watched me like it knew I wouldn't bother it. He'd talked about how we should watch out about that snake. If it had been near the house he would have killed it, but not there. He never killed them when they were in what he called their own territory. Except he said, "'Course it's all their own territory." The snake moved sluggishly and didn't rattle. Either it wasn't scared of me or it was too cool. That rattler didn't know Old Him wasn't ever coming there anymore.

If it had been me to do it, I'd have buried Old Him out there. Or maybe up on top of a really high mountain. At one of our picnic spots maybe, where you could see a long ways off. Of course you can see a long ways off down here in the desert, too.

Stars came out. It was almost as bright as moonlight. I recognized the whole sky, parts of it as Paiute and parts of it white people's: Draco, Cassiopeia's Chair, the Bears, Coyote's Daughters. . . . That was because of what he'd taught me. I thought, Are you up there? Up with the spilled white beans? All glittery? I said, "Pa." I said, "I want to tell you."

Except he knew. He'd always known. Even when I was right in the middle of doing a bad thing, he knew. I was the one who got him burned and right after that, when his hands got well enough, he caught crickets and tethered them with threads—to sing me to sleep, he said. He brought me a horned toad.

I tried all those things with Fayette. I'll bring him out here some starry night. Maybe it'll be so nice he'll say something.

Lotti took him out to where Pa used to go. Ma let her do it even though it was night. Lotti wanted him to walk there. She said they had to do it just the way Pa always did, except Pa got drunk. He wasn't going to walk. Not even for Pa. And it couldn't be for Pa. Nothing was for Pa anymore, even though everybody kept telling him, Your pa would have wanted you to do this or that or the other, but if he walked, things would be just the same—as if nothing had happened.

The first time Lotti tried to take him out there she started carrying him piggyback, but he knew that wasn't really real because she couldn't do that the whole way. He knew she thought if they got far enough, he'd have to walk. She gave up pretty quick and put him down by a prickery bush and rested up. She said, "What if I did what you're doing all day long? What if everybody did? What about then?"

They sat while it got darker and there was a little moon way over to the side. She'd have to start back or it would be too dark for piggyback. He was wondering if she'd do it in time, but then she did. So the next time they went, she put him on Crazy Colt.

They saw Pa's snake right off. He's not afraid of snakes except sometimes. Pa said, Keep an eye out, and he did. There's a snake noose right handy in the barn. Even Ma used it, though she doesn't like to. Pa caught one that was taller than he was.

Lotti said to cry. She said she was sorry she'd teased him and that he wasn't like a girl and never had been (though inside he knows he is). She said, did he see how Uncle T-Bone cried? She said, "Pa would have cried if you had died," but he's not sure about that. She said, "Out here nobody will know," but crying was for a long time ago when he was little.

A while ago Lotti had sat him up on Goldy even though Pa always said, "Don't ever sit on colts," but Lotti lifted him right on him anyway. She said he was small enough and it was just for a minute and Goldy was a house pet and wouldn't jump around. Goldy'd been sacked, and Lotti said he wasn't that much bigger than a sack. Goldy was nice and warm. He'd leaned forward with his head on Goldy's withers. Afterward he had golden Goldy-hairs all over himself.

It felt good on Goldy and now good in the hot water. Sort of in the same way. Lotti went in with her shift on, and he wore the bottoms of his longhandles. (Lotti was wearing a dress a lot lately and even an apron sometimes. She hardly looked like herself at all.) It was way, way after bedtime and he went to sleep in there just about first thing, leaning against Lotti. One time he woke up and saw her talking to the stars.

In the morning there was a nice red dawn and he was all crinkled because of so much water.

They watched the sun come up. Lotti said Pa would want them to. She said Pa was always looking at the sky and thinking about the weather. Well, maybe some. She didn't make coffee until after.

If that snake tries to get her, then he might yell out. If he still can. He should practice someplace where nobody can hear just in case he can't do it or if funny noises come out instead.

Lotti writes: I haven't had one single minute for writing since I can't remember when, nor drawing either, and I really shouldn't be writing now. I should be sewing up Fayette's torn nightshirt, and there's a whole basket of socks that need mending. Even more important, I should be figuring out how much hay we'll need now that we've cut down on our herds. Ma certainly isn't going to do it. She doesn't care about anything. I'm the one who had to say we should cut down. I'm the one who had to say we have to stick together. I said we ought to keep the ranch. Of course that was what I wanted. You can't tell what Ma wants. I didn't exactly want to keep the ranch for myself, but I need for it to be in the family and I need for us to stay a family.

Ma and the new baby are asleep. Well, everybody is, since it's the middle of the night. Ma hasn't named the baby even yet. I don't think she wants him to have a name. Maybe now that she sees it's not Old Him all over again, she doesn't care if he has a name or not. If it were me to name him, I'd call him Bill. I think this baby'd be happy being Bill, just as Fay and I would have been, and I think some of us ought to have normal everyday names like other people. (I kind of hope Ma reads this, except she won't. I'd leave it out if I thought she cared enough to look inside. It isn't like it used to be when I thought she might and, maybe, did—*if* she found it.)

I'm writing in here with Fayette. He still sleeps in the parlor away from the other children. I came in here because he had another nightmare. (He's gone back to sleep.) He has them lots of times now. He's gotten to be just like Old Him in that way. I keep hoping maybe he'll talk in his dreams—that would prove he can—but he just grunts or yells like Old Pa did. Funny what gets passed on. I wonder if Fay's dreams are the same as the ones Old Him had. A couple of times Ma had dreams that were almost exactly like mine. She said she was inside this big balloon and could see out and get about but couldn't touch anything.

I thought I was all worn out what with being out with beeves all day, but once Fayette woke me I got wide awake. I always used to think Old Pa's jobs were the most exciting and interesting. Well, now I've got all his jobs to do and most of Ma's and my own and Fay's, too. I guess if I had my druthers I'd still pick Old Him's.

Henri helped me today. We moved six bulls out from the big herd. I should have done it before, but I wasn't thinking things out. Those old bulls were getting to be bologna bulls, anyway.

I always boss Henri around, even now that he's as tall as I am and has a sort of mustache. (Even with the mustache he just barely looks fifteen while I look practically middle-aged. It's this awful body of mine.) Last week we spent two days in the hills bringing down the cows—the best to the winter pastures, but most for Uncle T-Bone to take with his to be sold. We get along, Henri and me—I don't know if he still distrusts me or not. I suppose one of these days I'll be marrying Henri. That seems logical—*if* I marry at all. I guess I wouldn't mind. I like how he has the look Ma always calls the Ledoyt look. Bony and ugly is what that is, but they always stand up nice and straight. Even Fayette always did—practically from the start—till now. Now, if he does move around a little bit (at least he takes himself to the outhouse by himself), he looks as if he's in a high wind or has an awful stomachache. I suppose, in a way, he has . . . and is.

So L. D. came this afternoon while Henri and I were out. He came alone this time. I *knew* he'd come at exactly the wrong time, though I wonder if there'll *ever* be any right times anymore! I've hardly had a chance to talk with him and probably won't have. He's sleeping in the stock barn. So is Henri. If L. D. would just wake up right now and see the lamp lit and wonder and come in to see if it's me . . . If he would, for just a little while . . .

I can't tell if I'm in love with chubby old L. D. or if it's that I'm in love with art, which I know I am. (I'm in love with his horse, too.) When I think about painting and drawing and L. D., I get all trembly and scared. Even a little sick. Sometimes I can't catch my breath, I want and want so badly. If I even have time to draw a little bit, it's not so bad. I just can't seem to stop wanting to, no matter how hard I try, and I really am trying. And after all, before I met L. D. what I wanted to be was a rancher. Of course I never *ever* wanted to be a rancher's wife.

Right now I'd like for L. D. to be sitting beside me and for both of us to be drawing. Maybe he could be drawing me like he did before, all shaded and crosshatched. Sometimes he used a crow-quill pen so he couldn't make any mistakes, and he *didn't* make any. And he could be trying to talk me out of being a nurse—except he doesn't know about that. But how can I even do either one? Not only there isn't any time, but there's no money either.

Well, that grandma said she'd pay for me to go to art school and that I should live with her while I go. (She and L. D. talk about me all the time.) First of all, I'm not sure how long I could stand that for, and second of all, they need me here, and then I need to be a nurse. It worries me that I haven't hardly had any schooling at all, though Ma keeps saying she's a better teacher than any of the ones around here. I couldn't get to be a nurse because of that, nor an artist either probably. I still haven't told that grandma about being a nurse. That's my secret. She'll make a big fuss—ladylike fuss, full of "land o'goshen" and "land sakes alive." I should tell her just to see what she'll say.

It's odd how the happy things (at least in my life) always seem to come along at the same time as the most terrible times. L. D. and me sitting on the porch drawing and L. D. teaching me. That was the best time of my life and the worst, too—almost the worst—what with Fay and him sick and me spoiling the best painting I ever saw, not that I'd seen even one real one before. I wonder what it would be like to have a happy time that was just plain all happy. I wonder what L. D. thinks of me. Aside from wanting me to get to be an artist and ride out in the mountains with a couple of mules, I mean. I wonder if he knows I'm only fifteen.

We all must seem pretty peculiar to him: Ma so exhausted, the baby still without a name, Fayette just lying there, and me with hardly even time to say hello. And my cooking! I couldn't even make L. D. a decent cup of coffee. This evening L. D. made it and he made Indian pudding before Henri and I got back. He's better in the kitchen than I am—as who isn't? I was a bad cook sort of on purpose—or that used to be the reason—but L. D. is like an artist even in the kitchen. When he tastes things he shuts his eyes. He makes me want to learn to cook properly—as if it might be in the place of painting. Of course it can't really be, but it would be a good thing if it could since I have to cook anyway. Probably the whole rest of my life will be cooking. I guess that's helping people about as much as being a nurse, too.

When I try to see us as L. D. might, I think we're like a whole family of crazy people. I don't really know exactly what crazy is, but I'll bet this is it. I know I don't feel like me at all. Mostly I just go through the day as though I wasn't here. Just my body does the work. It's as if I'm waiting for real life to come along again, just like I used to do. Real life! That's a laugh.

—•—

I'm the one who had to help Ma have the baby—all by myself. (If I'm going to be a nurse, I guess I'm getting plenty of practice.) That grandma was hardly any help at all. Aunt Henriette had planned to be here, but the baby came too soon. I could see Ma was in pain but she was quiet as could be. After the baby came, then she cried—a kind of crying as if you don't have the energy to really cry. I did everything just the way Ma said to. I've seen lots and lots of things get born—Old Pa and I had to help sometimes, with horses or the milk cows, not with our beeves—but this was different: a real little somebody, half him and half Ma and a little bit that's the same as me.

Aunt Henriette told Ma she ought to name him pretty soon. Ma said she wasn't ready. Aunt Henriette said, when would she be? And Ma started to cry again. Moan is more like what she does and sort of whispering it. She didn't say, Never, but you could tell that's what she was thinking.

Aunt Henriette heard me call the baby Billy and she said, "Not a bad *idée*," but she thought Ma might want something French. Aunt Henriette calls him Doré. She named him the same way Fay named Goldy. She called him that because of the little bit of goldish fuzz on his scalp. I don't think she really means for that to be his name, and who knows what color either of them, Goldy *or* Doré, will turn out to be when they grow up. So still, nobody knows what he's really named and nobody seems to care but me.

—•—

As soon as L. D. leaves I'll tell that grandma that I'm going to be a nurse just to see what she'll do. That'll be something to write in my journal, I'll bet.

Carol Emshwiller has been widely published in literary, feminist, and science-fiction magazines. She is the author of *Carmen Dog, The Start of the End of It All, Joy in Our Cause,* and *Verging on the Pertinent.* She lives in New York, where she teaches fiction writing at New York University.

Printed in the United States
4965